**pelting down steadily**

But Vanessa had no trouble keeping Taylor's Jeep in sight. She simply followed his red taillights.

Funny how different this road had seemed when she'd traveled it as a child. The surrounding marshlands had seemed like a magical forest, populated with pixies and animals that might actually talk to you.

Eager for her first glimpse of the old house, she braked abruptly when the drooping branches parted, and revealed a two-story veranda supported by white columns.

She was still staring when she noticed Taylor tapping on her window, a dazzling smile on his face. "The old place needs a good airing," he said as she rolled it down. "But this is your aunt Charlotte's old home."

*Home*, she thought. *For now.*

# ABOUT THE AUTHOR

Laurel Pace has been writing all her life, whether novels, short stories or poetry. Her first venture into professional writing came when she was producing commercials for an advertising agency and was called on to create copy in an emergency. She discovered that she enjoyed copywriting much more than production and decided to make a career switch. Laurel now makes her home with her husband in Atlanta, Georgia.

## Books by Laurel Pace

**HARLEQUIN AMERICAN ROMANCE**
192–ON WINGS OF LOVE
220–WHEN HEARTS DREAM

**HARLEQUIN INTRIGUE**
112–DECEPTION BY DESIGN

Don't miss any of our special offers. Write to us at the following address for information on our newest releases.

Harlequin Reader Service
901 Fuhrmann Blvd., P.O. Box 1397, Buffalo, NY 14240
Canadian address: P.O. Box 603,
Fort Erie, Ont. L2A 5X3

# ISLAND MAGIC

## LAUREL PACE

# *Harlequin Books*

TORONTO • NEW YORK • LONDON
AMSTERDAM • PARIS • SYDNEY • HAMBURG
STOCKHOLM • ATHENS • TOKYO • MILAN

For my mother,
quite simply the greatest

Published September 1989

First printing July 1989

ISBN 0-373-16312-6

# Chapter One

Whoever said "when it rains it pours" must have had the South Carolina Low Country in mind. Vanessa Dorsey had reached that conclusion after driving two hours in a torrential downpour that encased her car as if it were a gigantic opaque dome.

On second thought, maybe it was unfair to blame the inclement weather on the locale. Maybe *she* was responsible, Vanessa mused, giving herself a humorless smile in the rearview mirror. Maybe this deluge was just a reflection of her life for the past eighteen months. First the divorce from Jeff, then the loss of her advertising job when her chief account experienced a managerial shuffle, neatly eliminating her job in the process.

Things would start to improve on Parloe Island; they simply had to, she told herself. If she could ever find Parloe, that is. Vanessa frowned, narrowing her slate-blue eyes at the approaching road sign. She managed to decipher the words caught in the Thunderbird's headlights in time to signal a turn and wheel sharply to the left.

Relaxing her grip on the wheel, Vanessa eased back in the seat, but her eyes remained on the road.

So many years had passed since her last visit to Parloe Island—sixteen to be exact—she could hardly remember the dirt road leading to Great-aunt Charlotte's
house. The house was on the mainland side of the
island, not far from the Intracoastal Waterway; Vanessa could at least trust her memory on that fact.
During her summer visits, her rambling walks had often
taken her to the Waterway's drawbridge where she could
watch for the occasional passing boat and the water-
fowl it inevitably scared up from the shore.

Certain now that she had driven past her destina-
tion, Vanessa began to look for a place where she could
turn around. When she spotted a weakly illuminated
Union 76 sign, she pulled over and braked next to the
row of gas tanks.

Leaning on the steering wheel, Vanessa inspected the
aqua stucco building with the name Palmetto One-Stop
arching across its plate glass window. For the obvious
benefit of summer tourists, a billboard facing the road
advertised bait, tackle, and suntan lotion, but it was the
magic phrase Hot Coffee to Go that caught Vanessa's
eye. Switching off the car lights, she pulled up the collar of her leather jacket before making a dash for the
Palmetto's door.

A man with the ruddy face of a lifetime beach-town
resident slouched over the service counter, thumbing
through a magazine, but he looked up the moment the
bell suspended over the entrance jingled. Vanessa could
tell he was watching her as she blotted her jacket with a
tissue and shook the water from her dark curls, but she
pretended not to notice. She had spent enough of her
life in small towns to know the interest a stranger could
arouse, especially one who was female and not altogether unattractive.

"Wet enough for you out there?" The man behind the counter peered over the cigarette display and smiled, waiting for her answer.

"Too wet," Vanessa mumbled, giving the front of her navy gabardine slacks a perfunctory brushing. "Uh, would it be possible to get a cup of coffee?"

"Sure would." The man ambled to the far end of the counter where a Pyrex carafe steamed on a double hot plate. "Cream? Sugar?" His big, weathered hand gestured toward a plastic bowl of sugar packets and stir sticks.

"Just black, thanks." Vanessa already had her wallet in hand when she stepped up to the counter.

"Anything else you need today, ma'am?" the clerk asked, resting one arm on the cash register.

Vanessa's eyes swept the store's shelves, crowded with insect repellent and motor oil and pastel T-shirts that proclaimed I've Been to Parloe. Shaking her head, she glanced at the five-foot inflatable plastic alligator bobbing from the strings moored to the ceiling above the cash register. "Just some directions. I'm trying to find the old Dodderidge house."

The clerk's faded blue eyes were instantly alert. "You mean Miz' Charlotte's place?"

Vanessa nodded. "Could you tell me how to get there?"

"You planning on renting that big ol' house?" the clerk asked, sidestepping her question.

"No," Vanessa replied, a little more curtly than she had intended. "I mean, I will be living there. But just for a while. My sister and I inherited the house from our father's aunt," she added in an effort to still the man's curiosity.

"Don't tell me you're Miz' Charlotte's little niece!" the man exclaimed, slapping his broad palms against the speckled Formica counter.

Having reached her full five feet ten and three-quarter inches at the tender age of thirteen, Vanessa was unaccustomed to being described as little, but she managed to nod. When the man continued to beam at her as if she were a long-lost friend, she offered her hand. "I'm Vanessa Dorsey."

"Luke Johnson." The man's handshake was as exuberant as the smile lining his weather-beaten face. He held onto her hand for a moment as he went on. "Not a day Miz' Charlotte stopped by here for a sack of sugar or some eggs that she didn't mention you girls. Always talking about one of you going to college or being off in New York City. But, Lordy, I never expected to have you show up back here!"

*Neither did I.* Vanessa smiled, gently withdrawing her hand from Luke's grasp. "It's been so long, I'm afraid I've forgotten how to find the house," she prompted.

Now eager to be of service, Luke pulled a creased map from beneath the register and spread it open on the counter. "See, this is where we're at. Bet you didn't know the One-Stop had replaced Stovall's Mercantile?"

"No, I didn't." Vanessa remembered the general store with its noisy ice machine and jars of twisted licorice ropes. "So I suppose I go back toward the bridge?"

Luke's stubby finger followed a blue line squiggling across the map. "You'll see a sign on your left. Says Trade Winds Condominiums. I swear, this island is going to be nothing but hotels and condos pretty soon." He shook his head sadly.

"Do I go past the sign?" Vanessa asked firmly.

"Yep. About, oh, say, a mile or so—" He broke off when the door bell tinkled. His face brightened as he threw up a hand in greeting. "Hello there, Doc! How's the world been treating you today?"

A low chuckle preceded the newcomer's reply. "Not so badly that a good strong cup of coffee won't set it right. How about you?"

Still leaning over the map, Vanessa felt her shoulders sag. As if it weren't hard enough to keep Luke on track, one of his cronies had to choose this moment to drop by.

As she pushed herself away from the counter, her hand brushed the sleeve of a wet rain slicker, and she started. Looking up, Vanessa found herself staring into a face handsome enough to cause a woman far more jaded than she to take notice.

Wide-spaced eyes as gray-green and unpredictable as the Atlantic were set between a broad brow and a firm, slightly squared jaw. Regular exposure to the sun had permanently heightened the color of the man's strongly boned cheeks and high-bridged nose. The hood of his yellow slicker was thrown back, revealing waving hair the color of wet, golden sand. He was tall—tall enough to give Vanessa the rare pleasure of actually looking up at a man, for a change—but well-proportioned. Even the shapeless rain garb could not entirely conceal the husky contours of his shoulders and chest.

"Sorry if I dripped on you," the newcomer apologized. He smiled, the sort of cordial smile that normally passed between strangers, but on his shapely, curving lips that smile struck Vanessa as anything but bland.

"Oh, that's quite all right." She shook her head as she scoured her bag for another tissue, but her mouth drew into the widest grin it had managed since the rain's onset.

When Vanessa glanced up, she found the man's smoky jade eyes still focused on her. He caught himself as she met his gaze, but his expression was devoid of any self-consciousness. In spite of her cautious nature, Vanessa sensed an honesty in this man that was as unwavering as his straightforward gaze.

At that moment, Luke sauntered up to deposit another Styrofoam cup of coffee on the counter. "Bet you didn't know this lady here was Miz' Charlotte's niece?" the gregarious clerk wagered.

"You're Charlotte Dodderidge's niece?" The man sounded surprised.

"Great-niece," Vanessa amended, but she imagined he was having a hard time believing this angular Amazon of a woman was any relation to petite Charlotte Dodderidge.

"Taylor Bowen. I'm pleased to meet you." The man quickly withdrew his hand from the slicker pocket and offered it to Vanessa.

"I'm Vanessa Dorsey." His fingers were long and slim, as befitted a man of his height, but the hard palm pressed against her hand felt almost too worn and hardened to belong to a doctor.

Taylor Bowen smiled fondly. "Back before Dad retired from the practice, Miss Dodderidge used to bring her little poodle to our clinic for his shots every year. What was his name?"

*So he's a vet; that explains the calluses.* "Peekaboo," Vanessa provided.

"That's right!" Taylor chuckled. "He was a feisty little character. Like your aunt. I distinctly remember the nip he gave me the first time we met. Nothing vicious, you understand, just a warning to remind me who was boss. Anyway, we were really sorry when Peekaboo and your aunt moved to Charleston.''

"Aunt Charlotte hated to leave the island, but after a while the big house was simply too much for her." Vanessa smiled at the irony of finding herself slouching over the counter as if she were one of the One-Stop's regulars, happily swapping Charlotte Dodderidge anecdotes with Taylor Bowen.

"Miz' Dorsey's come to take over the house," Luke interposed, ever willing to advance a conversation.

"So you're going to be living here on the island?" Taylor's straight brows rose quizzically.

"For a while." Vanessa deliberately kept her voice even. Like anyone living in a quiet, uneventful place like Parloe, Taylor undoubtedly considered the arrival of a new resident noteworthy. It would be presumptuous, however, to imagine more than a passing curiosity reflected in those heavenly green eyes. "We haven't had tenants in the house for several months, and I'm between jobs right now. Parloe just seemed like a good place to get away from it all. For a while," she repeated, hoping she didn't sound as much like an unemployed fugitive as she felt.

"If it's peace and quiet you're looking for, you'll certainly find it on this island. I gather your real home is in a big city?" Taylor lifted the cup of coffee and pried the plastic lid free with his thumb. He took a sip, watching Vanessa through the steam rising from the cup.

"I used to live in Richmond," Vanessa volunteered, but caught herself before *until Jeff and I split up and sold the house* came tumbling out. An ingrained prudence left her wary of revealing her recent upheavals, even to a stranger as engaging as Taylor was.

"Well, I think you'll find Parloe's pace a sight slower than Richmond's. And you're off to a good start." A whimsical smile played on Taylor's wide mouth as he looked down at the coffee cup and replaced the plastic lid. "You've already found the general store, and you know who to call if your pet gets sick."

"Oh, I don't have a pet." Vanessa had no idea what had possessed her to say *that*, but she regretted it instantly.

Taylor's grin twisted to one side, as if he were mulling over her comment. "Maybe you'll decide to get one while you're here. To keep you company in that big old house." When he leveled his steady gaze at her, she was struck by the way his dark lashes seemed to amplify the exquisite green of his eyes.

At thirty-two, Vanessa had come to pride herself on the way she held up under fire. Perhaps that was the positive side of nine years of marriage to a textbook Type-A personality. Perhaps it was the inevitable outgrowth of a career in a business noted for its lack of mercy. Whatever the case, Vanessa Dorsey could not remember the last time she had allowed herself to be swayed by a passing emotion. But right now, she could see no harm in indulging the delightful sensation stirred to life by Taylor's playful insinuation.

"Maybe I will," Vanessa conceded, returning his grin. She saw no need to tell him that her life was far too much in flux for her to assume responsibility for a house plant, much less an animal.

Taylor nodded, but his expression had grown more thoughtful, giving Vanessa the odd feeling that he sensed some of the turmoil lurking beneath her smiling exterior. "I hope you enjoy your stay on Parloe" was all he said as he pulled his wallet from inside the slicker and laid a five-dollar bill on the counter.

"So do I," Vanessa remarked with more vehemence than she had expected. While Luke meticulously counted out Taylor's change, she glanced again at the map.

"You're welcome to take that map with you," Luke offered.

Vanessa glanced up and smiled. "May I? I'd be embarrassed to get lost on an island that's less than five miles wide."

Taylor had paid for his coffee, but he was taking his time snapping the front of his slicker. "You're having trouble finding the house?" he asked.

Out of the corner of her eye, Vanessa saw him slide the coffee cup onto the counter. An unexpected tingle surged beneath her skin as he leaned over the map, resting his hand close to her own on the counter's edge.

"It's been years since I visited Parloe," Vanessa admitted. When she looked up at him, she was certain those green eyes could melt stone if necessary, not to mention a woman's heart.

"Forget the map. I'll show you where it is," Taylor volunteered without hesitation.

"That's awfully kind of you, but I really wouldn't want you to go out of your way." Vanessa felt obliged to protest. "And the weather is so bad," she added, glancing at the streaked plate-glass window.

As she had hoped, Taylor was quick to reassure her. "It isn't out of my way at all. Ray Hunter lives up that way, and I need to check his sow that's about to farrow." Picking up the coffee cup again, he gestured toward the door. "Come on."

"Okay," Vanessa agreed. Zipping up her jacket, she thanked Luke for his help, collected her coffee, and followed Taylor outside.

"Just follow me. The turnoff is only about a mile short of the bridge." Taylor raised his voice, trying to compete with the rain drumming against the metal awning. Pulling the hood over his head, he gave Vanessa a doubtful look. "You don't have an umbrella with you?"

"If I had thought to bring one, it wouldn't be raining." Vanessa resolutely stuffed her hands into her pockets, but a shiver rippled through her slim shoulders.

He laughed. "Wait here, and I'll bring your car up for you. I'm dressed for this weather, and you're not," he said, heading off the protest already forming on her lips.

"I'll be fine," Vanessa countered. "A little water never hurt anyone." In spite of herself, she grinned, partly at the stubborn set of Taylor's mouth, partly at the novelty of the situation. She had attracted her share of male attention in her life, but men rarely rushed to help her. It had something to do with her height and her obvious independent streak. As Jeff had frequently pointed out, she was good at fending for herself. But even as she grabbed her keys and dashed to her car, she had to admit she had liked Taylor Bowen's old-fashioned chivalry. A bit too much.

Vanessa watched Taylor cross the parking lot in long, sprinting strides. Through the curtain of rain, she saw him wave before climbing into a smoke-gray Cherokee four-wheel drive. She waited for the Jeep to reverse and pull out into the road, and then followed.

Although the rain was still pelting down steadily, she had no trouble keeping sight of the Jeep's red tail-lights, thanks to Taylor's sensible driving pace. She shook her head and smiled to herself when he signaled and turned, right onto what appeared to be a path tunneling into a thicket of undergrowth. No wonder she had driven past the side road—if this rutted, muddy pig trail really deserved to be called a road at all. She grimaced as her front wheels plowed through a pothole, spewing sludge over the windows.

Funny how different this road had seemed when she had traveled it as a child, leaning out the front window of Aunt Charlotte's ancient Cadillac with the humid, fertile-smelling air blowing in her face. The surrounding marshlands had seemed like a magical forest, populated with pixies and animals that might actually talk if they trusted you enough. Now it looked just plain dismal, and Vanessa sighed with relief when Taylor at last signaled another turn.

This was it. Even sixteen years could not dim her memory of the sheltering magnolias that stood like a row of sentries along the drive to her great-aunt's house. Vanessa felt an almost childlike excitement stirring within her, and she leaned closer to the dashboard, eager for her first glimpse of the old house. She braked abruptly when the drooping branches parted, revealing a two-story veranda supported by white columns. She was still staring when the Cherokee's horn tooted.

Vanessa rolled to a halt behind Taylor's vehicle, but before she could collect her bag and alight, he tapped on the window.

Taylor thrust his wet head through the lowered window. ''Give me the keys, and I'll get your stuff out of the trunk." He reached for the keys she held, suggesting that this time he would not take no for an answer.

"Let's just grab the things in the back seat. I won't need anything in the trunk before the rain lets up."

Vanessa climbed out of the car and made a run for the front porch. Stepping out of her muddy shoes, she plundered her bag for the envelope containing the house keys. She had just found them when Taylor joined her on the porch with three of her bags in tow.

The hinges groaned as the solid oak door swung open. Vanessa took a tentative step into the hallway and squinted into the darkness. The clammy smell of mildewed upholstery and stagnant air engulfed her.

"Is the electricity turned on?" Taylor's low-pitched voice sounded comfortingly dependable.

"It should be. I've been paying utility maintenance bills since the last tenant moved out." Vanessa's hand groped the wall. The old light switch snapped noisily, filling the hallway with a dull, vaporous light.

"That's more like it," Taylor remarked. Vanessa was grateful for his cheery tone, but it seemed more incongruous than she liked to admit in the shadowy hallway.

"Where shall I put your stuff? Upstairs?" Taylor shrugged his broad shoulders, gesturing with the bags.

"Just leave them here. I need to explore a bit before I decide where I'm going to make camp." Vanessa clasped her arms and chafed them briskly. A house was bound to undergo some changes in sixteen years, especially one that had seen a succession of short-term tenants, but she was frankly taken aback by the hallway's gloomy aspect. She could only imagine in what sort of condition she would find the other rooms.

Taylor chuckled. "You sound as if you were leading an expedition into the jungle."

Vanessa turned and managed to give him a weak smile. "Well, I have to admit I wasn't quite expecting...this." Her hand swept the air and then dropped to her side.

"The place needs a good airing out," Taylor conceded, but it was amazing how his radiant smile could dispel the chill, even in such desolate surroundings. Heaving the luggage straps onto his shoulders, he led the way through the first door opening off the hall.

Vanessa followed, but when Taylor switched on the light, she recoiled. She immediately recognized her aunt's maroon velvet camelback sofa, in spite of an inch-thick layer of dust and the cobwebs connecting its scrolled legs. The coffee table's marble top was barely visible beneath its coat of grime. The Oriental carpet felt damp and sticky beneath her stockinged feet. Over the mantel, the gilt-edged mirror reflected a cloudy image of her aghast face.

Even Taylor's knack for making the best of things was being put to the test. "When was the last time you checked on things here?" he asked as he draped her garment bag over a dingy brocade wing chair.

"Since Great-aunt Charlotte died five years ago, a real estate agent on the mainland has been keeping the place rented. More or less. I haven't actually been down here to the island for sixteen years."

"Sixteen *years*?" Taylor gasped.

Vanessa was quick to defend herself. "I said it had been a while. I suppose it was a mistake to assume the agent would look after things. And of course, we haven't had a tenant since October. But I'm sure the house will look just fine after I scrape off some of this dust and wash the curtains." Her voice trailed off, hinting that she was far from convinced. She forced herself to smile, in part for Taylor's benefit, in part to counteract the irritating downward pull at the corners of her mouth. "I don't know. Maybe I'll just lock the place up and pitch a tent in the backyard," she quipped, but her flat tone belied her intention to make a joke.

"That doesn't sound like much of a vacation to me," Taylor commented so gently, she could tell he was trying to cheer her up.

"No, but neither does refurbishing a house from top to bottom. I'm afraid a complete remodeling job is simply beyond my energy level." *Not to mention my bank account,* Vanessa added to herself. Taylor might refer to her stay on Parloe as a vacation, but in reality she was taking refuge in the only place she could afford until one of her job prospects panned out. She would just have to keep her fingers crossed and hope the roof didn't cave in in the meantime.

Taylor had stooped for a better look at the fireplace's charred contents, then he suddenly stood up and walked to her side. A tremor raced up her arm as he reached out and gently squeezed her elbow. She dismissed the feeling as nerves. "The first thing you should do is to open the windows and let in some sunshine."

Vanessa swallowed and looked down at the strong hand clasping her arm. For a moment, she felt the craziest urge to lean her head against the sturdy shoulder that loomed so invitingly warm and close.

So much had gone sour in the past year; she had often felt as if she were struggling merely to keep going. She was strong enough to get through a crisis; she'd had ample opportunity to prove herself on that count. But at that moment, Vanessa felt like crying, and she felt like doing it on Taylor Bowen's shoulder.

Instead she faked a feeble little smile. "You're right," she said. "Sunshine, and maybe just a little soap and water." She managed a giggle, and Taylor's grasp on her elbow relaxed.

"You're sure you're going to be all right here to-night?" he asked, with a trace of surprise.

"Fine. I have some snack food in my tote bag, so I won't have to venture out again in this miserable weather. I intend to get a good night's sleep and then tie into the cleaning first thing in the morning," Vanessa said, hoping she sounded more optimistic than she felt.

Taylor nodded and lifted his arm, squinting at his watch in the poor light. "If you're certain there isn't anything else I can do to help, I guess I ought to get on down to Hunter's place before dark."

"To see about the expectant mama pig?" She gave him a sly grin.

Taylor chuckled. "That's one way of putting it."

"Well, in any case, I'm really grateful for your help," Vanessa assured him. She wanted to say more, but before she could formulate her thoughts into any kind of coherent phrase, Taylor had turned and walked to the door.

"Don't work too hard tomorrow," he cautioned her from the doorway. When he opened the heavy front door, wind gusted into the gloomy corridor.

"I won't," Vanessa promised.

On the porch Taylor snapped his slicker with one hand while he pulled up the hood with the other. He paused at the top of the steps as if he had forgotten something, and then turned. "Chin up. You're going to be surprised at how great this old place looks on a sunny day." He flashed her a thumbs-up, along with a smile that offered more encouragement than words ever could.

Vanessa returned the thumbs-up sign. She watched his retreating figure, mirroring his wave when he reached the parked Cherokee. Her eyes followed the bright taillight bars until they were obliterated by the thick mist.

She would be surprised, Taylor had promised. Vanessa wanted to believe him, although her practical mind warned her that the bright sun was likely to reveal only more work to do. Still, her arrival on Parloe had already brought its share of unexpected twists and, yes, quite pleasant surprises. Taylor Bowen, for instance. Was it too unrealistic to hope that, beneath the grime and cobwebs, Aunt Charlotte's estate still retained some of its past glory? For now, at least, Vanessa preferred to think so.

# Chapter Two

*Yeeeeee-oooooo!*

Vanessa's eyes shot open and then stared wildly into the predawn darkness. She held her breath, listening with every nerve fiber for a repetition of the eerie cry that had jolted her from her sleep. Next to the bed, not more than two feet from her head, her travel alarm kept up its scratchy tick, but nothing else disturbed the silence. Slowly, she eased up on one elbow, all the while berating herself for not having had phone service connected before her arrival. Here she was, completely cut off from the outside world. If there was something, *someone,* out there...

Another hoarse squeak broke the stillness. Vanessa started and then relaxed slightly. One thing was certain—whatever was making that sound could not possibly be human.

"It's just an owl. A screech owl," she muttered to herself, now feeling more irritated than frightened. "The marsh is full of owls and animals and things that make odd noises, and you're going to have to get used to it while you're here."

Pulling the blanket around her shoulders, Vanessa leaned over to the window to part the curtain and peer outside. The rain had long since ceased. To the east, the pale dawn cast a metallic pink glow over the Waterway's inlet; the oyster beds exposed by the low tide gleamed as if it were polished obsidian in the gray light.

At least the fair weather would give her a chance to test Taylor's sun-and-fresh-air theory. For no particular reason, Vanessa smiled as she dug a baggy sweatshirt and a pair of jeans out of her suitcase. Her optimism flagged, however, the moment she stepped into the dingy bathroom, and she hastily washed her face and gave her hair a slapdash brushing. She was relieved to close the door on the rust-stained sink and dripping faucets and start downstairs.

Of all the rooms she had inspected so far, the kitchen was by far the most tolerable. Too big and drafty by modern standards, it had somehow retained a good bit of its original atmosphere. Seated at the wooden work table, Vanessa finished off the oatmeal cookies from her tote bag and began to make a list of things to do. *Contact Ma Bell,* she wrote on a scrap of the cookie sack. That weird noise may have been only the cry of an impassioned muskrat, but telephone service was still a number-one priority.

*Stock up on groceries* came next on the list. In addition to the basic food staples, she would need one of everything from the cleaning products department, Vanessa decided. She was reviewing her list when a plaintive bleat suddenly came from behind the house. It was the same sound that had roused her from her sleep an hour earlier, and whatever was making it was not more than a stone's throw from the back porch.

Vanessa peeked out the kitchen window before opening the back door as quietly as possible. The sun had already burned away enough of the morning's mist to allow a clear view of the mossy yard, but the only creatures within sight were a few robins tugging worms from the wet soil. Tiptoeing down the steps, Vanessa scanned the surrounding woodland, then followed the brick walk leading around the house.

A muffled snort greeted her as she approached the listing frame building that had once been the Dodderidge stable and, in more recent years, had housed Aunt Charlotte's beloved Cadillac. The sagging Dutch doors stood ajar, wide enough for Vanessa to squeeze through, but she cautiously peered into the gloomy interior. Her frown dissolved into a smile the moment she caught sight of the shaggy donkey huddled between two bales of straw. The little creature stretched its thin neck when it saw Vanessa and let out another wheezing bray.

"Poor little guy!" Vanessa crooned, wrestling the door far enough back to admit some daylight into the garage. "You sure do have a funny voice for a donkey. Where did you come from?" she asked, extending her hand as she approached the animal. As she should have expected, the donkey did not see fit to reply, but its soulful eyes regarded her in a very kindly fashion. It snuffled with pleasure when her hand smoothed its fuzzy neck. *What on earth do you do with a donkey?* Surely an animal as large and substantial as a donkey belonged to someone? The owner would probably show up in no time, especially if she posted a found-donkey notice in the Palmetto One-Stop. Vanessa continued to scratch the donkey's ears while she considered the matter.

"I bet you'd like a bite to eat," she remarked, brushing loose donkey fur from her hands. Now that she had gotten a better look at the animal, it did appear to be alarmingly thin. "I'll be right back," she promised before dashing back to the house.

When she returned, she brought two sliced apples with her. "It's all I have left, but I promise to add donkey food to my shopping list." She smiled as the donkey daintily sniffed, then crunched into a slice of apple. The poor creature must have been famished, to judge from the greedy way it now attacked the apples. It continued to nibble at her fingers after the last wedge had been consumed.

"All gone." Vanessa giggled, holding up her hands for inspection. She abruptly stopped laughing when the donkey began to foam at the mouth.

She watched in horror as it mouthed its tongue and yawned, covering its muzzle with greenish froth. Was it choking? If it was, how on earth do you perform the Heimlich maneuver on a donkey? Maybe it was poisoned. But from what? Two Winesaps she had bought in the A & P?

Vanessa stooped and inspected the donkey's neck, hoping that a solution to the problem would suggest itself. She gave the animal's scruffy back a timid pat, but quickly withdrew her hand when the donkey wheezed hoarsely and seemed to gag.

Vanessa had no idea what was wrong, but she now feared it was serious. "Wait right here!" she commanded, pointing a warning finger at the animal. Turning on her heel, she ran back to the house and grabbed her handbag. That donkey needed help. Fast. Trying to keep a grip on her nerves, she jumped into her car and tore down the muddy drive.

When she reached the Palmetto One-Stop, she found Luke chatting with the dairy delivery man, but he cheerfully motioned her in the direction of the pay phone. She managed to rip five pages in the directory before she located the number of the Parloe Island Animal Clinic, the place Taylor Bowen had said he worked.

Lacing the metal phone cord through her fingers, Vanessa chewed her lip and waited for someone to answer.

TAYLOR BOWEN PLANTED BOTH HANDS on the counter and watched the first fragrant droplets fall into the coffee carafe. He was toying with the idea of substituting his empty mug for the carafe when the clinic secretary poked her graying head through the doorway.

"Mornin', Tay." Mary Beasley greeted him with her usual motherly smile. "It is morning, you know," she teased, peering over his shoulder at the half-full carafe. "Did you have a rough evening?"

"Hunter's sow finally delivered, after I wallowed around in the mud with her for an hour and a half. And then I got your call on the car radio about that mare caught in barbed wire up on the mainland. It was pretty late when I finally got her leg stitched up and could head for home." Shaking his head, he filled two mugs and handed one to Mary. "How did we ever manage without an intern?"

"You worked around the clock, just like your daddy did before you joined him in the practice," Mary reminded him as she emptied a packet of sweetener into her mug. She frowned at the scoop of creamer before dumping it into the coffee. "You know, you could stand to delegate even more of the routine work around here—you've said yourself that Diana is as competent as they come. If you like, I'll give her the routine farm calls and leave you the office business.''

"Let's see how the appointment schedule looks today," Taylor hedged, jiggling his mug as he sauntered toward the door.

"Just like your daddy!" Mary rolled her eyes in mock disgust. "That man always thought Parloe would sink into the swamp if he wasn't out there working his fingers to the bone twenty-four hours a day, and you're just as bad!"

Taylor was about to offer the stock defense that he was ultimately responsible for his intern, but the buzzing phone suddenly summoned Mary. When he caught up with her in the front office, her normally calm dark face was drawn with concern.

Taylor read Mary's expression in a glance. "A bad case?"

"A lady just called and said her donkey was choking to death." Mary nervously popped the ball point pen she held.

"Choking on what?" Taylor hesitated as he lifted the house-call list from the spindle.

Mary shook her head. "I asked, but she didn't know. She just kept emphasizing that it was a real emergency. She sounded really upset, Taylor."

"I'm on my way." Taylor had already pulled on his khaki insulated vest and was looking over the house-call list Mary had prepared. "If I leave now, I can probably still make that eight o'clock appointment. What's the address on this donkey case?"

"The old Dodderidge place."

Taylor looked up from the typed list and gaped at the secretary. "But that's impossible! Vanessa doesn't have a donkey!" he blurted.

"I only know what this person told me," Mary countered, holding up the neatly recorded phone message for his inspection.

Taylor frowned at the pink slip of paper for a moment, his fingers frozen in suspended animation on his vest's zipper pull.

Arms folded across her chest, Mary watched him with a puzzled look. "Excuse me, but is something wrong?"

"No, no, it's nothing," he recovered himself in time to assure her. Well, hardly *nothing*, he added silently, but there was no need to fill his secretary in on either Vanessa Dorsey or the complicated feelings she had aroused in him the previous afternoon. He had had enough trouble already trying to put their brief encounter into perspective.

"If this is an emergency, I'd better run," Taylor concluded. He quickly pocketed the phone message and then hurried out of the office, fumbling with the sticky zipper on the way.

"Don't forget your house-call list," Mary cried, running after him with the folded paper.

Taylor paused in the doorway. "Oh, thanks." He laughed a little sheepishly as he stuffed the list into one of his vest's many convenient pockets and loped out the door.

A choking donkey at Vanessa Dorsey's ramshackle old estate! Of all the surprises the morning could have dealt him, Vanessa's call was the one he would never have anticipated in a hundred years. She had been so quick to let him know she didn't keep pets, but in the past twelve hours she had somehow managed to acquire a donkey, of all things. He was chuckling to himself in spite of the emergency call when he wheeled the Cherokee into the magnolia-lined drive.

Before he had even cut the motor, he saw Vanessa running around the side of the old house. A sudden rush of adrenaline hit him with such force his head seemed to swell from the pressure. He was accustomed to this hyped-up feeling, dealing as he so often did with life-and-death situations. But the freight train of emotion thundering through him was fired by something more than the normal tension he felt when approaching a medical crisis.

*God, she's beautiful!* She seemed even taller than he recalled, with those long denim-covered legs that just stretched on forever, or at least as far as a man's imagination could follow. Her hair billowed out behind her in a dark cumulus cloud. As she neared the Jeep, he could see the rosy flush spreading across her cheeks. Her large, expressive eyes glowed like polished sapphires, rimmed by the fine black lace of her lashes.

"Thank heaven you're here!" Vanessa braced a hand on the Cherokee's hood and caught her breath.

Taylor climbed out of the Jeep and slammed the door. "We try to get to emergencies as quickly as possible. How is the patient doing?" He was surprised at how steady and professional his voice sounded, and he was proud of himself.

"I rushed right back here after I phoned your office, and he seemed okay. But then he started foaming at the mouth again. You don't suppose he's rabid, do you?" Vanessa twisted the hem of her sweatshirt nervously as she followed Taylor to the back of the Jeep and watched him unload a black leather bag.

Taylor grimaced doubtfully. "I'd be real surprised if that were the case. Has he eaten anything that might have been difficult to swallow?"

"He looked so hungry, I gave him a couple of sliced apples. Donkeys *can* eat apples, can't they?" Vanessa's luminous eyes registered such genuine distress that Taylor almost felt guilty for having posed the question.

"Normally. Let's have a look at him. Where is he, anyway?"

"In the garage." Vanessa set off at a trot, beckoning him to follow. She struggled with the sagging garage door. A squeaky bray resounded from inside the dilapidated building.

"If he's talking, he can't be too far gone," Taylor remarked, edging through the door.

Vanessa looked up at him and smiled anxiously. Concern had made her lovely face look even paler; her dark eyes were drawn into a tense line. In his chosen profession, Taylor frequently witnessed heart-rending scenes, and often had to console people who were forced to part with cherished pets. But never had he felt such an overwhelming urge to reach out, to reassure, to comfort. Something inexplicable made him want to murmur soothing words into that tumble of dark hair. Instead, he placed his bag on the packed dirt floor and walked quietly to the waiting donkey.

He could sense Vanessa's nervous presence behind him as he examined the shaggy creature, but he forced himself to concentrate on his patient. "Where did you get this little character, anyway?" he asked over his shoulder while his fingers gently probed the underside of the donkey's neck for signs of an obstruction.

"That's a good question. I heard him bray when I got up this morning. I suppose he wandered in from a neighboring farm. Is he going to be all right?" As Taylor gently prodded the donkey's mouth open, Vanessa leaned over his shoulder, so close he imagined he could feel her body's fragrant warmth through the bulky vest he wore.

"As far as I can tell *she's* going to be just fine." Taylor straightened himself and gave the donkey's neck a firm pat. "Actually, I think this moldy straw is probably the culprit." He held up a ragged strand of half-chewed straw that he had extracted from the donkey's mouth. He felt strangely pleased when Vanessa did not recoil in disgust, but examined it closely. "I've seen my own horse foam a bit when he's trying to get rid of a particularly unwieldy bite of hay."

"You have a horse?" Vanessa had stepped around the donkey and placed one arm on its scrawny neck. "For years, I asked Santa Claus for a horse, even after I quit believing in Santa, but he never came through."

Taylor nodded, not taking his eyes off Vanessa. Her face was free of makeup today, leaving a few tiny lines branching from the corners of her eyes and mouth. The faintest smattering of pale freckles danced, unconcealed, across her short, straight nose. Far from detracting from her beauty, they made her even more alluring—if that were possible.

"Well, maybe that explains where this donkey came from," he teased her. "Any idea what you're going to name her?"

Vanessa smiled down at the donkey and scratched its floppy ears. "She isn't mine," she corrected. "But if she were, I'd call her Emily. Anyway, I'm sure her owner will be around to fetch her pretty soon."

"Don't be so sure. Judging from her appearance, I'd guess Emily has been foraging for herself in the marsh for some time. I think you just may have acquired a pet." Taylor let his hand slide along the animal's neck until it collided with Vanessa's cool fingers.

"But I can't keep an animal," Vanessa objected, and he could feel her fingers tighten their grip on the donkey's mane.

"Why not? You certainly have room here."

"But someday I'll leave. What will I do with her then?"

"You just said her owner might show up," Taylor reminded her.

"*You* just said her owner might not."

"Then I'll help you find her a good permanent home before you leave," Taylor promised. Rationally speaking, he had no idea why he was so dead set on persuading her to keep the donkey, but his mind was already racing ahead in search of arguments supporting his case.

Vanessa blinked up at him for a moment, and she seemed to be pondering a much more complicated issue than Emily's custody. "I suppose you'll tell me what to feed her," she finally conceded, smiling as she withdrew her hand from the donkey's neck. "And she'll certainly need more room than this garage." She walked to the door and swung the top portion open wide.

Taylor secured the latches on his veterinarian's bag before joining Vanessa at the door. "It wouldn't be too hard to repair this fence." He leaned across the door's splintered edge and pointed to a tipsy row of fence posts. "There's plenty of usable lumber stacked up here in the garage. If you want some help, I could give you a hand on my afternoon off."

When he saw the unabashed pleasure enlivening Vanessa's face, nothing could have persuaded him to retract his offer.

"That would be very nice," she said simply.

Taylor eased his breath out slowly, measuring the time it took to exhale, as he looked into Vanessa Dorsey's eyes. There was nothing coy about their direct gaze, yet he felt himself being pulled into their midnight-blue depths as if by a powerful undertow. For the first time in his thirty-four years, Taylor was confronted with something within himself he could not entirely control. He felt an urge growing, a desire so palpable it almost made him wince.

Suddenly, he pulled himself up short. For God's sake, this was a business call after all! She had summoned him to perform a professional service, not to stand around gaping like an overgrown kid. Clearing his throat, Taylor pivoted and grabbed his bag. As he held the garage door for Vanessa, he thought he detected a glow lingering on her cheeks, but outside in the clear sunlight things immediately took on a saner, more levelheaded cast.

"So, where are you heading from here?" she asked lightly, folding her hands behind her back and idly kicking at a tuft of grass. Vanessa might feel a city girl's trepidation where salivating donkeys and farrowing sows were concerned, but those mannerisms reminded Taylor endearingly of his farmer clients.

"I'm going to worm some cattle on the mainland," he replied, and wished immediately he had lied and said "vaccinate" or anything less repellent than "worm." Vanessa's question had sounded so deliberately conversational, he was beginning to fear he had done something to alienate her back in the garage. A beautiful woman like her was probably thoroughly weary of men who gawked and started to breathe heavily when they were alone with her for more than thirty seconds.

He glanced over at her, trying to gauge her mood, but the curtain of glossy dark curls thwarted his scrutiny.

Vanessa scuffed aside the weed her toe had uprooted and watched Taylor shove his bulky medical bag into the back of the Cherokee. He hesitated momentarily, hand poised on the tailgate, as if he were taking mental inventory of the assorted ropes, halters, and cartons of veterinary medications. After a moment Taylor locked the tailgate and turned to Vanessa, hands buried in two of his vest's innumerable pockets. When he continued to look at her, she smiled and then caught herself. Here she was standing around making small talk while he tactfully waited to be paid.

"I guess I'd better get my wallet," Vanessa announced hastily. She took a couple of steps backward, nodding toward the house.

"We'll bill you," Taylor interposed quickly.

"Oh. Okay. Fine." Vanessa halted in her tracks. "You have the address?"

"Everyone on Parloe knows this address." When Taylor chuckled, it was as if his zest for life were brimming over into that husky, rippling laugh.

Vanessa found it impossible not to share in his laughter. "I forget the whole world isn't like New York or Richmond."

Taylor's eyes narrowed as they drifted across the sun-dappled lawn. "There's nowhere in the world like this island," he stated firmly, and, beneath his genial smile, Vanessa could see he was serious. When he turned, he looked at her directly. "So, what about it?" he asked, suddenly withdrawing his hands from his pockets and slapping them together briskly. "You still want a pen for Emily, I hope?" Taylor looked as if he would be truly disappointed if she said "no."

"Of course I do! I don't change my mind *that* quickly!"

Taylor's eyes twinkled with amusement, hinting that he had won precisely the reaction he wanted from her. "You raised so many objections, I just wanted to be sure you hadn't had second thoughts."

"Well, I haven't. I was just waiting for you to set a time," Vanessa assured him primly.

"One o'clock Wednesday afternoon," he shot back without even a moment's hesitation.

"It's a deal." Vanessa proffered her hand, intent on cementing their agreement with a handshake. At the touch of his pleasantly rough palm pressing hers, she felt a resurgence of emotion that refused to subside even after he had released her hand and climbed behind the Jeep's wheel.

The filtered sun burnished Taylor's thick, wavy hair as he stuck his head out the window. "Feed Emily oats," he advised her with a wink. "The kind you buy in a big sack. And Luke should have a bale of decent hay he'll sell you."

Vanessa nodded solemnly. "Oats and hay," she repeated dutifully. "Anything else I ought to do for her?"

"Give her lots of TLC. It's still the number-one wonder drug, you know." He cranked the engine and looked back at her.

"Yes, I do know," she replied, smiling demurely. "TLC it is, then! And the doctor will be back to check up on the dosage?"

"Wednesday at one. TLC check." Taylor knit his brow as if he were engraving the appointment on his memory. Then he smiled up at her again. His eyes softened, and Vanessa felt his gentle, caring gaze as palpably as if he had stroked her cheek or smoothed her hair.

As the Jeep lurched forward on the soggy drive, Taylor's hand reached out and threw her a jaunty goodbye wave. Vanessa stood with one hand shielding her eyes from the Parloe sun as she watched the vehicle disappear behind the Spanish moss and overhanging cypress. She smiled to herself and turned her face up to the warm, bright sun.

"Tender loving care," she repeated softly. If anyone was qualified to gauge that remedy, it seemed to be Taylor Bowen.

# Chapter Three

"Makes your sink sparkle like brand new *without scratching the surface like those old-fashioned cleansers.*" The actress's gratingly enthusiastic voice rose to a crescendo and then yielded to up-tempo music.

Dropping the frayed steel-wool pad into the sink, Vanessa focused a cold eye on the tiny television set perched on the end of the counter. She poked the volume control with a rubber-gloved finger, reducing the commercial's jingle to an inconsequential murmur. After spending most of the past two days scraping layers of dirt from the old house, she was in no mood to listen to some miracle-product huckster.

An energetic bray from the backyard redirected her attention to the open window. At the sound of Emily's now-familiar salutation, she smiled and pulled off her rubber gloves. Silly as it seemed, she had already grown attached to the little donkey in the short time since she had found her in the garage.

On her way out the back door, Vanessa grabbed an apple from the fruit bowl, intent on giving herself a break and Emily a treat. Taylor had said he would come over around one to help her with the fence, and she had wanted to have the house in presentable condition. Her definition of presentable had grown considerably more liberal in the past forty-eight hours, however, and she was relieved that Emily had called her away from the wretched sink.

The donkey tossed her head and leaned against the wobbly fence row that Vanessa had managed to prop up alongside the garage. She gave another excited bleat as her mistress approached, but instead of stretching eagerly for the apple, she set off in a stiff-legged trot around the garage. As Vanessa followed her, she heard the syncopated drum of iron-shod hooves against packed earth.

At the edge of the garage, Vanessa paused, lifting one hand to shield her eyes from the sun. To her surprise, she saw a horse and rider approaching on the drive. The sunlight filtering through the magnolias caught the sheen of the horse's coat, which was as black as midnight. As the trotting animal drew closer, Vanessa was startled to recognize Taylor sitting easily in the saddle, his muscular torso swaying in rhythm with the horse's canter. While imperceptibly guiding his mount with one hand, he led another horse, a smaller, light gray animal, behind them. As the trio rounded the curve at the top of the drive, the black thoroughbred let out an undignified whinny when it spotted Emily, earning a laugh from both Taylor and Vanessa.

"Steady there!" Taylor leaned back in the saddle and kicked his feet free of the stirrups. Vanessa's eyes followed his lithe movements as he swung one long leg over the horse's rump and then sprang lightly to the ground. When he turned, his smile formed a gleaming white crescent against his tanned skin. He greeted her with a hearty "Good afternoon." Then he added apologetically, "I'm a little early. I hope I didn't interrupt your lunch."

Vanessa grinned wryly and rolled her eyes in the direction of the house. "No need to worry on that count—I gobbled a peanut-butter sandwich hours ago. I was up before the birds this morning. And yesterday. *And* the day before that. Believe me, this is not spring cleaning, it's an archaeological dig."

"That bad?" In spite of his jocular manner, concern tempered the brightness of Taylor's smile.

Vanessa nodded wearily. "Very bad, but the end is in sight. I'll give you the grand tour today, and let you be the judge. Actually, it hasn't been all drudgery. I've unearthed a lot of memories under the cobwebs and debris, a lot of really good memories."

As she spoke, her gaze wandered across the mossy lawn to the hedgerow with its untidy thicket of box-wood interspersed with bright yellow forsythia. When she glanced back at Taylor, he was regarding her in-tensely, almost as if he could see deep within her.

"This place must be like a living family album for you," he commented quietly. "You're really lucky to have it."

"Yes, I am," Vanessa agreed. She had experienced so much bad luck in the recent past, it was nice to be re-minded there still was another kind. Then, too, she felt strangely compelled to share her thoughts with Taylor. By conventional standards, she scarcely knew him; all told, they could not have spent more than a few hours together. Yet Vanessa sensed he possessed an uncom-mon sensitivity, a gift for understanding the little nu-ances that ordinarily escape notice.

Pleased as Vanessa was to see Taylor again, she found her attention irresistibly drawn to the two horses he had in tow. "Are these your horses?" she ventured, tentatively extending her hand toward the gray's silky neck.

Taylor regarded the black horse with unconcealed pride. "This one is. The other one I borrowed for the day from a friend."

"May I touch?" Vanessa asked. When Taylor nodded, she carefully stroked the gray's neck.

Taylor grinned and looked down at the reins looped between his tapering fingers. "You can do more than touch. After we get this fence taken care of, I thought you might like to ride around the island with me."

Vanessa's hand froze on the mare's glossy neck. "Me? Ride?" She chuckled doubtfully. "Look, you can blame Santa if you like, but I've never been on anything except a pony about the size of a German shepherd. The best I have to show for my childhood horse phase is a very dog-eared copy of *Black Beauty*."

Taylor blithely dismissed her reservations. "That doesn't matter."

"It does if I end up in traction. I have responsibilities, you know. If I were in the hospital, who would feed Emily?" Seeing his mouth open, she held up her hand in warning. "I know—you don't have to tell me. But I'd just prefer to keep my aging body in one piece, thank you."

"Vanessa, I swear—" Taylor clapped one hand over the breast pocket of his denim jacket "—this gray mare practically comes with a written guarantee. All you have to do is sit up there and let her follow Knight and me. Come on," he wheedled. "I can tell you really want to ride, don't you?"

"As much as I did when I was eight years old," Vanessa confessed.

"Here's your big chance then."

"Okay," Vanessa agreed, trying to check her delighted smile, which contradicted her dire predictions. "I guess we'd better get on with this fence repair while I still have the use of all four limbs."

But as she watched him tether the two horses to the porch railing, she had to admit she was thrilled by the prospect of exploring Parloe on horseback. More appealing still was the thought of doing it with Taylor.

Even a task as uninspiring as repairing a collapsed fence seemed less onerous with the two of them cracking jokes and tugging at the split rails together. The work went fast, thanks to Taylor's practiced hand and Vanessa's newly discovered skill with a hammer. As someone who had spent most of her adult life in a dress-for-success suit, Vanessa was amused by the spectacle she must have presented, in her rolled-up painter's pants with a half dozen nails clamped between her teeth. She was pleased, too, by Taylor's quietly appreciative looks. If she had had any reservations about imposing on his limited free time, they had vanished by the time the two of them had restored the fence to its original sturdy condition.

Taylor and Vanessa leaned on one of the now firm rails and surveyed their handiwork proudly. Exertion and the brilliant Low Country sun had left them with a fine film of sweat, and Taylor's blue work shirt was plastered in dark patches to his chest and back.

"Let's see how Emily likes her new home and then have something cold to drink," Vanessa suggested. Stooping, she swung between the rails and walked to the garage where the inquisitive donkey had been confined during the fence work. The little animal bleated in delight when Vanessa unbolted the lower portion of the door and released her into the expanded paddock.

Taylor wiped his brow with the back of his hand and chuckled. "It's nice to know you're appreciated."

"It's nice to know there's iced tea in the fridge." Vanessa laughed as she led the way around the house.

At the foot of the back steps, Taylor paused and nodded toward the spreading elm that shaded most of the yard. "I bet someone put that swing up for you one summer when you were visiting your aunt," he remarked, pointing to the weathered slat that dangled from one of the elm's boughs. Now suspended by only one rope, the swing looked curiously pathetic.

Vanessa chuckled. "Guess again. According to Aunt Charlotte, that swing was around when *she* was just a little girl. No telling how old it is."

"You ought to fix it up," Taylor suggested, but Vanessa was already shaking her head.

"There are too many absolutely essential repairs I need to make. I'm not sure I should worry about an old swing." On the back porch, she turned to him, her eyes sparkling. "And speaking of repairs, be forewarned. This kitchen is not going to be featured in the next issue of *Better Homes and Gardens*."

"Good. At least I won't be afraid of messing something up while I drink my tea," Taylor told her as he scuffed his boots across the sisal doormat. He paused in the kitchen doorway, planting both hands on the frame. "Vanessa, this is really great!"

"You're just saying that," Vanessa demurred, clasping her hands behind her back.

Taylor's green eyes drifted from the starched gingham curtains billowing over the sink to the bleached pine hutch that filled a corner. They settled on Vanessa again. "No, I'm not," he insisted. "It's cheerful and cozy, and it looks as if...people really enjoy living here."

Vanessa smiled as she ran her hand along the hutch's surface. "Well, I do, at least. I was really happy to find a lot of Aunt Charlotte's things still stored in the attic." She pointed to the collection of hand-painted Provençal china and a ceramic pig in a sailor suit that doubled as a cookie jar. "It's nice to have them down here again where they belong."

Taylor had joined her beside the hutch. When he lifted the ceramic pig's head, Vanessa imagined the faintest odor of nutmeg, chocolate and brown sugar wafting from the cookie jar. Replacing the lid, he smiled down at her. She felt a sudden and undeniably sensual warmth suffuse her entire body, a sensation that, unlike the cookie aroma, could not be attributed to her overactive imagination.

"I don't know about you, but I'm ready for that glass of tea," she announced, making a break for the refrigerator. Wrenching two ice trays from the freezer, she balanced them on top of the tea pitcher and hurried to the sink. She opened the cupboard and pretended to study the assortment of recycled jam jars that served as drinking glasses.

*Easy does it,* she cautioned herself, reaching for a tall glass with red and yellow circus clowns pursuing one another around its rim. *You're attracted to him, and that's perfectly normal. You're divorced, which is almost the same as single, and you're entitled to male companionship. Just don't get carried away.*

Vanessa selected another tumbler, this one of dimpled blue Depression glass, and held it up for Taylor's inspection. "This is a pretty eclectic collection of glasses, but at least these two don't have screw tops."

She gave him the sort of bemused smile she had frequently relied on to humor apprehensive clients and recalcitrant ad copywriters.

Taylor's wide mouth pulled into a lopsided grin as he lifted the blue glass up to the light, but his eyes remained trained on Vanessa with disconcerting intensity. She slammed an ice tray against the drain board, trying to dislodge a few cubes and get her mind off the unequivocally masculine presence hovering at her elbow.

"Let me do that." Taylor took the tray from her unresisting hands and popped a half dozen cubes into each glass. Before she could grab the pitcher, he had dispensed two glasses of clear amber liquid. "Cheers!" He clicked his dimpled blue glass against her red and yellow clowns.

"Cheers!" Vanessa piped before taking a gulp of tea. She drained half the glass and then replaced it on the counter. Fanning herself with one hand, she leaned closer to the open window. "I've spent most of my life in the South, but I don't suppose I'm ever going to get used to the heat."

"This is turning into a very warm March, even for Parloe." The ice tinkled as Taylor shook his glass and then fished out a cube. "Ever try this?"

Vanessa watched him take her hand and turn it palm up. She jumped when he lightly touched her wrist with the cube. "It's not as good as plunging into the Atlantic, but it's the next best thing," he explained, rubbing the cube against her pulse point. "Feel cooler?"

"Yes! Like an iceberg," Vanessa lied. Since he had clasped her hand, she was sure her temperature had risen a notch or two, but she did her best to look cool and collected. When he finally tossed the ice cube into the sink, she seized the opportunity to reclaim her hand. "Let's go riding," she suggested. Not waiting for his reply, she led the way out the back door.

"I'm glad I won you over to my idea," Taylor said, catching up with her at the bottom of the steps.

"To the old ice-cube cure?" Somehow, it seemed safer to indulge in a little playful teasing now that they were outdoors.

Taylor gently tugged one of the short curls skirting her ear. "You know I'm talking about riding."

Vanessa returned his smile, but she sobered when they reached the patiently waiting horses. They were big animals, bigger than Black Beauty had ever looked, certainly bigger than that pygmy Shetland she had ridden at the Beaufort County Fair. She watched Taylor closely as he checked the girths and adjusted the stirrups for her.

When he seemed confident that everything was in order, he untied the gray mare and led her away from the porch. "Do you need a boost?" he asked Vanessa helpfully.

Vanessa gave the horse's neck a businesslike pat. "No, I don't think so." Gingerly twisting the stirrup, she inserted her foot, took a little hop, and then swung into the saddle with startling ease.

Taylor mocked her. "Are you sure you don't know how to ride?"

"Positive. And if you don't want irrefutable proof in about two seconds, you'd better get on Knight and lead the way before this horse decides to do it for us."

"Her name's Velvet," he told her. As soon as he had mounted he pivoted his horse alongside hers. Vanessa aped the way he grasped his reins, but when he urged the big black horse into a fast walk, Velvet automatically fell in step beside him.

Vanessa had always imagined there were some natural wonders that could only be appreciated from a certain vantage point: the Grand Canyon from an airplane, the Alaskan glaciers from the deck of a cruise ship. To that list she now added Parloe Island from horseback. She soon discovered the dense marshlands that appeared impenetrable from the road were in fact crisscrossed by a number of paths, some so narrow the horses went single file. On every side, they were surrounded by lush subtropical vegetation, as wild and unspoiled as a primeval forest. Even the birds perching in the overhanging trees seemed to take little notice of the slow-moving horses, allowing Vanessa an opportunity to observe them in their natural habitat.

According to Taylor, some of the trails had been in use since the island had been settled, and Vanessa had little difficulty imagining a Colonial lady riding sidesaddle through the thicket of palmetto and cypress, on her way to visit one of the neighboring indigo plantations. Occasionally, they would catch a glimpse through the interwoven branches of a white or—more often than not—weathered gray clapboard mansion..Then Taylor would regale her with a capsule history of the estate.

"You remind me of Aunt Charlotte," Vanessa commented after they had circled a deserted house and paused in its derelict orchard to give the horses a rest. "I used to love the stories she would tell about the different houses around here. She knew exactly when each one had been built, who had lived there, everything. How long have you lived on Parloe?"

Taylor swatted lazily at the tiny buzzing insect that had just strafed his nose. "My whole life. Oh, I guess I shouldn't count the years I spent in exile while I was in college and vet school.''

"And you've never gotten the urge to try elsewhere?"

Taylor leaned back, resting one hand on the back of the saddle, and gazed up at the natural bower overhead. "Never." Returning his eyes to Vanessa, he grinned slowly. "I can hear you thinking, Vanessa, all the way over here. You're wondering how I've managed not to die from sheer boredom, spending the better part of thirty-four years in a sleepy little place like Parloe."

Vanessa straightened herself in the saddle. "That's not what I was thinking at all," she insisted honestly. "It's just that nowadays so few people ever seem to stay put."

Still smiling, Taylor shook his head. "I can't imagine calling any other place home. This island is in my blood. You see, the first Bowen settled here over two centuries ago. Parloe gave him a far richer life than he could ever have enjoyed as the third son of an impoverished English baronet. A lot has changed since Grenville Bowen's arrival, but my family has never forgotten its debt to this island. That's the main reason my Dad went to vet school—up until he opened his practice, Parloe's poor folk had to rely on home remedies and luck to heal their farm animals. I'm proud to carry on his tradition." Lifting the reins, he clucked to Knight and reined the horse around a snarled mass of honeysuckle vines. "Come on. I'll show you something."

Vanessa's thighs tightened instinctively around the mare's back as the horses picked their way through the underbrush. She loosened her hold when the trail opened up again into a broad, grassy clearing, interspersed with spreading live oaks and dogwood just coming into bud.

"This is beautiful," Vanessa exclaimed. "It's such a lovely site I'm surprised no one has ever built here."

"My great-great-great-grandfather did, about two hundred and fifty years ago." Taylor rose in the stirrups and pointed to the middle of the clearing. "See those spaces where the grass is discolored?"

Vanessa raised herself in the saddle. Between two of the enormous live oaks she could barely discern an outline in the mossy earth.

"In the eighteenth century, the planters used a mixture of crushed oyster shell and lime to make a kind of cement they called tabby. Our family home had a tabby foundation, and it left a mineral deposit, so you can still see its outline on the ground. It's odd, isn't it, the tricks life plays sometimes. That house survived the ravages of three wars without a scratch, only to be struck by lightning twenty-two years ago. It burned to the ground in less than an hour."

"How awful for you and your family!" Vanessa looked from the barren clearing to Taylor, but he had already wheeled Knight around and was thrashing back through the undergrowth.

Pressing her heels against Velvet's flanks, she hastened to catch up with him. Taylor reined and turned in the saddle. He waited for her to join him before nudging Knight into a jog trot. Vanessa leaned forward, striving to make eye contact with Taylor, but the black thoroughbred's brisk gait thwarted her efforts.

"This trail connects with the main road," he told her after several minutes' silence. Taylor's normally relaxed Southern inflection had taken on an unfamiliar tightness, and his mouth was set in an uncompromising line. Visiting the site of the devastated house had obviously awakened painful memories for him—memories, Vanessa sensed, that he preferred not to discuss.

Soon the forest began to thin out, at last opening onto a paved road. To the right, a slender inlet fed into a sprawling basin where shrimpers and a few sailboats resided. With their nets pulled high, the fishing boats seemed to salute the passing riders.

"The ocean is out there somewhere, I suppose," Vanessa remarked when they halted at the curve of the road.

Taylor gave her an incredulous look. "You mean you haven't been to the beach yet?"

Vanessa was pleased to note the return of his usual jocular tone, but she quickly sprang to her own defense. "I haven't had time yet. I've been too busy cleaning house and fretting over a stray donkey."

Taylor looked down at Knight's thick mane and shook his head. "I'm only a vet, but I'm going to give you some doctor's orders. Put on your shorts, take off your shoes, and go to the beach. You don't want to spend your whole vacation fussing over that house. Get out and enjoy yourself, for heaven's sake."

"I intend to," Vanessa agreed. Although her stay on Parloe was not technically a vacation, she could not argue with the wisdom of Taylor's advice. Then, too, she was aware of how successfully their leisurely ride and quiet conversation had distracted her from her problems.

"Can we ride along the shore?" she asked, her imagination now thoroughly primed by the strong salt air gusting in from the basin.

"I'd rather not. There's a lot of construction along the beachfront, and the big trucks might frighten the horses." Leaning back in the saddle, he swung his mount around toward the inlet.

"Luke said condos were going up all over the island," Vanessa remarked, urging Velvet alongside Knight.

Taylor's dark frown made no secret of where he stood. "This place is being overdeveloped, like just about every other island along the coast. Of course, we've always had beach houses on the ocean, but they don't really create a problem. It's the big high-density developments that are ruining things."

"I suppose they do bring money to the island," Vanessa said.

Taylor nodded reluctantly. "Yes, that's true, up to a point. But they also eliminate some jobs. They also affect the water quality, and that in turn affects the shrimpers. A lot of fishermen are in trouble right now. Fortunately, a few citizens have decided to take action before it's too late."

Vanessa was about to ask what sort of action, but a chorus of high-pitched shouts distracted her. Around a curve in the road, a gaggle of children was weaving toward them on bicycles. To judge from the books and lunch boxes piled in the bikes' baskets, they were returning home from school, but they braked when they reached the two riders. To Vanessa's surprise, they all seemed to know Dr. Bowen, who graciously reined his horse long enough to chat about one child's new puppy and the calf another boy's family had just acquired. Vanessa had to suppress her amusement at the obvious curiosity Taylor's unidentified female companion aroused.

"Do you really know everyone on this island, or does it just seem that way?" Vanessa asked with a grin after they had waved goodbye to the children and turned off the pavement onto a shady trail.

Taylor shrugged. "Parloe is so small, I suppose everyone's path crosses sooner or later."

Vanessa nodded as she ducked to avoid a trailing strand of Spanish moss. "I know what you mean. The town I grew up in was so tiny, everyone not only knew everyone else, they knew everything *about* everyone else."

"You don't sound as if you liked that very much," Taylor ventured.

Vanessa sighed and looked down at the reins loosely curving over the pommel. "Montebello, South Carolina, is not a place for keeping secrets." In spite of her exaggeratedly light tone, she felt a knot tightening inside her, an old familiar pang that had lessened with age but had never entirely gone away. Even after all these years, she could remember exactly how it felt, walking up Main Street, trying to act as if nothing were wrong, trying to ignore the pitying glances, trying not to overhear the embarrassed whispering about Rich Dorsey's bankruptcy and his poor wife and kids.

"Well, that's one secret of yours that's out now. You're from a town called Montebello." Taylor had reined Knight so close to Velvet that his stirrup grazed Vanessa's. "You know, I really don't know anything about you, Vanessa, except that you're Charlotte Dodderidge's great-niece, and you're down here for a vacation."

Vanessa pretended to look straight ahead, but she could feel his penetrating gaze on her. Gathering the reins, she suddenly halted the mare and twisted in the saddle to face Taylor squarely. "And you're only half-right on that count," she told him, looking him straight in the eye. "I'm not between jobs by choice. I lost my job." She waited a moment for the information to sink in, but Taylor only nodded slowly, as if that were not the worst revelation he could imagine.

"You make it sound like a dishonorable discharge," he commented quietly.

Vanessa let the reins sag. "Oh, I don't know how dishonorable it was. After all, advertising is a precarious business. I just feel rather silly that I didn't follow my instincts and start looking before I had to. I had known for some time that my client had been approached by other agencies, but my account supervisor kept assuring me we had nothing to worry about. It turned out we did. When Federated Hospitals went to another agency, there went my job." Her hand fluttered listlessly in the air before dropping onto the pommel.

"That wasn't your fault, Vanessa. I'm sure you were doing a good job. At least it sounds as if you were a hell of a lot more savvy than this supervisor fellow." Taylor leaned over and gave her arm a firm squeeze. "You'll find another job. It just takes time."

"That's what my old colleagues keep telling me. Everyone swears he'd hire me in a flash if the circumstances were right. In the meantime, the bills keep mounting, and I'm still waiting for this agency to land another client and that account to get a bigger budget and so on and so on." Vanessa felt her color rising along with her anger. She had dammed up her frustration for so long, she had permitted it to take control.

Taylor's fingers pressed her elbow insistently. "You've been under a lot of stress, and you need a break. You'll feel better after a few weeks on the island. No problem's insurmountable."

Vanessa was already shaking her head before he had finished. She felt Taylor's cool fingers close beneath her trembling chin. Her eyes were brimming when they met his.

"Whatever has happened to you, there's one thing you should always remember. You're kind and strong and beautiful, and no one, nothing can change that. You're an amazing person, Vanessa, so full of life, with a whole wonderful life ahead of you."

His hands seemed to quiver against her now feverishly warm cheeks, but his luminous eyes were as unswerving as a tranquil gray-green sea. It was a sea she could plunge into, drift on, lose herself in. Everything around that sea seemed to stand still. The surrounding forest receded; the warbling and humming of nature hushed to an almost reverential stillness.

She really didn't know quite what to say, his kindness was so unexpected. But Vanessa felt certain about one thing: something had changed that day and life would never be the same again.

# Chapter Four

Vanessa flipped up the collar of her shirt, bracing herself against the brisk wind skidding across the dock. For as far back as she could remember, the dilapidated shrimping dock had looked as if it were in imminent danger of collapse. Yet here it stood, apparently none the worse for the intervening years, with one of Aunt Charlotte's rusted crab traps still dangling from its ancient pilings.

Shading her eyes from the sharp morning sun, Vanessa gazed across the Waterway. Through the screen of Spanish-moss-draped trees, she could just make out one of the trails Taylor and she had followed the previous day. Their ride had taken on a dreamlike quality in her memory—the two of them wrapped in the quiet isolation of the marsh with time suspended around them. At the thought of Taylor's sun-warmed face hovering close to hers, Vanessa instinctively closed her eyes.

"Miss Dorsey? Yoo-hoo!"

Vanessa's eyes shot open, and she wheeled to see a man waving to her from behind the house. As the man hurried across the lawn, she tried to place the vaguely familiar bespectacled face. "For a minute there, I was afraid you weren't home." His close-set eyes brightened behind his glasses as he waited for her at the end of the dock.

"I was just trying to enjoy a quiet Saturday morning." That came out sounding a trifle churlish, and Vanessa hastily forced a smile.

"I hope you remember me. Paul Tate. With Tate Realty." The man shifted his briefcase and offered his hand.

"Nice to see you again, Mr. Tate." *Of course!* Vanessa thought as she exchanged handshakes with the Charleston real-estate agent to whom Sandy and she had entrusted the house's management five years ago.

"I have just a few things for you here." Balancing the briefcase awkwardly on his knee, he rummaged through it. He handed Vanessa a paper-clipped sheaf of papers and then stepped back, smoothing his hairless crown with one hand. "As you can see, I had to have some repairs taken care of. The shutters needed rehanging, the back steps had rotted out, there were quite a few plumbing problems, a couple of broken windows, and, of course, plenty of yard work, as always."

Vanessa listened to his voice trail off as she scanned the bundle of photocopied receipts. "I hope you deducted any extra expenses from the rent."

" I did. That's why there were no proceeds left from the final month's rent."

Vanessa glanced up at the little man. "I understand."

Mr. Tate cleared his throat and nodded delicately toward the receipts. "I fear, Miss Dorsey, that the cost of repairs actually exceeded the rent I collected."

Vanessa lifted her head. "I'll reimburse you, of course."

"No rush, you understand." Mr. Tate hastened to remedy any perceived insult. He did a quick two-step to keep pace with Vanessa as they headed back to the house. "While we're on the subject of repairs, I think I ought to warn you that the roof is in very poor condition. You'll certainly want to have it replaced now that you'll be staying here."

"I won't be staying in the house," Vanessa cut in. "At least not for long."

"Oh." Mr. Tate glanced down at the grass-stained toes of his white bucks. "Well, I'd certainly be delighted to have an exclusive on the place now that you're ready to sell."

"I'm not ready to sell."

Mr. Tate halted so abruptly, Vanessa was forced to stop, too. "Excuse me, Miss Dorsey, but if I may ask, just what *do* you plan to do with the house?"

Vanessa stared blankly into the puzzled eyes peering from behind the horn-rims. "I haven't decided yet," she confessed. "Wait a second, and I'll write you a check for these repairs." She bolted up the walk to the house before the real-estate agent could pose any more annoying questions.

Just what *did* she plan to do with this great, shambling wreck of a house, anyway? One thing was certain—the house had no intention of holding itself together until she had made up her mind. Vanessa frowned as she checked Mr. Tate's computations and then wrote out a check that hurt.

Vanessa had to tell herself that Mr. Tate was only an innocent bystander when he pocketed the check and reminded her again of the roof's dire condition. These days, even though she had a fat savings account, she felt uncomfortable enough just buying thirty dollars' worth of cleaning products; bankrolling a new roof was simply out of the question, what with her mother's and her sister's need for supplementation.

In spite of her reservations, Vanessa trotted up the stairs to the attic before Mr. Tate's white Riviera had disappeared down the drive. As her flashlight swept the rafters, her heart sank. If anything, the real-estate agent had understated the problem; the roof decking was mottled with dozens of discolored patches while the floor showed traces of myriad dried puddles. Vanessa felt as if she carried the weight of the entire three-story house on her shoulders as she trudged down the steps. The roof needed immediate attention, and her only choice was to patch it herself. With this cheerful thought in mind, she stopped only long enough to sprinkle a few handfuls of oats into Emily's feed bin before jumping into her car and heading for town.

IF THE CONGESTED PARKING LOT was any indication, at least half the island's population had converged on the Palmetto One-Stop that morning. When Vanessa entered the store, she found the aisles thronged with customers and Luke frantically ringing up orders at the cash register.

"Good morning, Miz' Dorsey! How are you doin' today?" He waved a box of shredded wheat in greeting.

"Just fine, thank you," Vanessa fibbed. She hesitated beside the counter, scanning the rows of canned soft drinks and paper towels.

"If you need any help, I'll be with you in a jiffy," Luke assured her, nodding toward the brown paper bag he was rapidly stuffing with both hands.

"Do you have any roofing materials? Shingles, stuff like that?"

Luke nodded his close-cropped head toward the rear of the store. "Sure do! Back there, just past the freezer chest. Between the chicken wire and the PVC pipe."

Chicken wire and PVC pipe! If her former clients at Federated Hospitals could only see her now! Vanessa smiled ruefully as she scooted around a display of agricultural pesticides that partially concealed the ice-cream chest. Two small boys were leaning across the chest, their sneakered toes thumping dully against the cabinet's white enamel flanks while they dug through the assorted frozen treats. Puffs of frosty vapor rose around their reddish-brown heads, but the boys seemed oblivious both to the cold air and the woman trying to squeeze past them.

"Is that a Banana Swirl?" the smaller of the boys demanded. "I want the Banana Swirl!"

"Excuse me," Vanessa muttered. She was doing her best to get past the freezer chest without upsetting the canisters of weevil dust and potato-bug powder, but a flailing denim leg blocked her path. Clearing her throat, she tapped its owner's shoulder lightly. "Excuse me!"

A sharp-featured little face, dotted with freckles, turned to glare up at her. *A holy terror,* she thought to herself, falling back on her mother's pet term for the sort of snickering small boys who had delighted in smuggling toads into her Sunday-school class. Her mother had frequently thanked heaven for giving her two well-behaved girls to raise, and looking down into a pair of brown eyes that fairly glinted with devilment, Vanessa was beginning to see her point. Whomever fate had blessed with this pair of demons had more than a handful.

Still grinning, the boy slid to one side, just enough to allow her to pass. Then he strained on tiptoe, stretching across the chest in an attempt to seize the frozen-yoghurt cone that his companion held just out of his reach.

"No fair, Matt! *I* said dibs on the Banana Swirl!"

Glancing over her shoulder, Vanessa saw the other boy's smile widen with gleeful mischief. "Did not!"

"Did so!" The debate continued as she rounded the jungle gym of stacked PVC pipe.

Still shaking her head, Vanessa stooped and with a finger gingerly scraped some dust from the label binding a stack of fiberglass shingles. She had slipped a shingle from the bundle and was examining its gritty, gray surface when a bright, birdlike voice interrupted her thoughts.

"Looks like someone has a leaky roof."

Vanessa looked up into a pair of round blue eyes set in a round muffin face. "Someone certainly does." She smiled, taking in the woman's pale, unlined skin, which contrasted pleasingly with her thick, snow-white hair.

When the little woman grinned, she reminded Vanessa of a fairy godmother. "You're new around here, aren't you? The name's Cora Henderson."

Vanessa brushed her hand on her jeans before offering it to Cora. "I'm Vanessa Dorsey."

Cora chuckled, folding her arms across the front of her striped knit shirt. "Just moved to the island?"

"Last week, but I'll only be staying here for a little while," Vanessa explained.

The woman's feathery white brows shot up. "Well, if you're renting a house you certainly shouldn't have to repair the roof yourself," she declared indignantly. "Who are you renting from, anyway?" Her keen eyes darted around the store as if they hoped to discover Vanessa's lax landlord cowering behind one of the crowded shelves.

"Actually I own this house, but I'll only be living in it temporarily." She seemed to get into this conversation so frequently, Vanessa wondered why she had not yet found a less convoluted way of getting through it. "Do you live here year-round?" she asked, snatching at a ready-made opportunity to turn the tables. Although Cora's accent was difficult to place, it was definitely not the languorous drawl of a Low-Country native, and Vanessa guessed her to be one of the island's growing number of relocated retirees.

Cora nodded, but before she could share any details about herself, Luke descended on them. "So you've decided to fix up the roof now?" he asked brightly. "I'll bet that old house is going to be a regular showplace by the time you get it all remodeled."

"I didn't *decide* to fix the roof—I don't have any choice if I want to keep it from caving in," Vanessa told him.

"You're remodeling?" Cora's normally smooth face was furrowed in perplexity. "But I thought you said you were just..."

"I am *not* remodeling." Vanessa hastened to set the record straight. She tried to look as if she meant business as she pointed toward the nails. "Now, I would like a pound of those shingle nails and some roofing cement, please. And two packages of the fiberglass shingles."

But her no-nonsense manner had been totally wasted on Luke. Vanessa felt her shoulders sag as he launched into his now familiar account of her genealogy. Cora listened without comment while he went on about Miz'

Charlotte and her once glorious mansion, but the diminutive retiree's eyes seemed to grow even wider in puzzlement.

When Luke hefted the shingles onto his shoulder and led the way to the cash register, Cora fell in step behind him. She smiled as she deposited a carton of milk and a plastic garden sprayer on the counter, but Vanessa could tell she was still mulling over Luke's comments. "I'm glad to see you're interested in preserving one of Parloe's landmarks. Even if you don't plan to live here," Cora was careful to add. Not taking her eyes off Vanessa, she took the paper bag from Luke, briskly shook it open, and placed her two purchases inside it. "Since you own one of the island's historic homes, you ought to get involved with the Parloe Island Committee for Contained Growth."

Vanessa grabbed the bulky bundle of shingles, balancing her handbag and the sack of nails on top of it as best she could. "I'm sure it's a worthwhile organization, but I'm afraid I just don't have the time..."

"The group is just getting organized," Cora explained, snapping her straw purse shut. "But we're planning to meet twice a month at the Presbyterian Senior Center. Do you know where that is?"

"No, but..." The sack of nails began to slide to one side, and Vanessa hastily clamped it against the shingles with her chin.

"Just behind the church, on Scott Road. You can't miss it. All sorts of people are joining. We're going to lobby, write letters, and when we get wind of a new developer sniffing around the island, we'll keep tabs on him." Cora swung the door open and held it for Vanessa.

"Thanks," Vanessa managed to mumble in spite of the nails boring into her chin. "Your group sounds great, but you see I'll probably be moving fairly soon." She gulped and shifted her grasp on the shingles as much as she dared. Damn it! How could she defend herself with her jaw pressed against a bag of shingle nails?

"Hey, Vanessa!"

Still hanging on to the paper bag, Vanessa glanced in the direction of the gas pumps in time to see Taylor Bowen replace the cap on the Cherokee's gas tank. As she waddled toward her car with the load of shingles, he rushed to intercept her.

"Good Lord—you didn't tell me you were planning to replace your roof!" Taylor adroitly seized the shingles.

Vanessa lifted the lid of the Thunderbird's trunk. "It seemed more practical than turning the third floor into a swimming pool the next time it rains," she remarked drily, picking crumbs of shingle dust from her sleeves.

Taylor cocked a brow and grinned as he deposited the shingles in the trunk of Vanessa's car. "Come now. A little water never hurt anyone, or so someone told me once upon a time."

Vanessa glanced up and gave Taylor a tolerant grin. Conditioned as she was to keeping her problems to herself, she had been a bit shocked, in retrospect, by her emotional outpouring to him during their ride around the island. His tender reaction had further complicated matters, and she had spent much time trying to imagine how she would interact with this man who had glimpsed her soul, if only fleetingly, the next time they met. If she had been looking for a mundane, unromantic setting, she could not have found a better spot than the Palmetto One-Stop parking lot with Cora Henderson at her side.

Vanessa slammed the trunk smartly, but before she could think of a witty rejoinder, Cora spoke up. "Vanessa is restoring the old Dodderidge home," she announced proudly. "Isn't that marvelous, Dr. Bowen?"

"It certainly is." Taylor nodded agreement, his face the picture of polite interest, but the twinkle in his green eyes did not escape Vanessa's notice.

Cora shifted the brown paper bag onto her hip and dug into her straw bag. With a triumphant smile, she pulled out a folded piece of yellow paper and shook it open. "Now, isn't that luck? I just happen to have a flyer with me. Let's see. The group meets next Tuesday evening at eight," she read from the yellow paper before thrusting it into Vanessa's unresisting hands. "Everyone will be thrilled when I tell them Charlotte Dodderidge's great-niece is going to be there. I'm so glad we bumped into each other!" Cora was beaming as she walked across the parking apron to a red Volkswagen Rabbit plastered with bumper stickers promoting environmental causes. She was halfway behind the wheel when she paused to throw them a jaunty wave. "See you Tuesday!"

The fingers of Vanessa's right hand fluttered weakly. "'Bye," she muttered, although Cora was now well out of earshot. When she looked back at Taylor, she found his face stretched into an enormous grin.

"When Cora gets the word around that you're renovating the house, people are going to start regarding you as a regular pillar of the community." Leaning back against the trunk of her car, he raised an eyebrow knowingly.

"For the last time, Taylor, I am *not* renovating that house! I simply discovered some leaks," she went on in a more even tone. "I mean, I can't very well just sit there and let the roof fall in." She gestured irritably toward the trunk where the shingles now reposed.

Taylor nodded soberly, but his eyes still sparkled with amusement.

"And there's absolutely no point in my joining this Sensible-growth Society or whatever it's called," she added, giving the yellow flyer a testy shake. She tried to square her shoulders, which still ached from lugging the shingles.

Taylor feigned surprise. "Did I say anything?" he asked innocently.

"No, but you let Cora go on about my restoring the house," she reminded him.

"What was I supposed to do? Tell her you're going to dynamite the place?" When Vanessa stared across the parking lot in exasperation, Taylor continued, "Call it what you like, but the work you've done on that house so far has improved its appearance one hundred percent. For the first time since your great-aunt left, it looks like a house people would love to call home. Lace curtains in the windows, the lamps glowing cozily—" his mouth curved to one side teasingly "—a pet donkey out back..."

Vanessa rolled her eyes. "You've made your point. And now I suppose I'd better go home and get on with my 'restoration.' I'm sure Cora and everyone else would disapprove of any delays."

"I wouldn't. In fact I think your going home right now is the worst idea I've heard all day."

Vanessa regarded him suspiciously. "Really? I thought you were a gung-ho member of the lace-curtain-restoration camp."

"Oh, I am. But I think you should come sailing with me this afternoon. My dad lives on the basin, and I keep a little sailboat docked at his place. It's a rare occasion when I have a free day *and* a good stiff breeze, and I'm determined not to waste this one. Your roof will be there tomorrow and the next day and the day after that."

"Don't be so sure. It looked as if it just might disintegrate if we get another good rain."

Taylor frowned good-naturedly. "It isn't going to rain, not with our new intern covering for me at the clinic so that I can take the whole day off."

Vanessa felt herself being pulled toward the Cherokee by a force as inexorable as the tides governing Parloe's ever-changing shoreline. But something more complicated than the leaky roof held her back. If she feared becoming sidetracked on Parloe, distracting herself from her job hunt with house repairs and orphaned donkeys, how much more treacherous was her attraction to Taylor Bowen? And she *was* attracted to him. After that conversation they had shared, trying to couch their acquaintance in casual terms had become an act of utter futility.

"Thanks for the invitation, but I can't risk any more damage to the roof."

"Come on," Taylor wheedled. "Tell you what, I'll even give you a hand with the repairs if you'll put them off until tomorrow."

Vanessa blinked, taken by surprise by his offer, but she had already fished her keys out of her bag. She hesitated for a moment, squeezing the keys like a talisman against her palm, and then sighed. "I'd love to,

Taylor, but I really can't," she said as she slid behind the wheel. She stuck her head out the window and managed to smile before starting the ignition. "Have fun," she called, trying to sound lighthearted.

Taylor smiled back—looking a little crestfallen, Vanessa thought—and then stuffed his hands into the pockets of his bleached duck pants. She fumbled with her keys and shifted gears, only to look up and find him still standing there with his hands in his pockets. It was amazing how that simple gesture could make a man of such unequivocal masculinity suddenly look like a dejected little boy. Vanessa drew a deep breath. Then she shifted into park again before switching the ignition off.

"You've convinced me the roof can wait," she said, climbing out of the car. "After all, a little water never hurt anyone."

Taylor's hearty laughter carried across the crowded parking lot. "That was easy—a battle won without firing a shot."

Vanessa held her grin in check and lifted a warning finger. "But if it rains I'm going to hold you accountable."

"Fair enough," Taylor agreed happily. Dropping his arm around her shoulders, he guided her toward the Cherokee. "Why don't you leave your car here? I'll just take a minute to collect my boys, and then we'll be on our way."

Vanessa halted abruptly in her tracks. "Your *boys*?" she began, but Taylor had already released his hold on her shoulders and was heading toward the store.

When the One-Stop's door flew open, he waved energetically. "Over here, guys!" he called. As he turned back to Vanessa, he was beaming. "Vanessa, I'd like you to meet Matt and Denny."

Vanessa did her best to smile, but she could scarcely conceal her incredulity. For, standing there with their arms linked through Taylor's, their eyes still gleaming deviltry, their grinning mouths still rimmed with traces of Banana Swirl frozen yoghurt, were the two holy terrors.

# Chapter Five

Vanessa's eyes traveled uncertainly from one grinning, rust-sprinkled face to the other before she caught herself. "Uh, yeah, hi, fellows!" Her mouth angled into a lopsided grin. For some reason, she had never pictured Taylor as a father. His sudden revelation that he not only possessed children, but two of such a lively bent, came as a great surprise.

"Hi!" the boys chorused. They seemed not in the least fazed by the tall woman gaping at them, for they immediately refocused their attention on Taylor and the business at hand.

"Are we going back into the marsh to fish today?" the taller of the two piped up. "'Cause if we are, we need to get some bait."

"No, we don't, Matt!" the younger one countered. "I got my worms!" His small face screwed into a frown for a moment as he searched the pockets of his blue nylon jacket. Pulling a mass of jiggling, red-rubber lures from his pocket, he beamed in triumph. "See?" He held the worms aloft for Vanessa's inspection.

"Um. Nice."

Taylor settled a firm hand on each boy's shoulder. "No fishing today, fellows." Seeing their faces fall, he cocked his head to one side and eyed them skeptically. "Hey, all I've been hearing is 'when are we going sailing?' And now we have a perfect sail day, and you're suddenly dead set on fishing."

Denny wistfully studied the latex worms cupped in his hand. Then his face brightened. "Let's do *both*!"

"Yeah!" Matt chimed in without hesitation.

Taylor chuckled and gave their reedy shoulders a shake. "Maybe you can talk Dad into some fishing, okay? Now let's get moving, or we're not going to have time to do much of anything."

As though they were sprinters jumping the gun at the starting block, the boys broke free of Taylor's clasp and made a dash for the Jeep. Taylor watched them, a gentle smile softening the lean lines of his face, as they clambered into the back seat. Then he turned back to Vanessa.

"At their age it's easy to get carried away," he apologized.

Vanessa gave him an understanding nod. "How old are your sons?"

Taylor grinned down at his arms folded across his chest, as if he were enjoying some private joke. When he looked up at her, he looped an arm around her shoulders and gently tugged her closer to him. "For the record, Matt is ten and Denny is a couple of years behind him, but..." His voice dropped dramatically, and he leaned to whisper in her ear. "They aren't really my kids—they're my Little Brothers."

Vanessa frowned and pulled to a halt, resisting the pressure of his arm, while her mind grappled with the twenty-odd-year gap separating Taylor from his younger siblings.

Taylor could restrain his laughter no longer. "You see, I'm a volunteer with the county's Big Brother program. As you probably know, Big Brothers matches people like me with kids like Matt and Denny, boys who have lost their fathers and need someone to fill that role in their lives. We get together regularly on weekends, go riding or sailing. Sometimes we take in a movie or a ball game on the mainland. It's no big deal really, just simple companionship."

"That sounds pretty important to me," Vanessa corrected.

Taylor conceded a diffident smile, but before he could comment, a reddish-brown head jutted from one of the Jeep's rear windows. "We're ready," Matt informed them with a hint of impatience.

"Coming!" Taylor called. Tightening his clasp on Vanessa's shoulders, he led her to the Jeep and held the door open for her.

From the front seat, Vanessa watched his tall figure round the hood of the Jeep and then slide behind the wheel. As he inserted the key into the ignition, he glanced over his shoulder. "All buckled up? Remember, I don't want any of my crew to sail out the window if we hit a bump."

Denny was frowning over the uncooperative seat-belt catch, but he giggled at Taylor's whimsical remark. When Vanessa shifted in her seat, she caught a glimpse of the fond look passing across Taylor's face. It was a complicated expression, a tender amalgam of care and affection and, yes, wistfulness. *He's proud of them,* she thought, settling back against the seat with a gentle smile of her own.

"Did you tell your mom you would be eating with us this evening?" Taylor aimed the question at the back seat as he wheeled the Jeep onto the road.

In the rearview mirror, Vanessa could see both tousled heads bob in confirmation.

Taylor gave Vanessa a sly wink. "I hope Emily will understand if you stay for supper, too, Vanessa."

"I imagine she's pretty tolerant about such things. But then you never can tell." Vanessa frowned and pretended to consider the matter. "She's gotten used to having me there all the time, and you know how stubborn her kind can be."

"If she gives you a hard time, I'll have a word with her," Taylor volunteered.

Vanessa could feel Matt's feet pressing against the back of her seat. The sneakers scuffed impatiently against the vinyl upholstery as the boy leaned forward. "Who's Emily?" he demanded, no longer able to contain his curiosity.

"A good friend of mine." Vanessa shot a mysterious glance over her shoulder. Catching the open-mouthed consternation reflected on both boys' faces she broke down. "Actually, Emily is a donkey who is presently living with me."

"A donkey? That's neat!" Matt declared. His small feet performed a shuffle across the seat back. "Can you ride her?"

Vanessa chuckled. "No. At least, I wouldn't want to try."

"Taylor has a horse named Knight. I've ridden him, too," Denny offered proudly. "All by myself."

Apparently, some of the brothers' more memorable outings with Taylor had involved grooming and riding his horse, and Vanessa contented herself with sitting back and letting the two boys regale her with stories about Knight. She was nodding sympathetically over Denny's account of trying to lift and clean one of the horse's iron-shod hooves when Taylor pulled into a sandy drive, flanked by giant yucca and oleander. At the sight of a white gingerbread gable jutting up among the palmetto fronds, the boys immediately dropped their narrative and squirmed free of the seat belts.

Unwilling and unable to restrain their youthful enthusiasm, Vanessa held the seat forward to let them out of the Jeep. After she had alighted at a more sedate pace, she paused and looked around. It was a lovely setting for a house: far enough from the main road to be shielded from traffic and tourists, close enough to the basin to hear the gently lapping waves. The house itself, she now realized, was quite new. Although its Victorian cupolas and wide encircling veranda harked back to another era, the two-story sun room and double garage bore the unmistakable stamp of a modern architect's hand.

Vanessa smiled appreciatively as she spun around for another inspection of the naturally landscaped yard. When she turned back to Taylor, she saw a tall man ambling down the drive toward them.

"Something tells me if we don't get a move on, Matt and Denny will have sailed halfway to the Bahamas without us." The man chuckled as he clapped a large hand on Taylor's shoulder, but his gray-green eyes were focused on Vanessa. Although his dark blond hair gleamed with silvery streaks that could not entirely be attributed to the sun, his trim build would have been the envy of many men half his age.

Taylor smiled, with recognizable pride. "Vanessa, this is my father, Stewart Bowen. Dad, I'd like you to meet Vanessa Dorsey. Vanessa is Charlotte Dodderidge's great-niece.''

For once, Vanessa did not have to fight the urge to roll her eyes at the now familiar tag line that invariably accompanied her introduction. She guessed Taylor's father to be in his mid-sixties, just the right age to remember the vivacious Charlotte Dodderidge in her prime. He was the sort of man her great-aunt would have deemed a true gentleman and, like Aunt Charlotte, he probably valued old family lines. As she exchanged a firm handshake with the elder Bowen, she was struck by how much the island aristocrat he looked, in spite of his roomy khaki pants and frayed work shirt.

"I'm glad you could join us today, Vanessa. I often think of Miss Charlotte and that little rascal Peekaboo.'' Stewart Bowen chuckled softly, letting his eyes follow the grid of small footprints preceding them along the sandy drive. "Hold up there, fellows!'' he called, throwing up his hand as they rounded the house. "I hope Taylor has cautioned you that things can be pretty hectic when Matt and Denny are around. They're a couple of demons, no two ways about it.''

True to their reputation, the boys had already peeled the canvas cover from the dry-docked sailboat and climbed aboard. Legs braced across the narrow prow, Matt struck the swaggering pose of a buccaneer, while his brother crouched in the stern and thumped a vigorous drum roll against the craft's sides.

"All right, mates! Stand clear!'' Taylor commanded, striding up to the boat with uncompromising nautical authority. Both boys jumped to the ground, but they hovered at his side as he leaned over the small boat and checked its interior. Vanessa watched him examine the coiled rigging with the same methodical care he brought to his veterinary work. Giving a final firm tug to one of the lines, he waved to his father and Vanessa. "Come on, everyone, or you're going to miss the boat."

"The boat can set sail without this old landlubber, thank you." Dr. Bowen chuckled as he stooped to take inventory of the life jackets stowed beneath the boat's seat. Shaking open one of the pint-size jackets, he held it for Denny. "While you young folks are out there tossing around on the waves, getting soaked to the bone, I'm going to enjoy a nice, quiet hour or two of fishing."

Denny hesitated with his arm poked halfway through the orange vest's armhole. "You think you'll catch anything, Grandpa Bowen?" he asked in a deceptively meek tone.

As Dr. Bowen slid the vest around Denny's narrow shoulders, he shot Vanessa and Taylor a surreptitious wink. "Maybe. Maybe not. 'Course, if you get through sailing in time, you can always come down to the dock and try your luck with me. I'm sure there'll be a few fish left." Grinning down into the freckled face, he adjusted the life jacket's Velcro fasteners.

Denny seemed satisfied with the arrangement, for he now turned to the sailboat with renewed enthusiasm. Although the fiberglass boat was so light that Vanessa could easily have pushed it down the beach to the water alone, Taylor let both boys lend a hand. Crouching to roll up her slacks and remove her shoes—a task Matt and Denny had accomplished with lightning speed—she watched from a safe distance while the two boys churned up enough surf to launch a super-tanker. When the roiling waves had subsided, she waded out to join them.

"Have you ever sailed one of these things?" Taylor asked. The grasp of his hand contrasted pleasingly with the cold water surging against her bare legs as he helped Vanessa board the swaying craft.

Vanessa steadied herself against the mast, and grinned. "Back when I lived in New York, I once took the Staten Island ferry, just for the heck of it. I suppose that doesn't exactly qualify me as a sailor though, does it?"

"Never can tell." When Taylor stretched to run the sail up, his shirt tail flapped around his lean, bare midriff. "Here, loop this line around that hook." He handed Vanessa a coiled rope and then swung back behind the unfurled sail.

"Is that tight enough?" Vanessa kept a white-knuckled grip on the rope.

When Taylor's face reappeared from behind the red-and-white sail, it wore a broad smile. "That's just great. Matt, do you remember how to tie a knot the way I showed you?" But Matt had already relieved Vanessa of the rope and was busily weaving it into an intricate knot.

"See, it goes like this. And then you pull it through here." Matt gave the white nylon line a deft twist and then sat back on his heels.

Vanessa nodded appreciatively. In truth, the nautical knot remained as incomprehensible to her as a Chinese brain-twister, but she was quick to praise Matt's ability. Since her introduction to Taylor's Little Brothers on the One-Stop's parking lot, Vanessa had gradually amended her initial judgment of the two holy terrors. They were active boys, all right, and certainly capable of getting into scrapes if given half the chance. But in her short association with Matt and Denny, Vanessa had sensed that beneath the smeared frozen yoghurt and freckled-imp grins, they were a couple of good-hearted kids.

That Taylor shared this opinion of the boys was evident. As the light sailboat skimmed across the sun-glazed basin, he took pains to show them the various techniques required to pilot the boat, patiently answering every one of their innumerable questions. With the quicksilver attention span typical of bright youngsters, Matt and Denny's conversation ricocheted from one topic to the next with scarcely a pause for breath; one second Matt was recounting the history of Taylor's sailboat, the next minute their attention was riveted on the school of fish Denny had spotted rippling beneath the water.

When Vanessa pointed out a brown pelican wheeling overhead, both boys craned to follow the bird's dive-bomber descent. She felt strangely pleased, watching the boys giggle as the ungainly bird chopped through the water and then surfaced with a gullet full of fish. Although Vanessa liked children, so far her life had afforded her few opportunities to interact with them. Starting a family had been one issue that Jeff had taken elaborate measures to circumvent, and the pressures of her own career had convinced her to postpone motherhood until some indefinite time in the future. Yet, now she was startled to realize just how very much she wanted to be a part of this little group, wanted to contribute to and share in the elective family that Taylor Bowen had formed for himself.

Vanessa felt a warm surge beneath her sun-heated skin when Taylor smiled at her, wrinkling his nose against the glare. He had never looked more handsome, with the wind lifting his hair and sculpting the thin shirt against his well-muscled torso. But as she pondered her feelings, Vanessa realized that they stemmed from a deeper source than mere sexual attraction. Watching him gently shadow Denny's efforts to maneuver the sail, his face full of care and pride as his hands steadied the small shoulders, she felt an odd pinch in her throat. At that moment, she knew that if he were the homeliest man on earth, she would still have thought him beautiful.

Thanks to Denny's budding seamanship, they were able to guide the boat back into the cove surrounding Stewart Bowen's fishing dock. Taylor ran the sailboat into the shallows long enough for Denny to spring over the side and splash to the dock.

"Catch us something for dinner!" Vanessa called as the boat was once more swept out into the basin.

As soon as Dr. Bowen had hoisted him on deck, Denny nodded and waved eagerly to the retreating boat. He looked decidedly dejected, however, when the craft scudded to shore a half-hour later.

"I guess they weren't biting today, huh?" Taylor looked up from the tarpaulin he was pulling over the boat and surveyed the empty fishing line sympathetically.

"No, I guess not." Denny dropped the line onto the edge of the boardwalk leading to the house, and shrugged.

"Looks like we'll just have to make do with hamburgers, then," Dr. Bowen announced, giving Denny's reddish-brown cowlick a furtive brush.

Denny's fifteen-second fit of despondency vanished at the mention of the magic word. "Oh, boy! Hamburgers!"

Vanessa was squatting on the edge of the walk, scraping sand from between her toes. The weathered planks vibrated beneath her as Matt and Denny pelted past, their vast energy reserves not in the least depleted by two hours of activity in the bracing salt air.

At the bottom of the wooden steps leading up to the rear veranda, Matt paused for a second. "We've got chocolate-chip cookies, too, Vanessa!" she heard him call to her before he raced up the steps after his brother.

Vanessa looked up from lacing her sneakers to yell back. "Terrific!"

"Maybe you ought to reserve judgment until you've sampled one. Neither Dad nor I could be called the greatest cook in the world," Taylor commented quietly. He stooped to offer her a hand.

His hand felt surprisingly warm as it clasped her chilly fingers. "Matt and Denny seem to think you do a creditable job."

"Yeah, but they're prejudiced," he protested with a laugh.

"Maybe I am, too," Vanessa remarked, venturing a glance up into the suntanned face that inclined, ever so slightly, over her shoulder.

Taylor only smiled, but his fingers tightened around her hand in a silently eloquent squeeze.

When they reached the veranda, they found Matt already heaping charcoal briquettes into an outdoor grill while Denny supervised his brother's labors from atop the porch rail. Taylor moved swiftly to get the fire-building situation under control, but Vanessa lingered at the top of the steps. She looked around when a theatrical cough sounded from the doorway.

"Okay. Who's responsible for the smoke signals?" Stewart Bowen was grinning as he carefully guided a butcher-block service cart over the threshold.

"*He* is!" the boys chorused gleefully, but the blackened fingers they pointed at Taylor left their accusation open to question.

"Just as I thought." Taylor's father nodded and then turned to exchange a knowing look with Vanessa. "I think we'd best leave the barbecuing to the experts."

"I never pass up the opportunity to let someone else do the cooking." Vanessa chuckled as she accompanied Dr. Bowen into the big, country kitchen. Following his instructions, she rummaged through an oak hutch and found crockery, gingham place mats, and napkins. She had just finished setting the table when the door flew open, admitting a wave of burnt-charcoal fumes and the herd of hungry cooks.

"The hamburgers are done!" Matt's sneakers squeaked against the Italian tiles as he rushed to Dr. Bowen's side.

Stewart Bowen nudged the boy's shoulder in a fashion that could only be described as grandfatherly, but he quickly turned back to Vanessa, swept a chair back from the oak table, and held it for her.

Vanessa smiled as she slid onto the chair and shook out the blue-and-white-checked napkin. "Everything looks delicious." Her eyes traveled from the platter of charred patties to the two young chefs, but she couldn't resist a wink at the rather sheepish-looking Taylor.

In all honesty, Vanessa could find nothing amiss with the simple dinner they shared in the big, homey kitchen. Not even the slightly overcooked burgers or the two kids giggling and nudging each other under the table could detract from the warmth and geniality of the Bowens' table. Great-aunt Charlotte had always regarded hospitality as a hallmark of good breeding, and Vanessa felt certain that both Stewart and Taylor Bowen would have more than satisfied her criterion.

Vanessa was not surprised when the conversation eventually came around to Charlotte Dodderidge. "You know, I think Miss Charlotte would be really proud to know that one of Richard's girls was living in her house," Dr. Bowen remarked as he offered her the casserole of baked beans.

Vanessa nodded and scooped a serving of the molasses-lacquered beans onto her plate. "I like to think so."

"You may not know it, but your father and I palled around together one summer when he was down here staying with Charlotte, he and I and a bunch of other island kids. Used to fish off your great-aunt's dock together—that was back when the shrimp were so plentiful, folks used 'em for bait. Can you believe we kids tramped through the marsh *barefoot*? It's a miracle some water moccasin didn't sink its fangs into one of those scrawny little feet." Stewart Bowen leaned back in his chair and chuckled softly, his eyes focused on some indefinite point across the table.

"Mom won't let us go barefoot," Matt commented, but Dr. Bowen only nodded absently.

"I'm often sorry I didn't keep up with your father. He was always looking for an adventure, always seemed to have such big ideas. I guess he never outgrew it, though. He ended up with his own business, didn't he?" Dr. Bowen directed an approving smile at Vanessa.

Vanessa cleared her throat and quickly blotted her lips with the napkin. *He ended up bankrupt.* "Yes, he did." She stabbed the dill-pickle spear remaining on her plate and began to saw a chunk from it as if her life depended on it.

"Oh really? What sort of business? Advertising?" Taylor leaned toward her, casually jiggling the ice cubes in his glass.

"No. Appliances. He had a chain of appliance stores." *Until he went broke and the bank padlocked them.* The pickle tasted so sour, Vanessa felt her mouth pucker.

"That's so like Rich. He wouldn't be content with just one store—he'd have to own a whole chain." Stewart Bowen laughed and shook his head. Then his handsome face sobered. "I was terribly sorry to hear that he had passed away, very sorry."

Vanessa managed a nod and then reached for her glass. As the cola flooded her mouth, its syrupy flavor mingled with the pickle's brine. She swallowed with great effort.

"Are you all right, Vanessa?" Head cocked to one side, Taylor peered up into her face.

Vanessa was dismayed by his concerned expression and immediately reassured him. "I'm fine. Just take my advice—pickles and Pepsi don't mix." She smiled, coaxing the tension from her face.

Over the years, she had often tried to fool herself into thinking that her father's wild speculation, which had kept his family on a perpetual roller coaster, and the resulting bankruptcy, no longer troubled her. But those delusions never lasted for long, as the Bowens' innocent questions had plainly shown her tonight. At least they had been satisfied with the bareboned information she had volunteered, she congratulated herself as she helped Taylor clear away the ketchup-spattered plates. Tossing the potato-chip crumbs into the trash can, she reminded herself that, all in all, it had been a delightful evening.

True, Taylor had spent most of it presiding over the temperamental charcoal fire and bantering with the two boys, but Vanessa had been struck anew by the enormously potent appeal of this man who could share so generously of himself. Small wonder that Matt and Denny's grins faded—for the first time since they had scrambled into the Cherokee that morning—when Taylor announced that it was time for them to go home.

"Come on, guys," he cajoled, ruffling both sandy heads. "You don't want your mom to think we've gotten lost in the marsh, do you?"

"She knows you wouldn't *ever* get lost," Denny scoffed, but he obediently collected his rumpled, blue-nylon jacket.

At the front door, the boys paused to bid Taylor's father good-night. The elder Bowen's eyes were twinkling as he casually leaned against the door frame, folding his arms across his chest. "You know, I've been thinking that maybe you boys would like to come with me to that exhibition basketball game in Charleston next weekend. That is, if you can find the time."

A chorus of exuberant hoots quickly dispelled any doubt on that matter. Taylor gave Vanessa a private wink as he held open the door of the Jeep, but during the drive to the boys' home he seemed happy to remain in the background while they laid elaborate plans for their outing to Charleston.

"We crossed this road during our ride on Wednesday, didn't we?" Vanessa asked, peering out into the dusk-shrouded marsh.

"Uh-huh, on our way to the basin. For someone who couldn't even find her own home a week ago, you've learned your way around pretty quickly," Taylor teased.

For once, Vanessa felt no compulsion to think of a humorous retort. She only grinned as Taylor edged the Jeep off the road. He eased to a stop in front of a small brown-shingled bungalow with a rusted orange Beetle parked in its unpaved drive.

Like the vintage car, the house showed signs of age that were now all too familiar to Vanessa, but the window boxes filled with vivid geraniums helped to brighten its weathered exterior. Still, she could not help but notice how badly the fence sagged and how desperately the house needed painting. As she leaned forward to allow the boys out of the Jeep, the screen door squeaked on its hinges, and a woman stepped into the porch light's yellow pool. The woman leaned wearily against the door, but when she spotted her sons racing up the walk her tight face broke into a smile. When Taylor emerged from the Jeep, she threw up her hand and waved.

"Grace cooks the day shift at the seafood restaurant down by the docks," Taylor explained, resting one knee on the driver's seat. "I know she must be dead tired tonight, but I'm sure she'd like to meet you. We'll only stay a minute."

"Fine." Vanessa popped the seat-belt catch and climbed out of the Cherokee. But as she approached the low porch, she felt a poignant jolt of recognition. Something in the tired, almost melancholy smile of the boys' mother evoked an echo in Vanessa's mind, an old but unfaded memory of another woman's smile, fraught with care.

Matt had already disappeared into the little house, but Denny was leaning back against his mother's waist, his chin cradled in her large-boned hands. As Vanessa and Taylor mounted the rickety porch steps, she looked up, but the loving smile she had focused on her youngest lingered on her face. She relinquished her clasp on his small jaw and stretched her cardigan closed across her chest while Taylor made introductions.

"Grace, I'd like you to meet Vanessa Dorsey. Vanessa, meet Grace Burch, mom to the two greatest kids on Parloe and cook of the best batter-fried shrimp in the world."

"C'mon now, Taylor. I reckon my boys are pretty special, but if my cookin' was *that* good, I'd have long since moved on to one of those fancy restaurants in Charleston. Anyhow, I'm certainly pleased to meet you, Vanessa." In contrast to her sturdy build, the woman's voice was surprisingly delicate, almost girlish. Contrary to her initial impression, Vanessa now judged Grace to be close to her own age. Her fine-featured face was more interesting than pretty, its strong angles revealing the shadows of stress, but her dark eyes were bright and direct, with a flicker of that spirit Great-aunt Charlotte would have termed 'saucy.'

Taking a step backward, Grace tugged at the hem of her baggy cotton sweater and then gestured cordially toward the door. "You're welcome to come in and visit for a spell. I'm afraid you'll just have to excuse the mess. I've worked a couple of double shifts this past week, and haven't had much time to straighten up," she added, pulling the screen door open a few inches.

Vanessa gave Grace a warm smile, but a slight uneasiness stirred in her as she followed Taylor into the tiny living room. Stepping across the threshold, she felt as if she had traveled back twenty years in time, back to another neat but shabby house, full of castoffs and threadbare furniture, and she almost winced at the pain those memories evoked.

Matt had draped himself across the maroon sofa and was squinting at a television set poised on a cheap metal table. Taylor dropped down beside him and immediately began to share *Star Trek* trivia, but Vanessa hung back near the door. While she chatted with Grace, she pretended not to notice the drab furniture or the many worn spots in the faded carpet underfoot.

Although Grace liberally sprinkled her own conversation with references to "those two young rascals," she was obviously delighted to hear Vanessa praise her sons.

When Taylor ambled over to the door, he was trailed by Matt and Denny. "We'd better get going, Vanessa. If I'm not mistaken, it's already well past these young men's bedtime."

Vanessa smiled down at the boys and then at Grace, but as she stepped outside, she took a hungry gulp of the salt-flavored night air.

"Good night!" Taylor's voice sounded jarringly hearty as he leaned across the seat of the jeep they climbed into. Easing back behind the wheel, he caught Vanessa's eye. "Tired?"

"Just a little," Vanessa quickly reassured him, throwing in a bright smile for good measure.

"Matt and Denny are quite a pair, aren't they?" he remarked after they had driven some distance down the unlighted road. His chuckle sounded especially rich and throaty inside the dark Jeep. "I hope they didn't wear on your nerves too badly."

"Not at all. I found them lively—but very nice kids. I enjoyed being around them," she told him honestly.

"I suspect that you and your father have really helped them a lot."

Taylor squinted into the beam of an approaching truck. "I just wish we could find a way to help their mother. Since her husband was killed in a car accident, that poor woman has worked her hands to the bone and still only makes ends meet. It's really a shame. I feel sorry for her."

Vanessa felt an uncomfortable warmth seeping into her cheeks. She too had felt for Grace.

Taylor, fortunately, seemed oblivious to her discomfiture. "But you won't find anyone on this island with more pride than Grace Burch," he went on, shaking his head. "That woman's backbone stiffens at the very mention of charity. If I buy anything for the boys, I'm always careful to slip it in, very casually, so as not to offend her." He shook his head again as he shifted gears.

Vanessa watched her own face, suddenly illuminated in the windshield by the lights of a passing car, as its muscles tightened. She was careful to clear her throat before she spoke. "I imagine if you were in her position, you wouldn't take too kindly to people pitying you and giving you things," she suggested as lightly as possible.

"It isn't a question of pity," Taylor protested. As he checked the rearview mirror, the lines furrowing his brow were cast into relief by the clear moonlight. "If you care about people, you want to help them out. It's as simple as that."

*It's anything but simple.* Vanessa shifted in the seat and regarded the handsome man frowning at the road stretching in front of the headlights. She could well appreciate Grace Burch's reservations about accepting gifts, regardless of the good intentions that accompanied them.

After all, hadn't her own mother stoically refused even Great-aunt Charlotte's assistance after Dad's death? And how many times had Sandra and she returned from a summer on the island with new blouses and lace-trimmed nightgowns secreted in their suitcases? They had wanted the pretty things badly enough to heed Great-aunt Charlotte's admonition not to tell their mother, but they had felt guilty accepting them, all the same.

Vanessa glanced to the side and smiled gently. Dear, good-hearted Taylor! His face looked so direct and open and kind as his eyes followed the silvery-white ribbon dissecting the highway. Like Great-aunt Charlotte, he would never be able to understand that not only was it better to give than to receive, but also a lot easier.

The Jeep eased to a stop. Vanessa had to blink twice before she recognized the One-Stop's parking lot, deserted now save for her Thunderbird and a truck backed up to the diesel pump. The store windows glowed with a fluorescent intensity that contrasted with the unrelieved darkness blanketing the surrounding woods, but when she looked at Taylor, his face seemed to glow with a natural radiance of its own. Suddenly, Vanessa experienced a crosscurrent of conflicting emotions, a potent mixture of reawakened childhood memories and the yearnings of an adult woman.

Taylor had switched off the engine, and she could feel his virile warmth as he moved closer to her. At first his hand rested lightly, almost tentatively, on her shoulder. Then he reached over and opened the door for her. "I suppose we should say good-night?" His low-pitched voice rose in a question, but he leaned back slightly, as if he already knew the answer. "We'll want to get started early on that roof tomorrow." His hand gave her shoulder a gentle squeeze and then withdrew, but something in that quick grasp reassured her.

"I'd almost forgotten." Vanessa laughed softly, letting some of the tension ease from her limbs.

"Good night, then." Taylor cradled her hand lightly and let his lips drift across her forehead.

"Good night." Vanessa closed her eyes, the better to savor the caress of his lips and the complex feelings their pressure elicited. Then without further ado, she climbed out and waved as he revved his engine and drove off into the night.

# Chapter Six

"Hello?" A yawn blurred the drowsy greeting.

"Sandy? This is Vanessa."

"Van?" The voice brightened slightly, struggling to dispel its torpor.

"Yeah. Remember me? Your sister?" Vanessa teased. "I'm sorry if I woke you," she added contritely.

"Oh, that's okay," Sandy hastened to assure her. "I just pulled an all-nighter studying for an exam, but I certainly can't afford to loll away today in bed. Anyway, I've been expecting to hear from you. Are you settled, all comfy and cozy, in Great-aunt Charlotte's house?"

Vanessa's groan tapered off into a laugh. "Let's just say settled, and hold off on the comfy-cozy business for the time being. You would *not* have believed the way the house looked when I walked in here last week. Mildew and cobwebs all over everything, every faucet dripping, the furniture buried in dust. Yech!" Vanessa wrinkled her nose and giggled. "Oh, and I even found a stray donkey hiding in the garage!"

"Must be a real three-ring circus. Although, you don't seem too terribly upset about it." Sandra sounded amused.

"In a way it's been kind of fun, puttering around the house. The only real problem at this point is the leaky roof, and I have a friend coming over this morning to help me patch it." Vanessa allowed a hint of her buoyant smile to carry over into her voice, and she caught herself. Where Taylor was concerned, her feelings were so complex and confusing she scarcely knew how to explain them to herself, much less to someone else, even Sandra. For now, she preferred to keep her attraction to him private, and she moved to change the subject. "How does the summer-job scene look?"

"So-so, but for heaven's sake don't pass that on to Mom when you talk with her. I fudged a bit and told her I'd already anchored down a research assistant's job for the summer. Actually, it was just a gray lie—something is bound to come through before the end of the term. But I didn't want her to fret, and you know how she is."

"I bet she's tearing her hair out, scared to death that I'll never find another job, right? I hope you told her I was doing okay."

"I did, but she would probably rather hear it from you."

Vanessa clamped her lip between her teeth. "I've been putting off calling her until I had some good news to report. I really think that Steve's agency will probably have a job for me soon," she declared with a vehemence that was more than a little suspect.

"I hope so, Van."

"Trust me, Sandy. I swear I'll be able to fill in the gaps for your tuition next year." Urgency put a husky edge on Vanessa's voice.

"I want you to find a job for your *own* sake, Van! You really deserve a break. As far as school is concerned, I'll manage somehow."

"We'll see that you do better than just manage." Vanessa knew such promises bordered on bravado, but she was desperate to reassure her sister.

"Don't worry about me," Sandy scolded her good-naturedly. "I'll take hitting the books over repairing a leaky roof any day of the week."

"You do sound pretty hale and hearty," Vanessa conceded, unable to resist her sister's teasing. "Especially for someone who probably hasn't had more than two hours of sleep."

"Three hours," Sandra corrected with a laugh. "But it's been really good talking with you."

"Then I won't apologize again for waking you."

"I'll catch you next week. In the meantime, have fun hammering away on the roof."

"I'll try," Vanessa said, then quickly added, "'Bye."

She smiled across the room, watching the lace curtains billow and float on the light breeze. But as her eyes drifted slowly back to the desk, they fell on the folder of resumés and letters lying beside her typewriter. Vanessa slipped off the desk and gave the messy stack of papers a hard look. Although she had been quick to assure her sister that a job offer lay just around the corner, the reality of her situation was far less rosy. Since her arrival on Parloe, she had heard nothing from any of her contacts. The knowledge that poor Sandra was scrounging for a lab job that probably paid a mere pittance only added to her frustration. No, she could not afford to rely on luck and the fickle commitment of old colleagues; it was time to make something happen.

Vanessa unsnapped the typewriter lid, thrust a sheet of bond into the machine, and slapped the paper bail into place. Opening the file folder, she shuffled through her correspondence until she found Steve Czerny's letter. He had sounded fairly encouraging—perhaps not as encouraging as she had led Sandy to believe—but his promise to keep her in mind if he heard of any openings certainly warranted another strong follow-up from her. Fired by desperation, Vanessa had pounded out the better part of a page when the old-fashioned doorbell's brittle ring interrupted her.

"Coming!" Vanessa grimaced at the typo she had just made and then reluctantly got up from the desk. With head thrust forward and shoulders squared, she marched to the front door. When she flung it open, she found Taylor, toolbox in hand, beaming at her. Like an antacid tablet dropped into water, Vanessa's frown fizzled into oblivion, leaving behind only the trace of a sheepish smile.

"I was just composing one of my please-hire-me letters," she explained, peeking around the door as she held it open for him. Surely it was only her imagination, but somehow his lightly tanned face seemed handsomer, his rangy body outlined by the comfortable work clothes more sensual, his smile even less resistible than she recalled from the previous evening.

"If you like, you can finish it before we start on the roof. I'm in no hurry today," Taylor suggested affably. His green eyes swept the now spanking clean foyer appreciatively before settling on Vanessa with a directness that made her feel surprisingly vulnerable.

"The letter can wait. Let's get started on the roof." Creeping over a steeply pitched roof was not something Vanessa would have chosen to do for entertainment, but she was surprised at how much more appealing the activity appeared compared to hustling Steve for a job yet again.

"Hold on," Taylor called as she turned toward the porch.

Vanessa halted and looked back at him questioningly.

"We need to have a look at the attic first. Then we'll know exactly where to work when we get out on the roof," Taylor explained.

"Oh, okay. Remember, I'm a novice at this home-repair stuff. I don't know beans about roofing." Vanessa walked back into the house and paused at the foot of the stairs.

"Yeah, but just think—a week ago you didn't know beans about donkeys, and now you're practically an expert," Taylor reminded her with a waggish grin.

Vanessa pulled a face over her shoulder. Then she grabbed the bannister and sprinted up the stairs ahead of him, not pausing until she reached the dusty landing outside the attic door. Below her she could hear Taylor's plodding footsteps on the stairs.

As he emerged from the stairwell, he pretended to struggle with the toolbox, which, Vanessa now noticed, was quite bulky. "I didn't realize you wanted to race," he quipped, dropping the gray metal box just short of her toes.

Vanessa smiled serenely as she tugged open the attic door and switched on the light. Her cheerful expression vanished when she noticed the dark watermark disfiguring the bowed lid of Great-aunt Charlotte's brassbound trunk.

"Oh, no!" The aged planks groaned beneath Vanessa's feet as she rushed to the corner where the damaged trunk stood. Crouching beside the trunk, she ran her hand over the once-lustrous wooden lid and shook her head. "Why did it have to drip onto this trunk, of all things?"

Taylor fiddled with one of the cracked leather straps securing the lid. "Let's have a look. Maybe the rainwater hasn't soaked all the way through."

Sinking back on her heels, Vanessa let him loosen the brass buckles, now corroded with aqua-blue flecks. As the lid creaked open, the faded odor of dried lavender and cedar drifted up from the folded clothing.

Taylor tested the lid's quilted blue sateen lining and grinned. "You're in luck. It's dry as a bone."

Vanessa had dropped forward onto her knees; she looked over at Taylor and smiled before plunging her hands into the trunk. She pulled out a pale mauve satin pump, decorated with a delicate rhinestone buckle, and held it up. "Just look! Would you believe Great-aunt Charlotte wore these shoes at her coming-out party back in 1920?"

Taylor nodded, but he regarded the shoe with respect, as if it were a valuable museum artifact.

"I'll bet her debutante ball gown is in here somewhere. Gosh, I remember how Sandy and I used to love looking at this stuff. Great-aunt Charlotte would let us touch all we liked, but she never would allow us to try anything on. Now I can see why she didn't want two crazy kids stomping around in her silk skirts, but back then we just kept nagging her. She always said she'd let us wear the clothes when we were old enough. Somehow we never seemed to reach that age." Pawing through the layers of folded clothing, Vanessa chuckled. Then her voice dropped to a breathless whisper. "Oh, here it is!"

Vanessa carefully lifted the gown from the trunk. Rocking back on her heels, she unfurled the dress across her knees. The skirt was scarred by creases, set by more than half a century, but the violet silk organza still possessed a rich sheen. The tiny rosettes trailing from the square neckline to the wide satin sash sparkled with seed pearls. As her hand smoothed the fabric, she glanced up at Taylor and found him regarding her with a curiously tender expression.

"You know you could wear it now," he reminded her gently. "I think Great-aunt Charlotte would approve."

Vanessa smiled. Her fingers lingered on one of the rosettes for a moment, tracing its pearl-encrusted outline. Then she folded the bodice carefully. "I'm afraid I'm a bit old to be playing dress-up. And probably much too big ever to squeeze into one of Great-aunt Charlotte's dresses." Giving the skirt a resolute pat, she returned it to the trunk and then closed the lid.

As she scrambled to her feet, she noticed that Taylor was still watching her. His smile had taken on a wistful cast, but he said nothing as he pushed himself up from the floor.

Hands folded behind his back, Taylor began to stroll around the attic, gazing up at the ceiling. He squinted in the uneven light as he stretched to pat a damp spot overhead. "Why don't you fetch the wire from my toolbox so we can mark these holes?" he suggested, running one hand along a rafter.

Vanessa trotted to the attic door and quickly returned with the wire and a pair of wire clippers. Following Taylor's instructions, she dutifully snipped lengths of wire, which he then thrust through the numerous pinholes, splits, and cracks. The work was time-consuming, and by the time they had completed their

inspection of the attic and gone downstairs, Vanessa
was already longing to be done with the task. She gave
a comic groan when Taylor unlashed the extension ladder from the top of his Jeep and propped it against the
side of the house.

Writing that letter to Steve Czerny suddenly seemed
less tedious as she scaled the aluminum ladder, cautiously testing each rung before trusting it with her
weight. A brisk breeze had come up, and Vanessa was
certain she could feel the ladder sway despite Taylor's
assertions that he was holding it steady. Leaning
uneasily against the sloping rooftop, she resisted the
perverse temptation to look down. Soon, however, she
was preoccupied with squirting roofing cement into
crevices while Taylor ripped away and replaced the un-
salvable shingles. When she at last made her way, slowly
and painfully, along the gable's ridge to the waiting
ladder, her legs felt like spent rubber bands. She clung
to the edge of the gable until Taylor had made his descent and then followed.

"That ought to hold the roof through anything less
than a hurricane," Taylor declared, brushing asphalt
dust from his work pants.

Vanessa was so tired she could only nod. When he
playfully jostled her shoulder, she smiled wearily and
managed to give his arm a comradely shove. Taylor's
presence was as excitingly masculine as ever, but fatigue had mercilessly dulled her senses. Right now, they
might as well have been two blue-collar buddies, saun-
tering back to her kitchen for an after-work beer.

"How about some lunch?" Vanessa asked as she
trudged up the front-porch steps.

"Sounds great. I'll be right in, as soon as I make one
more repair," Taylor called from the yard.

Vanessa turned slowly and clutched one of the porch columns for support. "You *can't* be serious? What on earth needs repairing so badly that you have to do it right now?"

Taylor gave her a sly wink. "Take a look out the kitchen window, and you'll see."

Vanessa watched him tote the ladder around the corner of the house. She shook her head in good-natured exasperation as she opened the front door and walked to the kitchen. Leaning across the sink, she parted the starched curtains and immediately spotted Taylor. He had already anchored the ladder against the elm and was busy attaching fresh lengths of rope to the dilapidated swing. The heavy boughs swayed as he lashed the new ropes around them and then gave the swing seat a firm tug. He climbed down the ladder, turned toward the kitchen, and gestured proudly.

"I expect you to use that swing, Ms. Dorsey," he told her with mock severity as he entered the kitchen.

Vanessa looked up from the lettuce leaves she was patting between paper towels and chuckled. "Next thing, you'll probably want me to get a rocking chair for the front porch, one of those cane-bottomed things that squeak," she teased.

"That's not a bad idea!"

Vanessa blotted her hands with a red-and-white-checked towel. "I'm getting lazy enough without a rocking chair to encourage me. I'm supposed to be looking for a job, you know." She turned back to the sink and rinsed a tomato beneath the tap.

"I know," Taylor commented without turning. He had sauntered to the pine hutch and was bent over the stack of magazines and newspapers that had accumulated there in the past week. Pulling a magazine free, he held it up and read from the cover. *"Ad-dendum."*

Vanessa feigned a jaded laugh as she smoothed mustard onto a slice of rye bread. "The Bible of the advertising industry, the Word according to Madison Avenue." When she carried the two plates to the table, she found Taylor bent over the open periodical. With unapologetic disrespect, she deposited his plate squarely in the middle of the page he was perusing.

Taylor frowned slightly at the plate before sliding it to one side with exaggerated care. "Careful. You'll desecrate these sacred writings. You know, if I didn't know better, I'd say you weren't all that crazy about the wild and wacky world of advertising." He held his hand up to fend off any arguments. "I know, I know. Deep down inside, you really love the business. But sometimes you do one hell of a convincing job pretending you don't."

Vanessa smiled at her sandwich, thoughtfully regarding the lettuce frill protruding between the slices of dark bread. "Okay, you've made your point. Promoting industrial-strength artificially-sweetened tutti-frutti-flavored soft-drink mix doesn't give me the same rush it did ten years ago. I've lost my starry-eyed enchantment with hawking mini-microwaves and micro-minivans. But there's one hitch to admitting that publicly—advertising is all I know how to do."

"Surely you don't really believe that," Taylor chided.

Vanessa blotted her lips before holding up a cautionary finger. "Granted, I can tack shingles and feed donkeys with the best of them. I'll own up to playing a respectable game of tennis, and my needlepoint has earned me compliments on occasion. However, when it comes to making a living, advertising is it. Period."

"I think you're selling yourself short," Taylor countered. "Think about the basic skills you've used in your ad jobs—dealing with people, analyzing data, managing money. You could capitalize on those talents in other industries." He lifted his sandwich, poised for a bite, and then quickly added, "You can't deny that."

Vanessa leaned back and lapped one arm over the back of the chair. "Everything you've said is true. There's just one big problem with changing fields at this point in my life: I would have to take a big cut in pay. *You* can't deny *that*." When Taylor only frowned down at the magazine, she went on. "Look, if I was just worried about keeping up a Yuppie lifestyle, I probably wouldn't even look for another ad job, but..." She suddenly caught herself and sucked in a deep breath. "Well, there are other considerations." That her father's Social Security did not begin to cover all of her mother's expenses, much less Sandy's med-school tuition, was a permanent reality in her life. She had no intention, however, of discussing her complicated family relationships with Taylor or anyone else, and she moved quickly to redirect his attention. "Since we're on the delightful subject of jobs, see if you can find any worthwhile leads in that issue." Vanessa popped the remaining bit of crust into her mouth and dusted her fingers over the plate.

Taylor glanced up at her and grinned. "You mean you haven't read this thing yet?"

Vanessa shook her head and tried not to feel guilty. She knew that trade papers were an important listening post for job-seekers, but lately she had been too busy to give them more than a perfunctory glance. Of course, she had found time to ride around the island with Taylor, join him and the Burch kids for an afternoon of sailing, groom Emily every day, and a dozen other unnecessary but infinitely more attractive activities.

"Here's something that might interest you," Taylor remarked. "There's a big article about a new agency in Richmond that's apparently growing by leaps and bounds."

Vanessa brushed a few caraway seeds from her fingers. "What's the name of the agency?"

"Miller-Dawson-Burnette—"

"And Lasky?"

Taylor's mouth twisted to one side in amusement. "You've heard of them, I see?"

"Oh, yes."

"Well, according to this article they're really raking in the bucks. Maybe you should get in touch with them. Since you were working in Richmond before, you probably even know some of these people." Taylor's hand swept the page, indicating a prominent black-and-white photograph.

Carefully folding her napkin, Vanessa slid from her seat and rounded the table. Bracing her hands on the back of Taylor's chair, she leaned over the table and pretended to study the open magazine. "Uh-huh," she mumbled.

"Recognize anyone?"

"Yeah. This guy right here used to be my husband." Vanessa poked the photograph with one finger.

For the first time since Vanessa had known him, Taylor did a double take. His handsome face screwed into an incredulous grimace as he reread the picture's caption. "Jeff Burnette?"

Vanessa straightened herself and folded her arms across her chest. "Was, once upon a time, Mr. Vanessa Dorsey. Believe it or not, that's dear old Jeff. I changed my name back to Dorsey after the divorce," she explained.

Taylor looked back at the photograph, his mouth drawn into a skeptical curve. Then he flipped the magazine closed. "I'm sorry..." he began.

"Don't apologize," Vanessa quickly interposed. "I can scarcely open one of these trade papers without seeing his picture. It doesn't bother me anymore. Really. Jeff belongs to the past," she concluded as she reached for her empty plate. Painful as the divorce had been, she was pleased that she could now say that without qualms.

What *did* bother her, Vanessa realized as she placed the plate in the sink and then selected an apple from the fruit bowl, was the phenomenal success Jeff had enjoyed since he and his cronies had formed their own agency. Not that she resented his good fortune. She had her faults, but envy was not one of them. But every time she stumbled onto yet another article about Jeff's meteoric rise to the top, she could not help but be reminded of her own derailed career.

Vanessa rolled the apple in her hand and watched it blur to a shiny-red sphere before her unfocused eyes. She blinked, dropping the piece of fruit onto the counter as Taylor's hands gently slid along her arms and then closed over her wrists.

He smiled down at her, caressing her tight brow with his eyes. "Don't let it get you down, Vanessa." When he jostled her wrists, her hands dangled limply. "Ten to one, your picture will be in *Ad-dendum* this time next year."

Vanessa shook her head and sighed. "Oh, Taylor, that's not what I'm after. As far as I'm concerned, Jeff is welcome to my share of the glamour pie, too. He's a hard worker, and he deserves to reap the benefits of his labor. But..." She paused, frowning at the gingham curtain billowing against her cheek.

"You've always worked hard, too, and you feel cheated." Taylor's voice was low and undramatic, but Vanessa was so stunned by the accuracy of his statement, she suddenly spun around to face him.

"Sometimes I worry I won't be able to help my sister pay her tuition this year." She had let the admission slip out without thinking, was powerless now to retract it. Vanessa suddenly glanced down at the counter and eased her hands from Taylor's clasp. "But I don't want to burden you with my problems," she added under her breath, reaching across the counter to retrieve the apple.

Taylor took the apple from her hand and replaced it on the counter. "Sometimes it's good to share your troubles, and I'd be glad to listen. That's what being human's all about." He hesitated, then dropped his voice. "I guess I'd like to be there for you whenever you need me."

Vanessa was taken aback. But before she could react a high-pitched buzz sounded somewhere in their vicinity.

"That damned beeper! May I use your phone?" Taylor asked, not bothering to control the annoyance in his voice.

"Sure. It's on the desk in the study." Vanessa pointed toward the door.

From the hallway, Taylor's steps sounded brisk and businesslike. The interruption had been so startling, she felt as if she had been rudely awakened from a dream and were still struggling to make sense of the conscious world. Vanessa heard the study door rattle open as she turned toward the sink. She lifted a plate mechanically and had just begun to rinse it when Taylor reappeared in the kitchen.

"A farmer on the other side of the island has a cow down. My intern thinks surgery may be necessary, and I need to lend her a hand. I'm sorry to run off like this. I guess I was pressing my luck when I thought this would be the one Sunday with no emergencies." For a man who was normally the epitome of easy-going composure, Taylor now looked decidedly ruffled.

Vanessa gave him her most reassuring smile, along with a gentle pat on the back, as he hurried out of the kitchen. "I hope this cow recovers as quickly as Emily did," she said, following him down the hall.

Taylor paused for only a second at the front door. "So do I." His grin was quick and nervous. "Catch you later."

"'Bye. And thanks for the help." Vanessa waved to his retreating back, watching him clear the steps two at a time. She had stepped back into the hall when he suddenly turned and dashed back to the house. "What's wrong? Did you forget something?" she asked in alarm.

"I sure did."

Without further ado, Taylor strode across the porch, rested both hands on her shoulders, and kissed her squarely on the mouth. Then, as if startled by his own impulsiveness, he quickly released her. He smiled self-consciously before turning on his heel and sprinting back to the Jeep.

Still reeling from the impact of that kiss, Vanessa leaned against the door frame. As her eyes followed the smoke-gray Cherokee down the drive, a smile gradually spread across her face. She waited in the doorway until she could no longer hear the Jeep's racing engine and then retreated into the house.

In the study doorway, Vanessa paused. The typewriter was still waiting on the desk where she had left it, with her letter to Steve still clamped firmly around its platen. She needed to finish that letter, she reminded herself, but later, not now.

Pulling the study door closed, Vanessa stepped back into the hall and turned to the stairs. She followed the curving bannister all the way to its terminal in the dusty little top-floor vestibule. The attic seemed especially quiet when she pushed open the door, and, not wishing to break the hush, she tiptoed to the brassbound trunk. As she lifted the violet ball gown from its resting place, its skirts rustled, enough perhaps to disturb the few spiders who made their home among the rafters of the old house, and smiled gently. She was still smiling long after she had carried the dress downstairs and hung it in her closet.

## Chapter Seven

Based on past experience, Luke Johnson was probably not the best person to ask for directions, but after letting her letter to Steve Czerny lie on the desk for two days, Vanessa was determined to mail it that afternoon. When she dropped by the Palmetto One-Stop and discovered that stamps were among the few commodities the store did not stock, she had no choice but to rely on Luke's meandering instructions. Still, she supposed if she followed the shorefront drive long enough, she would eventually stumble on the post office somewhere "down yonder," as Luke had promised.

Her eyes relaxed their tight squint when she spotted a flag fluttering over the squat palmettos bordering the road. Smiling to herself, she parked the car and then hurried across the narrow parking strip flanking the post office. In spite of her initial skepticism, she was beginning to believe that the healthful benefits of salt air and a slow-paced rural life were more than mere travel-industry propaganda. Even the still-unresolved problem of finding a job seemed less overwhelming today. Taking a cue from Taylor's pep talk, she had gone so far as to pick up the Charleston newspaper at the One-Stop, just to look over the classified ads.

The post office was deserted save for the lone clerk and an elderly black woman with two large packages. While Vanessa waited her turn, she found herself comparing the streamlined, nondescript office with its red brick predecessor, which she recalled from her childhood. Built in the days before plexiglass and concrete block, the old post office had boasted a mosaic tile floor and a counter of varnished wood, worn smooth by the pressure of countless hands over the years. As she handed the clerk her letter, she continued to search the colorless walls in vain for any remnant of the older building's charm.

At least the Oasis Café across the street still appeared to be intact. Almost every shopping expedition with Great-aunt Charlotte had culminated in one of the Oasis's malt-scented green-vinyl booths. Pressing a stamp onto the note she had written her mother, Vanessa wondered if they still made the frothy, chocolate egg creams that she and Sandra had favored. Since she was already in town, she might as well check to see, just for old times' sake. A mischievous grin was already growing on her face as she tossed the envelopes down the mail chute and then pushed through the door.

The hum of a television set, its volume adjusted to a white-noise murmur, greeted Vanessa when she entered the little diner, and for a second she hesitated. If the years had transformed the Oasis into a characterless burger palace, replete with video games and laminated menus, she would prefer to leave now and preserve unspoiled the memory of those homemade egg creams. She was reassured, however, when a buxom young woman in a crinkled nylon dress hailed her from behind the cash register. Following the friendly waitress's advice, she seated herself in a booth next to the window.

Like a jet pilot taking stock of his control panel, she scanned the tabletop and was pleased to find not only an old-fashioned, domed sugar dispenser but a beaker of hot-pepper sauce as well. When the waitress bustled over and confirmed that they did, indeed, still make chocolate egg creams, Vanessa felt as if her universe were a little closer to being in order. Pushing aside the glass ashtray, she spread open the newspaper and happily awaited her treat.

She was bent over the listing of management positions, trying to figure where she might fit among the experienced pharmaceutical sales reps and bankers who appeared to be in such demand, when a dull thump against the window caught her attention. Looking up from the help-wanted ads, she was surprised to recognize Denny and Matt Burch mugging through the smudgy plate glass. Grinning, Vanessa jumped up from the table and dashed outside.

"Hi, fellows! What's up?" she asked as she joined them on the sidewalk.

"Oh, nothing," Matt volunteered, suddenly looking down at the frayed toes of his sneakers. His brother solemnly shook his head in agreement.

Vanessa forced herself not to smile too broadly. On Saturday, the boys had bombarded her with non-stop chatter, but now, without Taylor's confidence-bolstering presence, they had been seized with an attack of bashfulness. "Are you finished with school for the day?"

Both boys nodded, and Matt pointed around the corner. "We're waitin' for Mom, and she's waitin' to get the car fixed," he explained.

Vanessa craned to follow Matt's finger and could just glimpse a low, corrugated-metal building through the thick palm fronds. "Say," she commented as if a bright idea had just occurred to her. "Since you guys are going to be hanging around for a while, why don't I treat you to sodas?"

Matt and Denny glanced at each other for only a second before fixing her with two pairs of eager brown eyes. Both sandy heads nodded in agreement, but then Matt hesitated. "We'd better ask Mom first," he said, glancing toward the garage.

"That's a good idea," Vanessa agreed. "I'll come along with you, just to make sure she knows it's okay."

Vanessa followed the boys around the corner to the garage. The unpaved lot was cluttered with a motley assortment of vehicles, parked at odd angles to one another in no particular order, but she quickly spotted the Burches' orange Beetle. A gray-uniformed mechanic was bent over the old car's gaping maw; Grace hovered anxiously at his side, her cardigan pulled tight across her chest. As Matt and Denny rushed toward their mother, she turned reluctantly away from the car.

"Can we, Ma? Please!" Vanessa caught the tail end of their entreaty as she caught up with the boys.

"I'd really love to have Matt and Denny join me. It would remind me of the good old days when Great-aunt Charlotte took my sister and me to the Oasis," Vanessa added with a laugh. If Grace were as resistant to taking largess as Taylor had said, she might be wary of letting her sons accept a treat, and Vanessa hastened to avert her objections.

But Grace only nodded. "That's real nice of you, Vanessa." She smiled, but as she glanced up, Vanessa was startled to find the dark eyes red-rimmed and puffy.

"You two mind your manners," she admonished her sons before turning back to the disabled Beetle.

Matt and Denny raced back to the Oasis, with Vanessa bringing up the rear at a more sedate pace. While she folded up her newspaper, the boys scrambled into the booth and began to study the menu with the intensity of Talmudic scholars. After serious deliberation, Matt settled on a Double Fudge Marshmallow Shake while Denny opted for the Oasis Superspecial.

Between sips of her modest egg cream, Vanessa chatted with the boys and watched them lustily devour their orders. In spite of their high-spirited company, however, she found her thoughts drifting back to Grace's ravaged eyes. The woman had been crying; there could be no mistake on that count. But why? Vanessa poked the bubbles remaining in her glass with the straw and frowned. Perhaps the old car was on its last lap, a situation that was never pleasant, and one that, for a financially strapped family, could be disastrous.

"Was Emily mad at you when you got home Saturday?" Denny's feet tapped a rubbery arpeggio against the linoleum floor.

Vanessa blinked and looked up from her empty glass. "Oh, no. She was as sweet-tempered as ever. You'll have to come see her sometime," she added, winning a toothy grin from the little boy.

Just then the café door rattled shut, and Vanessa swiveled in her seat. She spotted Grace in time to pocket the check lying on the table. "I think these fellows are about finished, but I hope you have time for a cup of coffee." Vanessa slid along the seat, making room for Grace to join them.

"That's kind of you, but we really need to get home." Grace smiled with noticeable effort. "I have a million things piled up to do, ironing and stuff, you know," she added apologetically. "Which reminds me. You boys need to run over to the launderette, pick up our basket, and put it in the car."

"Is the car all fixed?" Matt asked, tilting the drained soda glass between his palms.

"For now. So get a move on—if we're lucky, maybe we can get the clean laundry home before the stupid old thing breaks down again."

Matt scooted out of the booth, followed by Denny, who paused for a final, prolonged slurp from his straw. As the boys rushed to the door, Grace called after them. "Don't forget to thank Miss Dorsey!"

The café door slammed, cutting short the chorus of thank-yous. Grace shook her head; when she looked back at Vanessa, she shoved up the sleeves of her cardigan and managed another smile. "Well, I sure do thank you," she repeated. "It was nice seeing you again."

As Grace turned to go, something prompted Vanessa to jump up from her seat. "You're sure you won't have that cup of coffee?"

Grace whirled. For a moment, a look of indecision played on her face. "No, I'd better not. The boys..." Her head jerked toward the street, but beneath the rigorously polite smile, Vanessa glimpsed a woman yearning for a friend to whom she could pour out her troubles.

"I understand. Some other time, then?"

Grace nodded, more eagerly than she probably realized, and then bolted for the door. From the window, Vanessa watched her as she hurried down the street to the neon U-Wash-It beacon that had just began to pulse in the gathering dusk. Heaven only knew what sort of expensive repairs that ancient car of hers had required, Vanessa mused as she gathered up her paper and walked to the cash register. The Burches' problems certainly did put her own into perspective.

The waitress was perched on a stool behind the counter, watching a game show on the small TV, but she slid to her feet as Vanessa approached. ''Ever'thing just fine?'' she asked, taking the check Vanessa held out.

''Great. I think I can safely speak for the Burch kids, too.'' Vanessa chuckled as she dug through her handbag.

The waitress shook her head and poked the register keys. ''I'll tell you what, their poor mama sure does have the bad luck!''

Pulling a bill from her wallet, Vanessa lifted a brow questioningly. ''You mean with her car breaking down?''

The waitress frowned, pawing through the bin of dimes. ''Lord, no! I'm talkin' about her losin' her job and all. Not that that old heap isn't enough trouble.''

''Grace Burch has lost her job?'' Vanessa's throat suddenly went dry.

''Just about.'' The waitress shoved the register drawer closed with a vengeance. ''One of those big-time developers just bought The Crab Cove—that's where she cooks, y'know. In a month or two, they're going to shut the place down, turn it into some kind of ritzy restaurant for the summer tourists.'' Her mouth twisted to one side in disgust. ''Seven, eight, nine, makes ten.'' She layered the bills onto the counter and then leaned back, resting one heel against the rung of the stool. ''I'm telling you, it's enough to make you cry.''

Apparently, it had already been enough to make Grace Burch cry, Vanessa reflected. Still too stunned to comment, she stuffed the bills into her wallet. What on earth would Grace do? If she couldn't work at the island's only restaurant, she would have to seek employment on the mainland. But that would mean relying on a none-too-reliable car. The longer she considered the Burch family's dilemma the more complicated it appeared.

The waitress planted both elbows on the counter and gave a mirthless laugh. "If we don't manage to put the brakes on this kind of thing, I'm goin' to be standing right behind her in the unemployment line. I never was much of a joiner, but I'm sure going to that meeting tonight." She paused, glancing up at Vanessa. "I guess you've heard about this group that's forming, trying to get all this crazy development under control?"

Vanessa cleared her throat. "You mean, the Parloe Island Committee for Contained Growth?"

"Uh-huh." The waitress gestured toward the bulletin board hanging next to the pay phone. Vanessa immediately recognized one of Cora Henderson's yellow flyers pinned squarely in the center of the board. "You're goin', too?"

"Well, uh, I'd thought about it." Vanessa peered into her handbag and rearranged a few articles. "I mean, I might drop by and see what's going on."

The waitress nodded approvingly. "The way I look at it, if this thing's goin' to work, we've all got to get behind it. Well, you take care, honey," she called as Vanessa retreated toward the door. "See you tonight!"

"Sure." Vanessa anchored the door shut behind her. "Maybe," she added to herself as she walked to the car.

Of course, there was really no point in her attending the meeting, Vanessa argued with herself as she drove back to the house. After all, she would probably have found a job and be long gone from Parloe before the group even got off the ground. If she hadn't felt so outraged over Grace's misfortune, she would never have told that waitress she was interested in the preservation group. But she had been angry; in fact, she was still very angry, angry enough to want to do something to set things right.

She had no idea exactly what that something might be. But after she had fed Emily for the evening, she locked the house, climbed into her car, and set out in search of the Parloe Presbyterian Senior Center.

"WHAT THE DEVIL, TAYLOR!" Stewart Bowen grimaced and recoiled at the open door of the Cherokee. "Just because you're a veterinarian, your car doesn't have to smell like a cattle yard!"

"I didn't have time to go home and change. And *we* don't have time to mess around here arguing." Taylor leaned over the steering wheel and beckoned impatiently.

Stewart Bowen eased gingerly into the Jeep's front seat. "This is a business meeting, you know. An informal one, but a business meeting, nonetheless."

Taylor shifted gears briskly. "It's just the boots, Dad. I've got some clean shoes in back that I can change into when we get to the Senior Center." He grinned at his father. "I promise I'll pass muster."

Stewart Bowen pretended to study the passing landscape. "Let's hope! After all, you're one of the folks who's supposed to be in charge of this outfit," he grumbled.

In truth, Taylor would have preferred a complete change of clothes, not to mention a hot shower and a decent meal, but a last-minute emergency call had cut short any hopes he had entertained along those lines. He had been relieved just to have the foundered mare back on her feet and resting quietly by seven-thirty, giving him scarcely enough time to race by and pick up his father on his way to the meeting.

When Taylor turned off the road in front of the big white church, the parking lot was already jammed with cars. After squeezing the Jeep between two pickup trucks, he paused long enough to toss the mud-caked boots behind the seat and put on a pair of Reeboks.

"Better?" Taylor asked as they hurried across the parking lot to a low red brick building.

Stewart Bowen glanced down at the scuffed but clean athletic shoes. "Considerably."

"I'm glad to see such a good turnout for the first meeting." Taylor held the swinging glass door for his father. "Cora's flyers must have done the trick."

The two men paused in the doorway to survey the packed meeting room. The Senior Center's supply of folding chairs had long since been exhausted, and the latecomers were now bunched along the wall.

"Go on, son. Don't worry about me. I may just hang back here where the air isn't so thin." Dr. Bowen gave Taylor's back an encouraging push.

Smiling to himself, Taylor worked his way through the crowd to the platform where the committee organizers had assembled.

"Dr. Bowen, are we glad to see you!" Cora's wide blue eyes registered unmitigated relief. "None of us can get this confounded microphone to work."

"I'll see what I can do," Taylor promised. Crouching beside the lectern, he examined the snarled cables and checked the connections. When he rose and switched on the mike, a piercing hum rose above the noise of the crowd.

"Wonderful!" Cora looked up from the box of mimeographed flyers she was sorting and smiled approvingly. "Why don't you go ahead and start?" she added in a raspy whisper.

Taylor nodded and stepped behind the lectern. He tapped the mike lightly, and a hush gradually spread over the auditorium. As he began his prepared opening statement, his eyes swept the crowd; he was pleased to recognize almost every upturned face as that of a friend, a neighbor or a client. As he continued to outline the committee's goals, however, he found himself straining for a better look at a certain lustrous, dark head thrown into relief against the far wall. After taking such elaborate pains to explain why she could not join the group, Vanessa was the last person he had expected to see here tonight. But there was no mistaking that ruffled cap of curls, looming just an inch or so over her neighbors' heads.

Taylor's eyes followed Vanessa as she leaned slightly to one side and whispered head-to-head with Winona Cherry from the Oasis Café. He waited for her to look up, and when she did he gave her a quick smile that he hoped did not detract from his presentation. Vanessa's shapely mouth quivered in acknowledgement, but her eyes remained trained on the lectern. When he had concluded his address with an appeal for volunteers for the various subcommittees, she was still watching with rapt attention.

As the drone of voices rose once more from the crowd, people began to trickle past the table where Cora had arranged sign-up sheets for the subcommittees. Taylor paused to pump some hands and clap a few backs before wending his way through the throng to the rear wall. Vanessa was saying goodbye to Winona and did not see him as he approached.

Taylor tapped her shoulder lightly. "Come here often?"

He felt her lurch in surprise before she wheeled on him. "Taylor! You startled me."

"You kind of gave me a surprise, too, but a pleasant one, to be sure," Taylor commented with a sly grin. "Did Winona browbeat you into coming to the meeting?"

He was startled when Vanessa's lips drew into a grim line. "No."

"Hey, I'm sorry. I didn't mean to rib you too much." Taylor jostled her shoulder gently.

Vanessa frowned and shook her head. "I came because of Grace."

"Grace Burch?"

When Vanessa looked up at him, her slate-blue eyes had darkened to the shade of a brewing storm. "You haven't heard?"

"No, I haven't. What about Grace?" Taylor demanded, now genuinely puzzled. Surveying the audience from the lectern, he had been surprised not to see the Burches, but he had assumed that he had somehow overlooked them. Now that he thought about it, however, the likelihood of Matt and Denny disappearing into any crowd seemed remote.

"The Crab Cove is being sold to some developers who plan to convert it into an overpriced tourist trap. Grace is going to lose her job."

"What?" Taylor blurted out. "When did this happen?"

"Yesterday. When I saw Grace this afternoon, I could tell she had been crying, but I thought she was depressed about her car breaking down. Later, Winona told me that the Crab Cove's staff had just gotten the word."

"Damn it!" Taylor flexed his hands, fighting the urge to smash his fist against the wall in sheer frustration. As he stared angrily across the room, he felt Vanessa's hand close over his.

"That's the way I felt, too," she said quietly, giving his fist a firm squeeze. "That's why I wanted to be here tonight, just to show support. Practically speaking, I don't suppose that will do much to turn things around, though." Her grave eyes followed the stragglers trailing out the door.

Opening his fist, Taylor took her hand in his and cradled it for a second. "Support *is* important. Not everyone has the time or resources to participate actively, but names on petitions and head counts at meetings do influence zoning boards. I appreciate your coming," he added. Looking down into those wide blue eyes, he wished he could find a more eloquent way to tell her how personally touched he was that she had joined with the islanders, with *his* people.

"'Scuse me, Doc, but I'd like for you to have a look at this." Raymond Hardy, the owner of the island's rental agency, nodded politely to Vanessa as he handed Taylor a bulging folder.

A quick peek into the folder revealed several surveyors' reports and a Corps of Engineers' rendering of the coastline. Taylor heaved a weary sigh and stuffed the folder under his arm. "I'll take a look at it tonight, Ray," he promised. "Sometimes I wonder if I'm the right person to get this thing rolling," he added to Vanessa. They were picking their way through the folding chairs that had been abandoned, helter-skelter, in front of the platform. "At first, we thought it would just be a matter of getting enough folks interested to form task forces. I guess we were pretty naive." Clutching the folder behind his back, he propped one foot on the platform's ledge and regarded the long table where Cora and two of her cohorts were poring over the sign-up sheets. "How does it look, Cora?"

Her bright blue eyes lingered on a clipboard for a second before looking up at Taylor. "Well, there's lots of enthusiasm for the group," she began carefully. "Although I'm not sure just what Luke Johnson had in mind when he volunteered for the Legal Task Force. Hi there, Miss Dorsey. Glad to see you could make it," Cora added, her pensive expression dissolving momentarily into a warm smile.

As Taylor scanned the well-thumbed paper anchored to the clipboard, he heard Vanessa murmur a reply. Since her outpouring about Grace, she had scarcely said a word; although she knew the Burch family only in passing, she seemed genuinely upset over their plight. Vanessa was such a sensitive, caring person that he imagined she would have little difficulty being drawn into other people's lives, but because the Burches were his adoptive family, he found her concern for them deeply moving.

Taylor tossed the clipboard back onto the table and then swung around to face Vanessa. "Well, it's a start, at least." He attempted a grin, but even his facial muscles felt weighed down with fatigue.

Hands jammed in the back pockets of her slacks, Vanessa walked to the table. She bent over the crazy quilt of notes, sign-up sheets, and flyers, twisting her head to one side as she read. "What are you going to do first?"

Taylor opened his mouth, expecting a simple, direct answer to pop out in response to her simple, direct question. Then he hesitated. What on earth *were* they going to do? A week ago, he would have been able to formulate a sketchy game plan, but now, confronted with a growing mountain of uncollated information and an eager horde of untrained volunteers, he was dumbfounded.

"I don't know," he confessed. "We need to start lobbying," he added in an attempt not to appear totally incompetent.

Turning, Vanessa rested a hip against the table's edge and looked up from the fact sheet she was examining. "Before you do that, you should firmly establish the group in the public eye, give yourselves an identity."

Taylor folded his arms across his chest and tried not to look too defensive. "I'm sure you're right, but remember, I'm a vet, not a PR man."

Vanessa nodded and glanced back at the fact sheet. "Government officials are much more likely to listen to an organization they've read about in the newspapers and seen covered on TV. Contained Growth needs an image," she announced, folding the printed page with decisive strokes of her long fingers.

Taylor blew out a long breath. "I won't argue with you, but we have to work with the resources at hand. So far, the group has a dentist, a vet, an attorney, a waitress, an auto mechanic," he ticked off his fingers methodically, "a lot of farmers, a few business people, and Luke Johnson, who qualifies as a jack-of-all-trades, I suppose, but no PR types."

"Did you forget about me?" Vanessa asked quietly, pushing away from the table.

For a moment, Taylor could only gape in disbelief.

"Okay. Advertising and public relations are not one and the same, but they're kissing cousins, at least. I could do for this group the same thing I've done in the past for disposable diapers and dishwasher detergent— structure a plan of action, pull together information, present it effectively, and get it in front of the people who can do us the most good." She gestured over her shoulder at the littered table.

"But I thought you said you couldn't get involved," Taylor began. "I mean you keep insisting you'll be traveling a lot and . . ."

Vanessa shook her head impatiently. "Look, Taylor, I'm making you an offer. Are you interested?"

"Hell, yes," he managed to blurt out.

"All right." As Vanessa turned on her heel, she looked even taller than usual. Stooping, she rested both palms flat on the table like a general analyzing a battle plan. "Someone who's familiar with everything will need to sort through this stuff and fill me in with background information. Do you think you might have time?"

When Taylor joined her at the table, he slipped an arm, ever so gently, around her waist. "You'll never find a more willing volunteer."

TRUE TO HIS WORD, Taylor had dropped by Vanessa's house the following morning on his way to the clinic and delivered a huge box of material. To judge from the neat files, each carefully annotated and cross-referenced, he must have been up all night, sifting through papers and making notes for her. Not that he'd looked the worse for wear. As he unpacked the contents of the box onto her dining room table, pausing frequently to expand on one of his notations, Vanessa had found her attention straying from the diagrams and files to the handsome man explaining them.

Still, she could honestly say that she had not volunteered to help the committee to impress Taylor. That she would be working with him was a secondary benefit, to be sure, but the overriding motive that fired her creative energy during the long hours of research and analysis derived from another source altogether. Late that night, as she sat alone in Great-aunt Charlotte's tiny study with the heavy damask drapes drawn and the hurricane lamp casting its rosy glow over her notepad, Vanessa felt as if she were striking a blow for Grace Burch and her two kids. Perhaps it was too late to save the Crab Cove from its unfortunate fate, but the Committee for Contained Growth could avert other disasters if it developed into a viable lobbying group. In her career, Vanessa had handled multi-million-dollar accounts, but never had she felt such urgency to succeed.

THE FOLLOWING MONDAY, she summoned the courage to phone Taylor and tell him she had a marketing plan for the Parloe Island Committee for Contained Growth. When he promised to stop by the next afternoon, she felt a heady wave of elation. She was eager to show him the fruits of her handiwork and hear his opinion. Then, too, she had experienced a general mood elevation, something akin to what she supposed athletes feel when they at last enter competition and put their training to the test. It might be unpaid volunteer work, but the task she had just completed for the committee had demanded the full range of her skills. For five days, Vanessa had been back on the job; she now realized how badly she had missed employing her talents and taking pride in the results.

That Taylor put no limit on his praise of her plan proved to be the icing on the cake. "You've done an absolutely amazing job," he repeated for the umpteenth time. They were both leaning over the dining table where Vanessa had laid out her various proposals. His green eyes glowed with pleasure as they skimmed her typed outline of a media strategy.

Vanessa strained to maintain some semblance of reserve. "The acid test comes when we put it into action," she reminded him.

Papers fluttered as Taylor threw the plan onto the dining table. "Don't you ever give yourself a pat on the back along the way?" he asked in exasperation.

Vanessa slid onto the edge of the table, her knee lightly touching his. "I'll go you one better than a pitiful little pat on the back. I've been hoarding a rather decent bottle of wine in the fridge, and I think this might be just the occasion to crack it."

Taylor leaned forward and gently nuzzled the curls looping across her forehead. "I have an even better idea," he announced, leaning back and taking both her hands in his. "Why don't you bring the wine with you tomorrow night when we have dinner with Cora and some of the Committee volunteers? She asked me to extend the invitation when I dropped by today. You know, everyone is really proud that you've taken a stand for the island."

"Parloe means a lot to me." Vanessa leaned back, not breaking his hold. When the phone rang abruptly, she pulled one hand free to steady herself and then hopped to the floor. "Don't go away," she warned him with a devilish wink as she hurried to the study.

"Just a *minute!*" Vanessa grumbled to the imperiously jangling phone. "Hello?" she barked into the receiver.

"Vanessa? Hey, babe, it's Steve!" The words shot through her distracted mind like a rocket blasting into the stratosphere.

"Steve?" Vanessa repeated slowly, buying time while she frantically tried to place the confident baritone. Suddenly, she felt a tingling wave of recognition sweep over her. "Steve Czerny!"

"None other! I got your letter last week, and I've been meaning to give you a buzz."

Vanessa gripped the phone for dear life, pressing the blood from her fingers, while Steve paused to deliver an aside. "Yeah, well, I don't give a damn what the photographer says, Marty," she heard him growl to someone hovering in the background. He cleared his throat before going on. "Sorry. Where were we anyway?"

"You got my letter," Vanessa prompted, trying not to sound like an overeager teenybopper.

"Oh, yeah. Look, Van, you need to get your sweet self down here as fast as you can. Like tomorrow."

"To Atlanta?" Vanessa gasped.

"Uh-huh. Some...how can I phrase this delicately? Some *personnel changes* are about to take place." Steve's voice dropped so suddenly, Vanessa felt as if he were about to tell her he was defecting to the People's Republic of China. "On the Lansing Brothers account, no less," he added, and she could imagine his lips drawing into a tight line beneath his bushy black mustache.

"You mean there's going to be an opening?" In spite of herself, Vanessa had let a trace of Steve's cloak-and-dagger delivery creep into her own voice.

"I mean you need to *be* here tomorrow for lunch, lady. Can you make it?"

Vanessa let out a noisy breath. "Oh, well, sure." Glancing down at her grass-stained sneakers and faded jeans, she silently blessed Alexander Graham Bell and all of his descendants. "I mean, I can probably take an Early Bird from Charleston."

"Great. I'm looking forward to seeing you again, Van. God, it's been a long time, hasn't it?" Steve's voice had risen once more to its normal straight-ahead pitch.

"It sure has." Vanessa paused and waited for Steve to toss an unintelligible command over his shoulder. "Uh, I really appreciate this, Steve."

"Hey, I'm trying to bring you on board to make myself look good, you know," he joked gruffly. "See you tomorrow."

After she had hung up the phone, Vanessa stared across the room with a dazed look on her face. She had been so deeply immersed in the Contained Growth Committee project for the past week, she had almost forgotten that the rest of Parloe existed outside her dim study, much less the big, wide world beyond, and she was still stunned by the unexpected call. *Steve Czerny had a good job prospect for her.* For a moment, she risked the fantasy of accepting the job offer. She would immediately dispatch a check to Sandra. Then she would phone her mother and . . .

Vanessa suddenly stopped short. As if an invisible hand had just pulled the plug from her psychic reservoir, she felt the excitement drain from her when she remembered that Taylor was still waiting in the dining

room. He would be glad to hear the good news, she reminded herself; this was just the sort of call she had
been waiting for. But as she walked to the door, she felt
her stomach curdle. When she entered the dining room,
an uncertain smile had congealed on her face.

Taylor looked up, his face instantly registering alarm.
"Bad news?"

"Oh, no!"

Taylor walked to her side and clasped her elbow,
peering down into her face. "You look a little upset,"
he persisted.

Vanessa shook her head and then quickly added,
"No, I'm just in shock, I guess." She gulped out a short
laugh. "Can you believe it? After all this time, I actually have an interview."

"An interview?" Taylor's hand still rested on her
arm, but his eyes widened quizzically.

"That was Steve Czerny, this fellow I used to work
with, on the phone just now. It seems there may be an
opening at Henson and Knowles—that's the ad agency
where he works. I mean, it's nothing definite, but he
wants me to fly down tomorrow. Just to talk." For
someone who prided herself on succinct communica-
tion skills, Vanessa was doing a terrible job relaying
basic information.

Taylor nodded. "Where is the agency?"

"In Atlanta." At that moment, Timbuktu would not
have sounded more remote.

"Atlanta?" Taylor was still smiling, but the lively
expression in his eyes dimmed.

"Yes." Vanessa laughed again and then swallowed.
She felt his hand slide away, and she wanted to say
something, anything, to break the weird ringing in her
ears. But neither of them seemed able to do anything

but look at each other as the full impact of Vanessa's revelation settled over them like an insidious, cold dew.

"Well, that's fantastic!" Taylor's brief comment sounded all the more brittle, thanks to the resolute smile that he held onto with bulldog tenacity.

"Here I am getting all nervous, and they probably won't even want me. I'll probably be digging through the Charleston classifieds again tomorrow night." Vanessa opened her hands and then clasped them again. Although Taylor only shook his head, she felt a bizarre urge to talk. Suddenly, there was so much she needed to explain—to him and to herself—if only she could get beyond these pitifully meaningless phrases.

Taylor's smile grew more enigmatic as he walked to the hall door. "Don't be silly. You'll ace this interview."

"I doubt that!" For some reason, Vanessa's vehement denial sounded more like a wish than a protest.

Taylor's eyes drifted across the ceiling before landing squarely on Vanessa's face. "Sure you will."

Shaking her head, Vanessa closed her eyes, as much to escape his disconcerting gaze as to emphasize her point. "This is probably just another pipe dream," she insisted. "Uh, look, I don't know about you, but I'm starving. How about some coffee and a sandwich?" Not waiting for his reply, she wheeled toward the kitchen.

Taylor's excruciatingly even voice stopped her in her tracks. "Thanks, but I'd better get going. I have some chores to do at home. I guess you won't be able to make it to Cora's cookout after all," he remarked without turning.

In spite of her best efforts, this conversation seemed doomed to boomerang back to the same leaden topics.

"No, I guess not. Please tell her how sorry I am." Vanessa followed Taylor down the hallway to the front door. "Tell her I'll definitely make it another time."

Taylor only nodded. He had already retreated onto the porch and was jangling his keys inside his cupped palm. "Good luck with your interview." His voice sounded flat as he pivoted and strode toward the parked Jeep.

Suddenly, Vanessa dashed down the steps. When she caught Taylor by the sleeve, he spun around, too startled to resist. Although the sea-green eyes reflected his surprise, their gaze was uncompromisingly direct.

Feeling herself waver for an instant, Vanessa swallowed hard. She fingered the rough denim of his shirtsleeve, then released it and stepped back, folding her arms across her waist. "This is hard for me, Taylor," she began biting her lip. "Please try to understand."

His fingers felt unnaturally cold against her chin. "Buck up, kid. You'll do great tomorrow."

*That's not what I mean, and you know it. For God's sake, don't play games with me, Taylor—not now.* Her hands flexed, yearning to reach out to his retreating back, force him to face her and the crisis at hand. She hadn't meant to but she'd developed a taste for Parloe, for him. But the words remained mutely lodged in her throat, and she did not move. When the Cherokee disappeared beyond the trees, it left a desolate silence in its wake.

## Chapter Eight

"Hey, lady! You forgot your magazine!"

Vanessa halted in mid-stride and turned to see the cabby brandishing a copy of *Ad-dendum* through the open window. Awkwardly juggling her briefcase and newspaper, she took the magazine and stuffed it under her arm. "Thanks."

"Anytime, ma'am." The stubble-faced cab driver was already cranking up the window.

Vanessa stepped back from the curb and took a quick inventory of her possessions. Everything appeared to be in order—briefcase, handbag, the *Atlanta Constitution*, and the dog-eared *Ad-dendum*, but given her harried frame of mind, heaven only knows what forgotten item she might have left on the airplane.

If she had only gotten a decent night's sleep, she could have flown down to the interview feeling refreshed and confident. Instead, she had thrashed and turned in bed for six hours, wrestling with the tangled quilt and her own conflicting thoughts. She had alternately cursed herself and Taylor for complicating an already difficult situation, but, lying there alone in the cool, dark bedroom, Vanessa had finally been forced to acknowledge the truth: her emotional attachment to him had been as inevitable as the circumstances that would now surely lead to their separation. That agonizing realization had tormented her until she had at last fallen into an exhausted slumber shortly before dawn.

Irritably shaking back her sleeve, Vanessa checked her watch. It wouldn't do to appear too eager by showing up at Steve's agency a good hour before lunchtime. Maybe she would at least *look* less like a zombie if she got a good dose of caffeine into her. At any rate, she needed to sit down somewhere alone and collect her thoughts before arriving at the agency. She had worked with Steve long enough to feel easy with him, but she knew nothing about the other executives with whom she would be talking. They would all be scrutinizing her today, evaluating her skills, sizing up how well she fit into the corporate team. If she was to earn high ratings, she needed to think clearly and stay focused. And she certainly did not need Taylor's bittersweet smile hovering in the back of her mind like a restive ghost.

Fortunately, the lobby coffee shop in Henson and Knowles's building looked fairly peaceful; she could have a cup of coffee and take another look at the clippings she had assembled on the agency's recent activity. Vanessa had secreted herself in a corner booth and was bent over an article on H. & K.'s acquisition of the Whitney-Spawn real-estate account when a bemused voice interrupted her reading.

"Vanessa? Good Lord, it *is* you!"

Blinking, Vanessa looked up from the folded magazine page and twisted around in the booth.

"Don't bite! It's only me, your old pal Nikki Pappas."

At the sight of her friend's feigned look of wide-eyed terror, Vanessa burst out laughing. "Nikki! It's great to see you! I hope you have time to sit down." She quickly snapped her briefcase shut and placed it under the table. "How are you getting along? It seems like ages since we actually talked."

Nikki slid onto the vacated seat. "It *has* been ages, dear one, six years to be precise, since we took the Big Apple's ad scene by storm. Things at the agency just weren't the same after you moved to Richmond."

"It's nice to know I was missed," Vanessa remarked with a demure smile.

"You were," Nikki assured her. "But, hey, the last I heard you were holed up on some primitive island. You didn't say anything in your letter about moving to Atlanta."

"That's because I haven't moved here. I've just flown in today for an interview." Vanessa briefly recounted her telephone conversation with Steve Czerny. "Do you know anything about the situation at Henson and Knowles? I gathered they were having a shake-up, but Steve was pretty evasive."

Nikki shrugged and plucked at one of the spiky brown wisps framing her brow. "No particularly juicy gossip that I can recall. I can vouch for one thing— they're really doing a lot of business. I've done some free-lance copywriting for them from time to time, and I think H. & K. would be a pretty decent place to work. That is, if you take care to give Jason McNair a wide berth."

"Who's he?" Vanessa tried to attribute the queasy stirrings in her stomach to the diner coffee, but she leaned a little further across the table as Nikki went on.

"Probably the most distasteful man I've ever met in my life. Not only is he a real snake, but a snake that is absolutely impossible to please. I had nightmares for a month after writing for one of his accounts.'' Nikki rolled her dark eyes dramatically and braced her outspread arms against the back of the booth.

"Come on, Nikki. You've said that about every account man you've ever worked with,'' Vanessa reminded her drily.

Nikki folded her arms on the table and grinned. "Yeah, I guess you're right. Anyway, Jason the Snake notwithstanding, I think you'll like H. & K., and I think they'll like you."

Vanessa breathed a husky sigh. "I've got my fingers crossed. This has been the longest dry spell I ever care to endure. I feel as if I've been crawling across the Sahara, pursuing mirages. But enough about me. What have you been up to lately?"

Nikki sniffed and propped her chin on her hand. "Oh, the same as always—still free-lancing the same old copy for the same old shops, still dating the same old guys. I did paint the condo from top to bottom. I picked a nice, lusty shade called Sunset Peach for the bedroom—wishful thinking, I guess." Chewing the tip of her thumb, she eyed Vanessa carefully. "I don't suppose you have anything exciting to report in the romance department."

Vanessa toyed with the spoon resting on the edge of her saucer. "No, not really." She was not skilled at deception, a deficiency that would be particularly obvious to a perceptive friend like Nikki. Still, she could not afford to pour out her heart about Taylor and all the painful consequences of that infatuation right now, not with an important interview looming in less than half an hour. Talking with Nikki had helped put her into a work-oriented mode, one she intended to stay in, at least for the next few hours.

"Well, I'd better hustle, or I'll miss my next appointment." Nikki stooped to retrieve her portfolio before pushing herself up from the table. "Give Jason McNair my fondest, if you happen to see him. And good luck with that interview."

"Thanks, Nikki." Vanessa smiled up at her friend.

On her way out of the coffee shop, Nikki tossed a jaunty wave over her shoulder. "Oh, and, Vanessa—" Dangling her portfolio from one hand, she leaned around the swinging door.

"Yes?"

"Hold out for an office with a view."

Vanessa might have argued with Nikki's estimation of her negotiating position, but she could find no quarrel with her friend's infectious high spirits. During the time they had worked together in New York, she had learned to rely on Nikki's gallows humor to put the agency's latest crisis into perspective. When she had lost her job last year, she had often wished Nikki was around, just to share a couple of Bloody Marys and cajole her out of the doldrums. Perhaps her old friend's appearance in the coffee shop was a good omen.

At the very least, chatting with Nikki had helped her relax a bit, Vanessa realized as she stepped out of the elevator into Henson and Knowles's lushly carpeted reception area. Straightening her shoulders, she introduced herself to the receptionist. Before the woman could announce her arrival, however, the elevator door slid open again and Steve Czerny charged out.

His bearded face exploded into a delighted grin. "Hey, Van! You look great, lady." Steve managed to give Vanessa a quick hug, in spite of the handful of papers he held. "Gimme a sec to get rid of this production garbage, and then we'll head back to my office."

Tossing the papers onto the reception desk, he paused long enough to give the beleaguered-looking secretary instructions and then turned back to Vanessa. "Have a decent flight?"

"Okay, I guess. At least I got here in one piece." Vanessa watched Steve's stocky shoulders shake with laughter as he strode ahead of her down the corridor. In her high-heeled pumps, she had to take an extra skip between steps to keep pace with him.

As they rounded the corner into his office, the desk phone was already ringing off the hook. Cursing under his breath, Steve paused in the doorway and shouted down the hall. "Muriel, hold my calls!" He pulled the door shut behind him, tugged at his already cockeyed necktie, and glared around the room for a moment, as if he were trying to spot an eavesdropper hiding beneath the stacks of proofs, storyboards, and ratings statistics. Then his face loosened into a grin. "Whew! This has been a crazy day, and before it gets any crazier, I think we'd better get the hell out of here. Just give me a chance to call a couple of the guys I want you to meet."

Perched on the edge of his littered desk, Steve cradled the phone beneath his chin while he waited for someone to pick up. "So, tell me what you've been up to."

With her back turned to Steve, Vanessa pretended to examine a poster-size print of a cat-food ad while she racked her brain for an acceptable answer that would not be an outright lie. "I've been working on a freelance marketing project," she mumbled, blinking at the smug-faced cat dressed in a judge's robes. "The verdict is in on Kuddle Kitty Kitten Kibbles," the headline proclaimed. But looking at the miniature gavel the cat was wielding in his paw, Vanessa got the uneasy feeling he was passing sentence on her for twisting the truth. Actually, her volunteer work for the Contained Growth Committee *could* be called marketing, she thought defensively, turning away from the unsympathetic feline.

Fortunately, Steve was now engrossed in rapid-fire conversation. When he at last threw the receiver onto its cradle, he sprang off the edge of the desk and straightened his tie. "All set," he announced. He shot a wary eye toward the closed door and lowered his voice. "Uh, look, maybe I oughta give you a tip about..."

Vanessa's ears instantly pricked up, but before Steve could share his information, an aggressive rap on the door cut him short. "About what?" she rasped, but the door had already swung open, admitting two men and an attractive gray-haired woman. Vanessa managed to put on a suitably professional smile and exchange solid, confident handshakes as Steve handled introductions.

Vanessa instinctively liked Vivian Chase, who nodded graciously when Steve explained that she handled public relations for one of his account group's clients. She was surprised to learn that the shorter of the two men, a stubby fellow with a boyish shock of blond hair, was George Olsen, Account Supervisor for the Lansing Brothers' bathroom-tissue account. But she almost lost her composure when Steve made his final introduction.

"Jason McNair is account supervisor for the Burberry Bay condensed-soup line *and* Whitney-Spawn Properties." Steve delivered the information with a dramatic flourish, winning an insolent smile from McNair.

"From what I read in *Ad-dendum*, landing Whitney-Spawn was quite a coup," Vanessa heard herself say, but as her eyes studied the arrogant, large-jowled face, she had no doubt about whom Steve had wished to warn her. Looking into those calculating eyes, she vowed never again to accuse Nikki of exaggeration.

Thank God, Lansing Brothers is Olsen's account, and not McNair's, she kept thinking as their party piled into the elevator and glided up to the elegant top-floor restaurant. Meeting Nikki had been more than an omen—it had been providential. She continued to congratulate herself silently while they followed a black-jacketed waiter to a window table offering a panoramic view of the city. Armed with Nikki's warning, she could safely avoid blundering into a confrontation with McNair.

Just how easy it would be to lock horns with the contentious account supervisor was apparent even before the cocktails had been served. Vanessa had to bite her tongue as she watched McNair rudely interrupt Vivian Chase to give his own version of a recent new-business campaign.

"Russ Dominick developed the concept for that presentation," Vivian managed to comment. "If you worked in Richmond, you probably know Russ, Vanessa."

"Dominick's original concept stank," McNair snorted before Vanessa could respond.

"That's your opinion, Jason," Vivian countered. "And anyway, the client loved the final storyboard, which is all that counts."

McNair gave Vivian a contemptuous glance that clearly questioned her judgment, but the waiter arrived with their order, mercifully short-circuiting the discussion for the time being. Vanessa was grateful for the food; somewhere between Steve's office and the restaurant, she had acquired a formidable headache, one that she optimistically attributed to an empty stomach.

But her temples were still throbbing when the last plate had been cleared and the coffee served. Although the lunchtime conversation had progressed amiably enough, centering on Henson & Knowles's recent successes, Vanessa felt the strain of staying constantly on guard. She was all too aware of the undercurrents flowing beneath the casual comments to let herself relax. Until she better understood the complicated force fields at work in the agency, she would watch closely and weigh each word with care.

Apparently, she had acquitted herself favorably in George Olsen's eyes so far. When he managed to draw her into a side conversation, he seemed eager to hear her opinion of his strategy for the next Wonderpuff Tissue campaign.

"Basically, it's the same sort of blitz that Steve tells me you masterminded for Chick-a-Doodles," George explained, drumming his pudgy fingers lightly on the edge of the table.

"With Chick-a-Doodles, we felt that anything less than all-out saturation would be a waste of money." Vanessa was pleased when George nodded and squirmed around in his chair to face her, but before she could outline the history of the ad campaign, an abrasive voice intruded on their conversation.

"You worked on the Federated Hospitals account, didn't you?" Jason McNair remarked loudly enough to get the attention of the entire table.

For a moment, Vanessa stared at him across the table. That McNair would not have known such basic information about a serious job candidate was inconceivable, but as she studied that smug, heavy face she realized he had posed the question for one reason only: to put her on the spot.

"Yes, that's right," she said evenly. If McNair hoped to embarrass her, he was going to be sorely disappointed.

McNair nodded, letting his dark eyes drift across her impassive face. Those were shark's eyes, she thought, cold and empty and full of gratuitous malice.

"Everyone's heard about the Dalton Agency getting the Federated Hospitals account," McNair remarked in a voice loud enough so everyone could hear. He pretended to be absorbed in the matchbook he was turning between his fingers. "But I'm always curious about what *really* happened. And since you were right there," he poised the matchbook on the edge of the ashtray, "at the center of things, you're the obvious person to ask." The smile he gave her was pure poison.

Even a prisoner of war is required to give only his name, rank, and serial number; unfortunately, the Geneva Convention does not extend to hapless job candidates. Staring at her opponent, Vanessa struggled to keep cool. "There were some management changes at Federated, and some of the new people had worked with Dalton before." She spoke very slowly and distinctly, as if she were explaining a simple concept to a not-very-bright pupil. *Got it straight, Bozo? Or do I have to spell it out for you?*

McNair produced a deprecating laugh, the sort of evil snicker with which old-time movie villains announced their heinous intentions. "Come on, Vanessa. It was your account—you must have known why they were dissatisfied enough to take their business elsewhere. You can be straight with us."

Vanessa felt her hand stir where it rested limply on the table, seized by the urge to grab the glass of ice water and throw its contents in his face. Rotund little George shifted at her side, checking his watch and then tossing back the dregs of his Scotch and soda. Vivian Chase muttered something about an appointment she had later that afternoon, but Vanessa could tell they were all watching her, waiting to see how she would handle McNair's baiting.

Vanessa folded her hands on the table and took a deep breath. Beneath the table, she felt Steve's foot press hers; when she glanced at him his black eyes telegraphed their support. "The truth is pretty dull, I'm afraid. As I just told you, Dalton profited from the management shuffle at Federated. The new managers had worked with that agency before and decided to bring them in."

McNair leaned back in his chair, glaring skeptically. "Well, that's very interesting" was all he said. Not that he needed to say anything more; with a few well-chosen comments he had succeeded in indelibly underscoring her association with the Federated Hospitals debacle.

The rest of the luncheon was mercifully brief, or so it seemed. By that point, Vanessa had lost the ability to gauge time. Like an automaton programmed for unfailing courtesy, she smiled and shook hands with everyone, even Jason McNair, before the party broke up in H & K's reception area.

Vivian Chase gave her a cunning wink before she ducked into the elevator. "I'll look forward to working with you," she called just before the door slid shut.

Vanessa nodded to the closed door, acknowledging the polite gesture. George Olsen, too, was perfunctorily nice, albeit in an obvious hurry. Even Steve seemed relieved when his secretary pounced on him with a dozen pink phone-slips and the loudly whispered announcement that "the Old Man wants to talk with you."

Steve rolled his eyes heavenward, or more precisely, in the direction of Hamilton Knowles's eighteenth-floor suite. "Damn it! And I was really hankering for us to sit down and have another cup of coffee together. Guess we'll have to take a rain check." He shrugged dramatically.

Vanessa did her part to put this last stage of the interview out of its misery. "I have a plane to catch, anyway."

"We'll touch base soon. I expect George will want to get you down for a meeting with the Old Man pretty fast." He rolled his eyes again before quickly bussing her cheek. "Have a good trip, Van."

Vanessa felt as if she had one last crumpled smile left, and she used it then. "Thanks, Steve. And thanks for calling me."

"Sure thing," he called to her over his shoulder as he set off in a run down the corridor.

PEACHTREE STREET was already clogged with the first glut of rush-hour traffic, but for once Vanessa was too exhausted to worry about getting to the airport on time. She tumbled into the first cab that responded to her limp wave and sank into the back seat.

*What a mess I've made of my life! I can't do anything right anymore. After bumbling through things with Taylor last night, I manage to fly down here and blow the interview. If only that man, McNair, had behaved like a decent human being. If only I had been clever enough to defend myself. I've been unemployed for almost five months now. Five months! Some day I'll run out of money, and then what? God, if Sandra has to drop out of school, I'll never forgive myself.*

Her head seemed to swell with miserable thoughts, throbbing until she felt it would burst. Fumbling through her handbag, she managed to find a purse pack of Tylenol. *My first success of the year,* she thought as she forced the caplet down her dry throat.

By the time she reached the airport, her headache had abated somewhat, but it surged with renewed fury when she checked in and discovered that her flight was delayed in Dallas.

"They've got some real stormy weather out there, heavy rain, lots of lightning," the airline clerk told her, solemnly shaking his head. "Thank goodness, everything's okay here."

*Speak for yourself,* Vanessa thought. "I suppose I'll just check back in an hour or so?"

"That'll be fine, ma'am."

The nearest cocktail lounge was already overflowing, and Vanessa almost overlooked the single vacant stool remaining at the bar. Perhaps a glass of wine would make her feel a little better, or at least help her to relax. As she sipped the cool white wine, however, she became increasingly aware of the noise surrounding her, of the weary-eyed business travelers slumped listlessly over their drinks, of the vague impersonality that characterizes all airports.

Sitting there with her wine, Vanessa wanted nothing more than to be home. But then she didn't really have a home anymore, did she? Great-aunt Charlotte's place might be a grand old house, but a home was much more: shared laughter, a fire crackling in the grate, someone to sit in front of that fire with, snuggling and letting the soles of your feet scorch to a crisp. When she got back to the house, it would be as still as a tomb; there would be no fire—never mind that it was April—and certainly no one to share anything with. Her throat constricted—it was surely the wine—and her eyes began to sting—a result of the pervasive cigarette smoke, no doubt.

Vanessa was staring out into the blurry concourse when a shadowy image flashed across her consciousness. Blinking, she conjured up a shaggy gray head with floppy ears and a pair of soulful, dark eyes. Emily might be only a donkey, but she loved and depended on Vanessa, a responsibility not to be taken lightly. Poor little creature, she would be getting restless now, wondering why her supper was so late. The way things were going, who knew when Vanessa would get home?

Pausing only long enough to throw a few bills onto the bar, Vanessa ran to the nearest row of pay phones. She and Taylor might not be communicating as well as one could hope, but he would surely be willing to run by the house and feed Emily. As she waited for the call to go through, she felt a ripple of anticipation. It would be good to hear that rich, melodious voice of his, regardless of what he had to say. She was almost overwhelmed by the magnitude of her disappointment when Mary Beasley answered the phone and told her Taylor was out making calls.

"We've already closed for the day, actually. I was just catching up on some paperwork," Mary explained.

Vanessa glanced down at her watch, and grimaced. "I'm sorry to disturb you so late," she apologized.

"Oh, that's all right," Mary cheerfully assured her. "Taylor will be phoning in, if you'd like to leave a message."

"Just tell him my flight has been delayed, and ask him to feed Emily, please."

"I certainly will. By the way, how did your big interview go?"

Vanessa winced as she imagined a tight-lipped Taylor relaying the news about the interview to his secretary. "Just fine," she lied. "Uh, thanks loads, Mary," she hastened to add, eager to deter any further questions.

"Sure."

When Vanessa hung up the phone and turned back to the crowded concourse, she had never felt more alone in her life.

## Chapter Nine

"Gol'darned stubbornest animal on the face of this earth!" Millard White lapped a ruddy arm over the fence and eyed the ram with unabashed admiration. "Guess old Billy and me get along so good 'cause we're so much alike." The burly farmer chuckled waggishly and stretched to scratch between the goat's curving horns.

"Squirt this medicine inside his hoof twice a day, and the infection should clear up very quickly." Taylor was bent over his veterinarian's bag, but he reached up to hand Millard a yellow squeeze-bottle.

Millard squinted over the list of ingredients fine-printed on the side of the bottle and shook his head. "I don't know what all this fancy stuff is, but I reckon it's a sight better than the homemade cures my daddy used. I'll tell you, it was a blessed day when Doc Bowen set up his practice on this island, sure was." The farmer cradled the yellow bottle in his rough hands and glanced down at it awkwardly. "You know, these days most young folks head for the big money in the big cities. It's a rare one who'd throw in his lot with a bunch of dirt-poor folks and their mangy animals here on Parloe.

We're all real glad you decided to follow in your dad's footsteps. I don't know where we'd be without you."

Taylor's shoulders rose in a diffident shrug. "Dad sacrificed so much to establish his practice, I could never abandon it. If Billy's foot doesn't improve, give me a call," he reminded the farmer as he snapped the bag shut and straightened up.

"Sure will, Doc. You take care now."

Taylor managed to smile, pleasantly enough considering how tired he was, and wished his client goodbye. After spending the entire morning in surgery, he had driven twenty miles up the mainland, dispensing swine-flu vaccine and antibiotics and advice at a dozen rural homesteads. Now, as he climbed into the Jeep, the first thing he did was to double-check his list of calls, just to be sure the White place was indeed his last stop for the day. When the car telephone sounded, his heart sank.

"Hello?"

"Is it the connection, or did a mule just kick you in the stomach?" Mary Beasley asked with a bemused chuckle.

"Millard White's goat did his best to give me a hard butt, but I managed to outwit him," Taylor informed her.

"Good for you," Mary put in drily. "I have a few messages for you, if you can take them now."

"Any emergencies?"

"No, not really. You need to call back a couple of Committee volunteers this evening, and some fellow wants you to talk about Big Brothers at a Rotary luncheon next month. But there's only one item that needs your immediate attention."

Taylor resisted the impulse to groan. "Another house call?"

"You might say, but this one should be a snap."

At that point, even writing a prescription would have required more energy than Taylor felt he could spare, but he dutifully reached for the pen and notepad he kept on the dashboard. "Where is it?"

"Vanessa Dorsey called and asked you to feed Emily." When Taylor said nothing, Mary went on. "Her flight has been delayed. Apparently, she's going to get home awfully late."

"Oh, really?" Taylor's lips tightened as he clipped the pen onto the pad and pitched it back onto the dash.

A moment of silence intervened before Mary spoke again. "Poor thing, she sounded as if she'd had a really horrible day. Said the interview went fine, but I don't know..."

Was Mary's tone really so accusative, or was it just his imagination? "Yeah, well, advertising is a tough business, Vanessa knows that." A month ago, Taylor would not have believed he could sound so churlish. "Okay, Mary, let me get off the phone. I'll stop at the Dodderidge place on my way home and feed the donkey."

"Thank you very much." He detected a hint of frost in Mary's voice as she hung up.

Taylor had known Mary Beasley since his boyhood when she had first joined the clinic as his father's secretary; he respected her opinion, both as a co-worker and as a friend. But there was absolutely no way she was going to make him feel guilty now.

Mary had a propensity for motherly intervention, and he had probably discussed Vanessa too freely. Still, he had been careful to conceal his emotions, even when he had mentioned that Vanessa would probably be moving on soon.

He'd known it was futile, yet he couldn't help being drawn to the tall, warm-hearted woman. The two were mismatched—he was rooted to Parloe, she to the wider world. He'd encountered the same situation with other women, but Vanessa was the only one who seemed to matter, at least at this point in his life. Oh, heck, maybe it was his age... They hadn't even exchanged kisses!

Besides, what did Mary expect him to do? Cling to the hope that all Vanessa's interviews would bomb and she would remain permanently jobless and marooned on Parloe? And anyway, even if he could control her fate to suit his own needs, wouldn't it be grossly unfair?

As Taylor guided the Jeep onto the magnolia-lined drive of the Dodderidge estate, a surge of memories engulfed him, threatening to undermine the tight rein he held on his emotions. Through the open window, he could almost smell the chilling scent of smoldering ash, still hanging in the trees in the wake of the fire that had destroyed his own home so many years ago. He had been just shy of ten years old, too young to understand the magnitude of his family's loss. That his father had mortgaged the Bowen's ancestral home to establish his long-dreamed-of veterinary practice had been beyond little Taylor's comprehension. Even at that tender age, however, he had sensed his father's pain, the shame of a proud man forced to ask for help.

As Taylor climbed out of the Jeep, a dark shape stirred in the shadows shrouding the garage. Emily's plaintive bleat carried across the yard, rising and falling in the familiar seesaw that Vanessa always found so charming.

"Okay, Emily. I'm coming," he called to the little donkey trotting along the fence. "Take it easy, girl."

Taylor patted the animal's soft neck, pushing her gently away from the gate. Walking to the stall, he could feel her warm breath through the back of his shirt as she followed him, matching her neat little steps with his. The creature was more like a dog than a donkey, he mused, but then Vanessa babied her shamelessly.

"Here's a little extra for you, since you had to wait so long for your supper." Taylor shook an additional handful of oats into the donkey's feed bin and then replaced the lid on the grain barrel. A contented crunching filled the garage, occasionally interspersed with the rustle of a small hoof pawing the straw.

"You're going to miss her, too, aren't you?" Taylor murmured softly, reaching to brush a wisp of hay from the donkey's mane. The large, dark eyes remained fixed and uncomprehending. *They're the lucky ones, those that don't know what's in store for them.*

Tossing aside the blade of dried grass, Taylor walked slowly to the door. As he latched the lower half of the double door, he glanced up at the full moon. Its opalescent globe was marbled with threads of cloud; with luck, the rain would hold off until Vanessa was safely home.

The least he could do was to turn on a few lights for her, Taylor thought as he followed the path around the house. He groped behind one of the freshly painted shutters and located the key hanging on a concealed hook. When he opened the front door, he paused for a second, relishing the familiar odor of old wood, lemon oil, and the faintest remnant of Vanessa's perfume. As if to curb the emotions awakened by that evocative potpourri, he switched on the light.

He had not expected to feel like an intruder as he pulled the drapes and adjusted the table lamp in the small front parlor, but something prompted him to move quietly, almost stealthily. Everywhere, the vestiges of Vanessa's life were visible—a pair of sunglasses lying on the mantel, the toe of a sandal peaking out from beneath the hassock, a book left open, facedown where she had put it aside—and he took care to disturb nothing.

He was on his way out of the house when he noticed the dining-room door standing ajar. Through the narrow opening he glimpsed the big mahogany table. Vanessa's proposals for the Contained Growth Committee were just where they had left them, neatly stacked on the table next to the enormous box of material he had given her. She had worked fanatically hard on the project, had put aside her own concerns and applied every ounce of professional skill she possessed to develop the group's plan—with impressive results. Vanessa had problems of her own, but she had not let them blind her to the needs of others.

Suddenly, Taylor felt a wave of shame as he recalled the last time he had stood in the dining-room doorway. When Vanessa had told him about her upcoming interview in Atlanta, he had been so self-centered, he had only thought of what that job prospect meant to him. Worse still, when she had tried to discuss things with him, he had deliberately held her at arm's length, used her discomfiture to cushion his own disappointment.

*I want to be there for you when you need me.* His whispered promise echoed in his mind, taunting him. She had needed him then, needed his support and understanding; he could not have failed her more miserably. Suddenly, Taylor turned away from the empty dining room. The hall was plunged into darkness as he snapped off the light and fled into the night.

THE LEFT FRONT WHEEL sank into a pothole, jarring the Thunderbird so roughly that Vanessa almost expected both doors to fly open. Normally, she prided herself on her familiarity with the dirt road and the skill with which she circumvented its many snares. But tonight her only concern was to get home as fast as possible, never mind the toll her haste took on the car. She felt as if she had spent the better part of eternity slumped in a blue vinyl chair at the airport, leafing through vapid magazines and checking her watch. With the house now less than a quarter of a mile away, she had to fight the urge to flatten the accelerator.

The first thing Vanessa noticed when she wheeled the car up in front of the house was the gray silhouette of Emily's head, thrust over the closed lower door of the barn. Taylor must have gotten the message she had given Mary Beasley. Stepping out of the car, she could see a nebulous glow from behind the parlor curtains. He had apparently switched on a few lights for her, too. Well, Taylor could be really thoughtful; he had already demonstrated that on several occasions.

Vanessa heaved her briefcase out of the car, braced it at her side and nudged the car door shut with her knee. Yes, Taylor was thoughtful and charming and sweet and sexy and utterly incapable of understanding her predicament. When she had tried to talk with him yesterday, he had repelled her with unyielding smiles and perfunctory congratulations. She supposed that the remainder of their association would be conducted through the same invisible barrier. Her shoulders sank a little lower as she trudged up the steps.

She was fumbling with her keys, struggling to balance the briefcase against her hip, when the front door unexpectedly opened of its own accord. For a split second, Vanessa froze, clutching the briefcase like a shield in front of her. Had Taylor left the front door unlocked after he turned on the lights? Or had someone else . . .

The hall floor creaked, as if someone were gauging his steps as he approached. Then a tall figure loomed in the unlighted foyer. Dropping the briefcase, Vanessa turned on her heel. She was dashing toward the porch when a low voice stopped her in her tracks.

"Sorry if I frightened you, but I did want this to be a surprise." The hall light clicked on, and Vanessa turned to find Taylor stepping into the doorway.

"Well, it sure as hell was a surprise!" Vanessa managed to gasp as her heart rate slowed to normal. She noticed not only that Taylor was smiling warmly, but also that he wore . . . a *tuxedo*. In his right hand he held something that looked suspiciously like a champagne glass.

"Welcome home." With two long strides, he bridged the distance separating them and presented her with the glass. Then he stepped back to await her approval.

Vanessa eyed the pale platinum liquid skeptically. "Champagne?"

"Why don't you taste it and see?" A trace of the old Taylor, the one who teased and cajoled with such disarming skill, glimmered to the surface.

Vanessa shook her head, taking care to hold the glass steady. "Oh, no. I've been drinking *alone* in that godforsaken airport lounge for what seemed like forever. I'm not taking so much as a sip unless you join me. I suppose you have another glass?" When she grinned slightly, her facial muscles relaxed as if by magic.

"Not only do I have another champagne glass..."
Bowing slightly from the waist, he gestured toward the
door, beckoning her to enter.

Vanessa cast an uncertain glance at Taylor, but she let
him escort her into the hall. From behind one of the
closed doors, she could hear soft music. A tantalizing
fragrance, redolent of thyme and rosemary, hung in the
air.

"What on earth is going on here?" Vanessa demanded, but Taylor only grasped her elbow and guided
her into the dining room.

For a moment, Vanessa could only stare in mute
amazement. Gone were the stacks of folders, the yellow legal pads, and the felt-tip pens with which she had
hammered out the committee's proposal. The mahogany table was now covered with an ivory linen cloth,
etched with creamy scrolls of Battenburg lace. Nestled
in a cluster of pink carnations, lighted white tapers cast
their sparkling light on the bone china, silver and crys-
tal arranged at one end of the table. Yet more candles
lined the mantel where the arching mirror multiplied
their flickering.

Suddenly Vanessa turned and looked up into Taylor's face. "You did all of this?"

"Uh-huh." Looking down at his shoes, he laughed
apologetically. "You know, sometimes I'm good for a
little more than supervising pregnant sows and dyspep-
tic donkeys."

"That's not what I meant!" Vanessa countered. She
turned back to the room, clasping both arms across her
chest. "This...this is simply marvelous!"

"I was hoping you'd be pleased."

Vanessa spun around to face him again. "How could
I not be?" she chided.

Taylor was still smiling, but his jade-green eyes grew earnest. "Mary told me she thought you sounded disappointed about the interview."

Vanessa shook her head and lifted a hand to still his regrets. She might as well come clean. "'Disappointing' is too mild a word—try 'disastrous.' Believe me, one of those guys was such an impossible jerk, I don't know how I would have managed to work in the same building with him. It's just as well they didn't like me all that much." On reflection, she realized that her deliberately frivolous explanation contained more than a kernel of truth.

"Maybe. Actually, what I meant to say was that I'm sorry about the way I acted yesterday."

"Oh, Taylor!" Vanessa released her arms and then clasped them again, letting her eyes drift across the shimmering mantel mirror. "There's nothing to be sorry about."

"Yes, there is," he insisted. "I was surly and unpleasant. You wanted to talk, but I didn't want to hear what you had to say. Or at least I thought I didn't. I guess all I could think was that you would be going away forever, and . . . I just don't know if I could stand that." She felt his hand close over hers, drawing it into his sure grasp.

Vanessa looked down at their entwined hands. "I don't know if I could, either," she said softly. She pressed her lip between her teeth to quell its trembling.

Taylor worked his thumb free and gently stroked her wrist. "Since I saw you last, I've thought a lot about so many things that have happened to me, about life. But, you know, when I saw you get out of the car tonight and walk up those steps, I realized that one thing really mattered to me. I want to be with you, Vanessa."

The pressure of his thumb increased as his hand eased along her arm.

Vanessa clamped her hand over his, halting its progress with a tender squeeze. "Well, we are together, tonight." She smiled down at the two hands—one long and slim, the other broader and darkened by the sun. She tightened her hold over those strong, tanned fingers, trying to steady herself. She had not been prepared for his simple yet deeply touching admission, even less so for the havoc it wrought with her emotions. So many complex factors ruled their fates, dictated their fortunes, but right now she did not want to think about anything but the magical, candlelit world Taylor had created for them alone.

Taylor seemed to understand. Stepping back, he chafed her wrist playfully. "Let's enjoy ourselves, then. Have you eaten?" he asked in a lighter tone.

"No, not unless you count two bags of honey-roasted nuts."

"I don't." His hand slid behind her back, prodding her toward the table. "I think I can top airline fare, thanks to your Great-aunt Charlotte's chafing dish and a little help from the Crab Cove's kitchen staff."

As she approached the table, the smell of herb-seasoned seafood beckoned her, but when Taylor pulled out a chair, she balked. "Wait a minute. I can't sit down like *this*—" her hand grazed the front of her rumpled suit "—with you like *that*." Her eyes traveled the length of his well-fitted tuxedo. "Give me a minute to change, okay?" She had already retreated to the door. She waited for him to nod approvingly before dashing down the hall and up the stairs.

In her bedroom, she kicked off her pumps while her fingers wrestled impatiently with the zipper of her skirt.

Swinging open the closet door, she seized Great-aunt Charlotte's violet ball dress and pulled it free of its stodgy denim and cotton neighbors. The still-crisp fabric rustled deliciously as she wriggled the gown over her head. Smoothing the beaded overskirt, she turned in front of the mirror. On Great-aunt Charlotte, the hem must have trailed near the ground, but, thanks to the easy styling of the 1920s, Vanessa was pleased with the effect of the softly draped folds falling just below her knees. She tarried only long enough to slip into her own high-heeled sandals, and then hurried downstairs.

Taylor was waiting in front of the fireplace with his back to the door, but he turned when he heard her enter. His green eyes gleamed, capturing the quivering candlelight, as he regarded her with undisguised admiration.

"Do you like it?" Vanessa lifted a tier of the violet silk and then let it fall. It was a gesture right out of a fairy tale, but in a dress like this one it seemed perfectly natural.

"You're beautiful, absolutely beautiful!" Taylor's voice was husky. "You're like a vision."

"But this is real," she reminded him. When she took the hand he held out to her, she squeezed it tightly, savoring its palpable warmth.

But *could* such a dreamlike setting—the candles, the flowers, the music—be real? Could real champagne possibly sparkle with such effervescence? Without some magical ingredient, the aromatic seafood dish would surely not have tasted so delicious. And did real-life men and women ever look into each other's eyes with such tenderness? Could a flesh-and-blood man ever anticipate a woman's wishes so completely, communicate his own desire to fulfill them so ardently?

*If this is a dream, then let me dream it forever.* As they talked over dinner, sipping the tingling champagne and sharing quiet laughter, Vanessa felt as if she had left behind the ordinary world with its petty distinctions between real and imaginary. Once, during a lull between records, they heard the antique grandfather clock chime from the hall, but neither of them bothered to count the strokes. For now, time was too trivial a concern to intrude on their intimacy.

When a medley of sentimental favorites from the Forties dropped onto the turntable, Taylor rose and pulled Vanessa to her feet. Leaning her head against his firm shoulder, she closed her eyes and let him guide her across the polished hardwood floor. She could feel her filmy skirt swish against her legs as they swept through the door and down the hall. The music seemed to follow them, growing sweeter and more mellow in the distance. On the porch, the cool air kissed her bare arms, and Taylor instinctively pulled her closer. The night seemed to well up around them, suffusing them in its heady fragrance.

She had no idea how long they danced. One tune blended into another, until she was only aware of his solid chest beneath her cheek and the strong hands that held her a willing captive. Once, she heard him murmur her name, but she only sighed in response. Even when the rain began, she refused to open her eyes. She felt a damp spray as they glided along the porch rail, but Taylor turned, shielding her from the shower with his body.

Suddenly, the air seemed to shudder, rent by an angry clap of thunder. Vanessa unwillingly opened her eyes. When a jagged streak of lightning tore across the sky, she shivered.

Taylor's encircling arm tightened around her shoulders. "Maybe we should go inside. You're getting wet." He carefully smoothed a droplet from her exposed shoulder. Then he bent his head, letting his lips follow the trail left by his fingers. Turning her arm upward, he nuzzled the cleft of her elbow. The thunder rumbled menacingly, but this time Vanessa did not flinch. Nothing could distract her now from the exquisite sensations his lips had aroused.

Stepping backward, Vanessa let him guide her into the house. But now they followed a different music: the rhythms of their own bodies, swaying together in a timeless dance. Overhead the hall light caught them in its yellow shaft, flickered, and then fell dark.

"The power is gone," Taylor whispered into her hair.

"But we have the candles," Vanessa murmured back.

Although the record player had now been silenced, Taylor led her into the dining room in graceful turns. As they waltzed past the mantel, he paused to extinguish one candle, then swept her into another turn before halting to blow out the next flame. Finally, only one lighted taper remained. Taylor lifted the silver candlestick and presented it to Vanessa. For a moment, she held it aloft, watching the irregular play of light and shadow on his face. When he lifted her into his arms, the flame wavered for a moment, then surged once more, clean and bright. With her cheek pillowed against his shoulder, Vanessa watched the patterns their shadows cast against the wide aureole of light that filled the stairwell.

In the bedroom he paused and took the candle from her. Still pressing her close against his chest, he placed the candle on the antique dresser and then lowered her onto the bed. Lying back against the quilted counterpane, Vanessa stretched her arms, unfurling the violet silk until it framed her body like a butterfly's gossamer wings. The bed shifted slightly as Taylor rested one knee next to hers.

Not moving, she watched him shed the black tuxedo jacket. When he leaned over her, she could see the straining contours of his muscular chest beneath the fine white fabric of his shirt. "You're so beautiful." His lips lightly traced her hairline. "So magnificent." His warm breath punctuated each kiss he bestowed on her temple. "Sometimes I can hardly believe you're real." His tongue teased her earlobe, then flirted along the curve of her jaw.

Vanessa lifted her hands and stroked his hair. She had wanted to do that for a long time. When he murmured his pleasure, she pulled him toward her. Now she was leading him, guiding his face to her own. When their lips met, she opened to him, his urgency fanning her own.

Taylor let out a long breath and pushed himself back, bridging her legs with his knees. She shivered with delight as his hands slipped inside the gown's square neck to caress the tops of her breasts. While one hand continued to explore the full curves of flesh, the other withdrew to lift her slightly. When he began to undo the tiny buttons along the back of the dress, she did the same to his shirt. She could feel the cool air against her back where the dress now hung open. Taylor impatiently pulled his shirttail free and then cast his shirt aside. His bronzed skin gleamed in the candlelight, the muscles stretched taut over his lean ribs.

"Oh, Taylor!" Vanessa could not contain herself as she felt the silken bodice drift away from her shoulders, then her breasts, slipping like a whisper down the length of her body. Her skin felt unnaturally hot beneath his hands as he peeled away her stockings and cast them aside, along with the dress. She reached for him, but he pushed her gently back onto the bed. The sound of her quickened breathing swelled as she watched him discard his remaining clothing.

Something in her wanted to hold him away long enough to relish fully every inch of his masculine beauty; another part of her yearned to draw him to her, feel his warmth and weight on her, discover his body with her own. Taylor let her struggle with these conflicting impulses for only a moment. When he stretched out beside her, she turned toward him eagerly. His hands cupped her breasts, fondling them as his lips teased the flushed nipples into rigid points. Deep within, she was aching now, racked with an almost unbearable desire for him. When his hand slipped lower along her body, she yielded readily to the pressure, opening herself to him.

Vanessa wrapped her arms around his neck. As his body's heated rhythm intensified, she rose against him until they moved as one. For a single moment, they *were* one, united in an ecstasy that transcended normal physical laws. When they at last relaxed their hold on each other, Taylor smoothed her cheek. Smiling tenderly, he held his damp palm up, and she realized that she had been crying. *Tears of joy,* she thought, smiling back at him. And such boundless joy it was, a delight that went far beyond bodily release, one that sated the heart and soul as well. How could anyone ever find words to describe such sublime feelings?

"I love you," Taylor whispered as he burrowed his face into her hair.

Snuggling against his chest, Vanessa knew Taylor had found them.

## Chapter Ten

Dear Steve,
I want to thank you for arranging the interview for
me at Henson & Knowles last week. I certainly appreciated the chance to...

Frowning, Vanessa leaned back in the chair and
folded her arms across her chest. *Appreciated the
chance to be humiliated in front of your colleagues?*
How about *appreciated the chance to shadowbox with
Jason McNair. That Jason is some guy, isn't he?* Since
breakfast, she had been sitting at the desk, trying to
compose a respectable thank-you letter to Steve Czerny.
So far, she had come up with one satisfactory line:
"Dear Steve." At this point, she was beginning to
wonder if there was anything she could say that would
seem appropriate in the wake of such a debacle.

She had just ripped out the spoiled paper and inserted a fresh sheet when she heard a car's tinny engine
sputtering up the drive. Vanessa leaned across the desk
and parted the curtains. She smiled in surprise at the
sight of the rusty orange Beetle rattling to a halt in front
of the porch. The little car rocked as Matt threw open
the front door and jumped out, with Denny hot on his

heels. From the front door, Vanessa could see their mother getting from behind the wheel.

"Boys, mind those plants!" Grace Burch rushed around the car, just in time to steady a sagging cardboard box that Matt was wrestling out of the back seat.

"I swear, if you two aren't the world's worst," Grace was complaining as she mounted the porch steps. Looking up, she smiled, and Vanessa was pleased to note that her face looked considerably less strained than it had during their last encounter. "Good morning, Vanessa. I hope we aren't disturbing you, but we wanted to drive over and bring you some tomato plants." She jerked her head toward Denny, who was holding the box of seedlings. "We've got more than we need."

"How thoughtful of you!" Vanessa hurried to relieve the small boy of his burden. She eyed the little plants appreciatively. "Gee, I've never grown my own tomatoes before. In fact, I've never grown anything edible in my life."

Grace stepped back and buried her hands in the back pockets of her cotton slacks. "There's not much to it. Just stick 'em in the ground and give 'em a little fertilizer and water."

Vanessa grinned. "That sounds simple enough." She stooped to deposit the box on the seat of one of the porch chairs. "It's a shame we people aren't that easy to care for."

"It sure is," Grace concurred with such weary vehemence that Vanessa instantly regretted her blunder. What she had intended as an offhand joke had struck a nerve with the beleaguered widow, and she quickly changed the subject.

"Won't you come in for some coffee? I just brewed a fresh pot."

Grace glanced at the beat-up old car and then shrugged and smiled. "Sure. I'd love to."

Denny balked at the top of the porch steps. "Where's Emily? You said we could visit her someday," he reminded Vanessa.

"Yeah!" Matt chimed in. "Can we give her an apple? We've got some apples in the car."

"Apples are one of Emily's favorite snacks," Vanessa told them. She walked to the porch rail and pointed the boys toward the pen where Emily was quietly grazing. As they raced around the house, the little donkey looked up and brayed, winning delighted shrieks from both boys.

"Take care, both of you!" Grace hollered after them.

"Emily is very gentle," Vanessa reassured her as they walked down the hall to the kitchen. "I don't think she would ever bite or kick a child."

Grace chuckled. "It's not the donkey I'm worried about."

Vanessa invited Grace to have a seat at the kitchen table and then took two mugs from the cupboard. "I'm sorry the kitchen is so untidy," she apologized over her shoulder as she filled the two cups. "I've just been so busy lately I haven't done much cleaning." She cast a rueful glance at the assorted plates and saucepans piled in the sink.

"You've got a real nice place here, nice and cozy," Grace remarked. "And anyhow, I expect the work you've been doing for the Committee is a lot more important than washing dishes and mopping floors. When I ran into Cora Henderson at the One-Stop the other day, she just couldn't say enough good things about all you've done."

Vanessa carefully slid a mug across the table to Grace and then seated herself. "At least we managed to get the press releases in the mail this weekend. I hope we see some results. Soon," she added, spooning an extra pinch of sugar into her mug.

"So do I." Grace hesitated, letting her eyes drift around the room. Although she took her coffee black, she had been stirring it steadily for several seconds. "I really want to thank you," she went on hesitantly. "I mean, for taking a stand for the island and giving us a helping hand, even though you're just passing through. I've been so mad lately, felt fed up with everything. The more I think about what's happening to me and my boys, the angrier I get, but there doesn't seem to be anything I can do to set it right. I keep looking for a way to fight back." She clutched the spoon tightly, turning the skin over her knuckles a waxy white. "But so far I haven't found one. Sometimes I wonder if I can do anything anymore, you know what I mean?" She fixed Vanessa with her probing brown eyes.

Vanessa nodded slowly. "Yes, I do," she said quietly. *More than you can imagine.*

"I would just love to do something to set these developers on their heels. But about all I know is how to cook—that's what I've done all my life. It's been good enough, up till now, but . . ."

Vanessa leaned across the table and touched Grace's wrist gently. "There *is* a lot you and everyone else can do," she insisted. Looking into her companion's thin face, she recognized the frustration and self-doubt reflected there, feelings that mirrored her own all too closely.

Grace was shaking her head. "I don't know, Vanessa. If it wasn't for those two boys, I often think I'd just give up." Her soft voice trailed off.

Vanessa's fingers closed over the thin wrist and gave it a firm squeeze. "I've felt like that a lot since I lost my job last year."

Grace looked up abruptly, and her eyes widened in disbelief. "*You* lost your job?"

"Yes, I did. I've been unemployed for, let's see—" she shifted her arm for a glance at the date on her watch, "—almost six months now. I keep wondering if I'll ever find another job, keep asking myself if anyone in the world will want to hire a reject like me. But I just hang on to my hopes." She heaved a sigh. What had begun as an attempt to comfort Grace had evolved into a confession, but she was startled at how good it felt to share some of her own frustration with a sympathetic listener. "If I only had myself to worry about, I don't think I would feel quite so desperate. But I'm helping my sister finish her education, and Mom depends on me, too."

"I had no idea." Grace's voice was hushed.

Vanessa nodded and then managed a wry smile. "Well, I wouldn't have known about the Crab Cove's changing hands if Winona hadn't told me. I guess we're both pretty good at keeping our little secrets."

"I guess we are." Grace chuckled over her raised mug. She was about to take a sip of coffee when a series of bloodcurdling yells echoed from the front yard. "I swear, someday I really am going to skin those kids alive," she muttered, scooting her chair back.

Grace stormed down the hall, with Vanessa right behind her. "All right, just what's going on out here?" she demanded as she threw open the front door.

Taylor halted at the bottom of the porch steps and held up both hands in self-defense. "Take it easy, Gracie. We were just having a little fun."

Grace was obviously as surprised as Vanessa to see him there, flanked by the two grinning boys, but she quickly recovered herself. "Fun, huh? Sounded more to me like someone having his head chopped off."

Taylor fastened an arm around both reddish-brown heads and gave them guillotine-style squeezes, eliciting suitably ghastly cries from the boys.

"Enough!" Grace pleaded, and Taylor released the giggling boys.

Vanessa had been watching the clowning from the door, but she now walked out onto the porch. "This is a pleasant surprise." She propped one hip against the railing and smiled down at him.

Since that magical evening on her return from Atlanta, every aspect of their relationship had undergone a profound transformation. The most mundane conversation now carried a subtle charge of excitement; the most casual glance or smile, a deeper meaning only they were privy to.

"I was making calls in your neck of the woods, so I decided to drop by and share the good news with you."

Vanessa could tell that Taylor was deliberately taking his time. "What news?" she prompted, almost in chorus with Grace.

Taylor hooked two fingers through his belt. "Oh, just that the Committee is about to become a legitimate news item. Seems that your press release caught the eye of the news director at one of the Charleston TV stations. As luck would have it, I had worked with one of their reporters on a public service announcement for the Big Brothers last year, so..." He paused, resting a foot on the bottom step. When he looked up, he laughed to see both Grace and Vanessa leaning eagerly over the porch rail.

"So?" Vanessa prodded him.

"So Jack is coming out here Friday morning to shoot a feature on the problems we're facing." He suddenly grabbed a hand from both Vanessa and Grace and gave them a good tug. "Ladies, Parloe Island is about to become a hot news item."

"That's wonderful!" Vanessa gasped, and Grace let out an unrestrained whoop that rivaled her sons' most earsplitting yells.

"I thought you'd agree. But before we open the champagne, we need to take care of a few details. Diana has been interning long enough to cover for me at the clinic on Friday, so I can be available when the television crew arrives."

"If you need any help getting things organized, you know you can count on me," Vanessa volunteered.

"Thanks. I've already phoned Ray and Cora, and they're willing to talk about the Committee's goals on camera." Taylor was still beaming, but Vanessa could tell his mind was racing ahead to the pragmatic details of putting Parloe's best collective foot forward.

Vanessa eased off the railing. "You should let them interview you, too," she suggested.

Taylor shrugged. "If they want to, fine, but Jack seems to think the segment would have more impact if some of the people directly affected by the rampant development could tell their stories—you know, shrimpers, the older beach-house residents. I've already asked a couple of my clients if they would talk with Jack, and they're more than willing to sound off. Trouble is, their objections sound a lot like my own."

Frowning, Vanessa chewed her lip. "We need some-one who's been directly hit."

Grace had been listening without comment, but she now pushed herself away from the porch rail. "I'll do it," she said quietly. When Taylor and Vanessa turned toward her in unison, she cleared her throat. "I'll talk with that TV reporter."

"You will?" Taylor looked more than a little sur-prised.

Grace raised her chin, drawing herself up to her full height. "And why not? I reckon I have a complaint about as big as anybody's on this island."

Taylor scrambled to recover himself. "It would be great if you would talk with the reporter! But I want you to understand that I wasn't dropping hints, trying to pressure you. I know when we first started organizing the Committee, you said you needed some time to think before you volunteered to do anything," he reminded her gently.

"Well, I've done my thinking." When Grace squared her shoulders, she looked as if she were ready to take on the most formidable opponent single-handedly. "Might as well let off steam in front of a TV camera as any-where else, I guess."

"You'll be doing more than letting off steam, Grace. What you have to say will make a real impression on people. Believe me, you'll be doing something impor-tant that we'll all thank you for," Taylor assured her.

Grace shook her head, brushing aside his praise. "No need to thank me, Taylor." As she cast her eyes toward Vanessa, an almost imperceptible smile flickered across her face. "I've been waiting to have my say for a long, *long* time."

AS IT TURNED OUT, the islanders could not have wished for a more articulate spokesperson than Grace Burch. When Vanessa arrived with the television crew at the Burches' bungalow on Friday morning, however, she found the young widow in a state of nervous anticipation.

"What if I get all tongue-tied and make a mess of things?" Grace whispered to Vanessa, fidgeting with one of her button earrings. Her dark eyes anxiously followed the sound technician and camera operator as they lugged their equipment up the rickety porch steps.

"You won't," Vanessa assured her calmly. "And anyway, if you do, they can just start all over again."

Grace rolled her eyes. "Oh, Lord! This might take all day."

"You'll do just fine. And you look great," Vanessa added truthfully. Grace had chosen a simple, blue cotton-jersey dress for the occasion; with her fluffy brown hair swept off her face and a touch of lipstick, she was a surprisingly attractive woman.

True to Vanessa's prediction, Grace started to relax as soon as the reporter began talking with her. Indeed, as she nodded and responded to his questions, she seemed entirely unaware of the camera recording her reactions. The reporter had brought a prepared list of questions, but soon abandoned it in favor of simply listening to Grace's unembellished, yet heartfelt account of the Crab Cove's planned transformation and the effect it would have on her and her family.

"It's not that I'm against progress. Everything changes over the years, and this island's no different. But it's my home—always has been—and I want a say in its future. That's only fair, isn't it?" she concluded, fixing her probing dark eyes straight on the camera.

Even the reporter seemed affected by her straightforward delivery. "I certainly appreciate your talking with us, Mrs. Burch. This is just what I was looking for—something to inject a human element into the story." The young man held onto Grace's hand for an extra second before summoning his crew and rushing out to the waiting news van.

Vanessa longed to congratulate Grace, too, but she had time for only a quick thumbs-up and a warm smile as she hurried to catch up with the crew. The reporter wanted some footage contrasting the old Parloe with the new, and Taylor had suggested they shoot a scene that included the Dodderidge house. Vanessa was filled with a quiet pride as she signaled to the news van and turned up the drive to her house. She had always loved Great-aunt Charlotte's ancestral home, but only in the past few weeks had she come to realize how deeply she treasured her memories of the carefree summers she had spent on Parloe. Listening to Grace's compelling plea, she had felt as if Grace were speaking for her, too.

Taylor was waiting on the porch steps. As soon as he had greeted the reporter, he drew Vanessa aside. "How did Grace's interview go?" he asked eagerly.

Vanessa was watching the camera operator stalking back and forth in front of the house, but she inclined her head toward Taylor. "She was absolutely wonderful. If the other interviews went even half as well, these people have gotten a top-notch story from Parloe."

When Taylor released a deep breath, Vanessa got the impression he had been holding it since the crew's arrival. "You know how much Luke hates condos, and when Jack asked him about the Tradewinds project, he got a little long-winded. But, all in all, I think we've pulled this off without a hitch.'' Vanessa felt his hand lightly stroke her arm.

Vanessa covered his hand with her own and gave it a quick pat. ''I'm just glad this is their last stop, and I can almost quit worrying that something will go wrong. About ready?'' she called as the reporter approached them.

Jack Marshall was pulling on his coat, but he looked up and smiled. ''I'm ready if you are.''

Vanessa brushed the wrinkles from her short white skirt and then clasped her hands. While squiring the crew around Parloe, she had been too absorbed in the countless details affecting the news feature's production to give much thought to her own contribution to the segment. Now that the time had come for her to appear before the camera, however, she felt woefully unprepared.

''There's so much I wanted to say. Now I wish I had made some notes,'' Vanessa muttered under her breath to Taylor.

Through her light cotton sweater, she felt his hand smooth her shoulder. ''Just think of what Great-aunt Charlotte would want a TV audience to hear,'' Taylor whispered encouragingly.

Vanessa smiled at the vision of her strong-willed relative briskly leading the television crew on a tour of her estate, but she took inspiration from the fantasy as she chatted with Jack Marshall. Great-aunt Charlotte had been a gifted storyteller, ever willing to enrich her nieces' knowledge of their heritage with lore about the old house. By the time she and the reporter had completed their circuit of the grounds, she had shared many of her great-aunt's anecdotes with him.

Jack looked tired but pleased as he shook hands with Taylor and Vanessa on the front lawn. "You've given me so much interesting material. I'm sorry we can't include all of it in the feature. I can't thank you enough for overseeing things today, Miss Dorsey. Normally, I have to act as my own location manager, and it's a rare pleasure to have someone keep the gears rolling as smoothly as you did. The Committee is certainly lucky to have an advertising professional among its members."

"Anything for the Cause," Vanessa joked to deflect his lavish praise.

"I hope we can run this piece next week, but I'll give you a call when we have a definite air date," Jack called to Taylor as he hurried to the news van and jumped into the front seat. Before he had even pulled the door shut, the van raced down the drive, bouncing perilously over the deep ruts.

Taylor and Vanessa watched the van slip behind the curtain of Spanish moss obscuring the road and then turned back to the house. Arm looped around Taylor's waist, Vanessa guided him along the mossy brick walk leading to the backyard.

"You've put in a full day's work," Taylor remarked. "You must be really tired." His hand, resting on her shoulder, massaged her tight muscles, easing out some of their kinks.

The pleasurable sensations elicited by his fingers brought a smile to Vanessa's face, but her gaze remained fixed on the flaming sun that hovered over the waterway. "Tired but pleased. Why don't we sit on the dock and watch the sunset?"

Taylor only nodded his approval, but he continued to stroke her shoulder as they followed the meandering footpath to the dock. High tide had filled the inlet with frothy gray water that surged around the weathered pilings. Taylor caught Vanessa's hand to steady her progress along the creaking boardwalk. At the end of the dock, she sank down onto the platform, pulling him alongside her. Hands joined, they watched the brilliant orb sink toward the horizon. As the dark trees reached up to receive the dying sun, Taylor's fingers tightened around her hand.

"I'm really grateful to you for talking with Jack on camera today, Vanessa." Taylor's low voice had an unfamiliar hesitancy.

"Please don't thank me, Taylor," she began, but the pressure of his hand quickly silenced her.

"When our house burned, I was Matt's age, too young to realize the significance of what had happened. Oh, I'd been brought up on plenty of stories about my Bowen forefathers, about all the weddings and births and struggles that house had witnessed. But at the time, all I knew was that my life had undergone a big change." Taylor paused for a moment, his eyes focused on the shimmering infinity where the sky met the earth. "For a while, we never seemed to stay in one place very long, were always moving from one relative's house to the next. That first Christmas after the fire, the folks from the church brought us big boxes full of clothes and food. Dad was gracious, but even then I could tell it bothered him to have people feel sorry for us. What I didn't know at the time was that we were really hanging on by a shoestring." He paused and glanced down at their intertwined hands.

"You see, Dad had mortgaged the house to set up his veterinary practice. Borrowing money on the estate would have been unthinkable to all those aristocratic

Bowen ancestors, but by the end of the last century the house was about all the family had left—the house and a lot of pride. Of course, even if we'd had the money, we could never have rebuilt that historic house. But I felt really proud today when I heard you talking with Jack. So much of what you said—about Parloe's history and what we stand to lose if we let it be swept away by so-called progress—well, those are the things I would have wanted to say if that had been the Bowen house.''

"I just hope someone outside this island will listen to our story.'' Vanessa leaned her head against his shoulder, letting her eyes follow the rosy sphere melting into the marsh.

"*Our* story? You wouldn't have said that a month ago, you know,'' Taylor reminded her in a gentle voice.

For a moment, Vanessa avoided looking at him. "A month ago, it wasn't my story,'' she said softly.

"But now it is?''

"A lot has changed, more than I ever imagined possible in so short a time. Somehow I've started to think of Parloe as home. Maybe I've just gotten tired of being homeless.'' She chuckled to disguise the tremor in her voice. "I guess I've begun to realize that home is more than having a title or a lease with your name on it. Home is the place where you feel safe, where you can be yourself, where you can reach out and touch the people you care about—'' her voice dropped to an almost inaudible whisper "—the people you love.''

Taylor lifted his hand, pulling hers along with it. She felt his lips graze the tips of her fingers. "I think you've left something out,'' he murmured, his breath gently caressing her hand.

"I have?'' Vanessa looked up at him, not resisting as he pulled her to his chest.

Taylor nodded, letting his free hand drift across her hair and down her cheek. "Home is where you find the people who care about you." He lifted her chin and held it steady. "The man who loves you."

*And I love you, Taylor. More than I've ever loved anyone or anything. More than I ever dreamed it was possible to love.* Vanessa closed her eyes; at that moment, she did not trust herself to speak, so intense were her emotions. With a touch more eloquent than words, her hands rose to clasp his neck, drawing his face so close she could sense its contours. Behind the red veil of her closed eyes, she discovered each feature anew: the fine, straight nose nuzzling her cheek, the pronounced cleft of his upper lip outlined by her exploring tongue, the pleasingly rough-textured jaw beneath her palm.

"I want to make love to you, Vanessa." His husky voice caught, causing her to open her eyes.

And love her he did, with every touch and look and gesture. For it was love that held their arms and eyes interlocked as they slowly walked to the house and climbed the stairs to the bedroom, reveling in the anticipation. Love gently led their bodies, guiding their limbs on the big four-poster. Love alone could have inspired the unsung song that lifted and carried them into the uncharted heights of passion. And only the deep, ageless, unfathomable mystery of love could have satisfied her entire being so completely.

They lay quietly in each other's arms for some time, watching the light fade behind the chintz curtains. When Vanessa shifted to one side, pulling a lock of hair from beneath his encircling arm, Taylor rolled to face her. For several seconds, he only looked at her, an incredibly tender smile softening the strong planes of his face. She watched as he slid his hand across the pillow and cupped her cheek, carefully tracing the slope of her nose with his thumb, as if he were committing it to memory.

"You have such a pretty little nose." His smile gleamed, expansive and white, in the thickening dusk.

Vanessa laughed softly. "It ought to be pretty—it's certainly the only thing about me that's little."

Taylor shifted his face against the pillow and frowned skeptically. "Oh, I don't know. After all, size is relative." Pushing himself up on his elbow, he fished beneath the cover for her hand and then held it up, flattening the palm against his own. "Take this hand, for instance. You might think it's big, but next to mine...well, see for yourself." He rotated his wrist and regarded the two hands closely.

Vanessa lolled back against the pillow and laughed, but she offered no resistance when he worked her onyx ring from her finger and slid it onto the tip of his pinky. "Fits you perfectly, but I can barely squeeze it down to the first joint."

Vanessa nimbly retrieved her ring and replaced it on her finger. Flipping onto her stomach, she grinned up at him. "You've proved your point." She hesitated and cocked her head toward the hall. "Uh-oh. There goes the phone."

Taylor groaned as he swung his legs over the side of the bed. "Ten to one it's Diana with a veterinary emergency."

Vanessa snatched her robe from the back of the rocking chair and pulled it over her head. "Better now than thirty minutes ago," she called over her shoulder before dashing downstairs to the study. The desk seemed to vibrate with the phone's insistent ringing as she grabbed the receiver.

"Vanessa?" The breathless voice was so agitated that, for a moment, Vanessa did not recognize it. She blinked in surprise when the speaker caught her breath and went on. "This is Sandra. Thank God you're home."

Vanessa was instantly concerned. "You sound really shaken up. Are you okay?"

"It's Mom, Vanessa."

Vanessa's mouth went dry; when she tried to swallow, she felt as if someone were forcing sand down her throat. "Has something happened to her?"

"That's the problem: I don't know. When I tried to call her just now, Mrs. Wilkinson from next door answered the phone. She said Mom had passed out while she was working in the garden this past Thursday. I tried to get the details, but you know how Mrs. Wilkinson is when she's flustered. Can you believe she didn't even think to call you or me when this happened?"

Vanessa interrupted. "Where is Mom now?"

"She's in the hospital. I phoned Dr. Spellman, and his secretary told me he wanted to run some tests. I'm afraid I couldn't get much more out of her. Oh, Van, I'm so worried!"

Hearing her sister's shaky sigh, Vanessa wanted to hug her and make everything all right. "I'll drive up to Montebello tonight. Try to hang on, honey. It may not be as bad as we think," she added in a voice depressingly lacking in conviction.

Sandy swallowed, and Vanessa could imagine her trying to smile. "Call me as soon as you know something, okay?"

"You know I will. Try to get some sleep tonight. Promise?"

"I promise."

After Vanessa had hung up, she stood staring across the room. When Taylor walked up behind her, she took his hand without turning. "That was Sandra. Mom blacked out and is in the hospital," she began in a hoarse whisper. Suddenly, she broke off and wheeled around, burying her face against her shoulder. "Oh, Taylor! What if she's had a stroke? What if...it's really bad?"

Taylor murmured softly to her, gently stroking her hair. But for once even those skilled hands could not soothe away the anxiety gnawing at Vanessa's heart.

## Chapter Eleven

Vanessa had never enjoyed driving the little-frequented state road that connected her hometown with the Interstate, and she was enjoying it even less on this pitch-dark night, alone with her disquieting thoughts. She had been adamant about leaving for Montebello that evening, had resisted Taylor's pleas to wait until morning, thrown a few random things into a suitcase, and set out without stopping to have dinner. She had no idea how many miles she had logged since exiting I-95, but the thick forestation closing around the road now seemed smothering. Occasionally, the headlights picked out the bright eyes of some small animal crouching in the underbrush, and Vanessa would shudder.

When the Montebello water tower at last loomed over the treetops, she reduced her speed. The county hospital lay on the outskirts of the city, a ponderous red brick fortress dating from the 1930s. As Vanessa pulled into the parking lot, a siren wailed from the emergency entrance, reminding her of her last visit to this comfortless place.

She had been only twelve then, relegated to the custody of neighbors in the wake of her father's heart attack. Given the upheavals of that year—the collapse of

Dorsey TV and Electronics, the sudden move to a tiny frame house on the other side of town, the constant tension overshadowing their once-carefree family—her father's illness seemed just another in a series of calamities. Vanessa didn't know much about heart attacks then, but she was getting very good about calamities. When he came home from the hospital, she assumed they would somehow rearrange their lives to accommodate his weakened condition, just as they had learned to share the rented house's single, tiny bathroom and make do with one car. But weeks passed, and her father didn't come home. On that awful night when she and Sandra were hustled out of bed and brought to the hospital, Vanessa knew what had happened, long before she heard her mother's anguished sobs echoing down the corridor.

Tonight, the memories were still potent enough to tie a knot in her stomach as she approached the hospital admissions desk. Vanessa almost gasped with relief when the nurse informed her that Mrs. Dorsey had been discharged the previous morning.

*If she's gone home, then it can't be too bad.* Vanessa kept repeating the incantation over and over to herself during the drive to her mother's quiet neighborhood. The small white-brick ranch house looked tranquil enough as she turned into the drive. In the soft, dawning light, she could see the clusters of jonquils bunched along the rock walk; the terra-cotta birdbath was full and so were the numerous bird feeders swaying in the dogwood trees.

There were no lights burning in the house, and Vanessa took care as she inserted her key into the front-door lock. Tiptoeing across the carpeted living-room floor, she recalled the first time she had seen the house.

It had been shortly after her promotion to full-fledged account executive in New York; with more than enough money coming in, she had insisted that her mother shop for a home of her own. She had never regretted her contribution to the purchase of this cozy little house.

The tentative shuffle of slippered feet from the hallway caused her to pause.

"Corinne?" Her mother's voice sounded groggy as she called Mrs. Wilkinson's name.

"No, Mom. It's me."

The hall light snapped on, and her mother squinted into the dark living room. Standing in the door, she looked very small and frail in her loose-fitting nightgown. "Vanessa! Honey, what are you doing here?"

"I came to see about you."

Her mother gaped for a moment. "But how did you know?"

Vanessa hurried across the room and wrapped her arms around her mother. "When Sandy tried to call you, Mrs. Wilkinson told her you were in the hospital. Are you all right?" Her mother had never been a robust woman, but as Vanessa hugged her narrow back, her shoulder blades felt gaunt beneath her hands.

Her mother patted Vanessa's back reassuringly. "I'm fine, dear. Turns out it was that new blood-pressure medicine I had just started taking. As soon as Dr. Spellman took me off that poison, I perked right up. I'm sorry that Corinne gave you girls such a fright. I had asked her not to tell anyone."

"You ought to know better than to try keeping things from us," Vanessa chided. "Are you sure you feel okay? You look a little pale." She held her mother at arm's length and scrutinized the thin-featured face.

"Who wouldn't look like a ghost after two days of awful tests and sterilized hospital food? I swear I'm fit as a fiddle." Her mother tugged at Vanessa's hand, pulling her toward the kitchen. "Why don't we have some coffee?"

As they walked to the cheerful pine-paneled kitchen, her mother pretended to complain. "You worry too much, child."

Vanessa smiled, sliding a cane-bottomed stool from under the bar. "Yeah, well just don't forget where I learned it."

But if she had acquired her mother's propensity to fret over problems, both real and imaginary, Vanessa realized that she had also gained much to treasure from their relationship. As the two women sat at the breakfast bar, sipping their decaf and talking quietly, they revived a host of memories—some funny, some poignant, all precious. They were laughing over the time Vanessa's mother had sat up all night sewing sequins on a prom dress when the mantel clock chimed from the living room.

"I can't believe it's ten already." Vanessa placed a hand over her cup before her mother could refill it with coffee. "I promised to call Sandy when I got here. She'll be thrilled to hear that you're okay. And I need to call a friend, someone who's looking after Aunt Charlotte's house while I'm away."

She slid off the bar stool and hurried to the phone in the hall. Although she wanted to tell her mother about Taylor, she decided to play things down for the time being. Her mother had been crushed when she and Jeff had divorced, and Vanessa did not want to arouse any premature expectations.

Predictably, Sandra was overjoyed to learn that their mother was not seriously ill. She chatted with Vanessa for a few minutes, long enough to tell her about the summer job for which she would be interviewed the following week. Perhaps it was superstitious on her part, but Vanessa did not mention her own disastrous interview at Henson and Knowles. The less said about some things, the better, she thought while she waited for her mother and Sandy to conclude their conversation.

As Vanessa had hoped, when she phoned Taylor, he picked up on the first ring.

"I had my fingers crossed that it would be you." A slight edge of apprehension tempered the pleasure in his voice.

To put him at ease, Vanessa quickly filled him in on her mother's condition. "We've been talking nonstop since I got here," she concluded. "Actually, I'm long overdue for a visit. Next Sunday is Easter, so I think I'm going to stay down here for the rest of the week. Would you mind taking care of Emily, just through the holiday?"

Taylor almost scoffed. "Of course I wouldn't! Have a good visit with your mom and don't worry about anything here."

"Those sound like doctor's orders," Vanessa teased.

"They are. And I want you to plan on having dinner with me the night you get home, no excuses," Taylor told her sternly.

"I'll drive back the Monday after next. How does that sound?" she asked in as demure a tone as she could muster.

"Perfect. Just perfect."

EVERYTHING WAS WORKING OUT perfectly, Taylor mused the following Wednesday as he drove to the Burches' bungalow. His good luck had started at the very beginning of the week when he had announced his plans to take Matt and Denny to a movie in Charleston; school was closed that week for the spring recess, and both boys had been clamoring to see *Invasion from the Gamma Galaxy.* Diana, bless her soul, had volunteered to cover for him at the clinic on any day Taylor chose; after promising the young intern that he would return the favor, Taylor picked Wednesday. And now Wednesday had dawned, mellow and balmy as only a spring morning on the South Carolina coast can be.

Both Burch boys were waiting for him on the front porch, but they bolted down the walk the second they spotted the Jeep.

"Let's go!" Matt cried as he scrambled into the back seat. He crouched behind the seat, pointing an invisible laser gun at his brother's sandy head. "*Kerchow!*"

"*Perchoing! Choing! Choing!*" Denny swiveled in the seat and fired a volley of his own.

Taylor held up a hand to ward off the pointed fingers they aimed at him. "Hey! If you guys disintegrate me, who'll drive to Charleston?"

Matt brandished his cocked hand. "We were just going to freeze you. Then we'd thaw you out again," he explained with a giggle.

"Oh, well, that's good to know. Just the same, maybe you'd better hold your fire and buckle up." Taylor squinted at the sun-glazed windshield and pulled onto the road. "Since we're going to be in the city fairly late, I think we should stop by and check on Emily on our way, don't you?"

Any other delay would have surely earned a duet of disappointed sighs, but at the mention of Vanessa's pet donkey, both boys nodded their eager consent. For some reason, helping him care for Emily in Vanessa's absence had become a favorite chore for the young-sters, especially Denny. But then, perhaps he had sub-consciously influenced them, Taylor speculated, prejudiced as he was toward anything associated with Vanessa.

For her part, Emily certainly welcomed the com-pany. As the boys leaped out of the Jeep and raced across the yard, she egged them on with her undulating bray. While Denny proffered a freshly plucked handful of grass beneath the donkey's snuffling nose, Matt hurried to refill the water tub anchored next to the ga-rage.

"I like Emily. She's a neat donkey," Denny de-clared, looking over his shoulder at Taylor. Turning back to Emily, he gave her neck an energetic pat. "Va-nessa's neat, too."

Taylor propped one foot against the fence and eyed the reddish-brown head closely. Was his imagination getting the best of him, or was this tousle-headed kid sounding him out? "I agree," he remarked. Scuffing his toe against the fence post, he waited for Denny to ask if he meant Emily or Vanessa.

But Denny only turned and gave him the toothiest grin that would fit on his small freckled face.

"Let's hit the road." Taylor lightly clapped Denny's shoulder and beckoned to Matt. In time, he would re-veal some of his very special feelings for Vanessa to the boys, in an appropriate manner, under appropriate cir-cumstances. He wouldn't have much choice, he re-flected; keeping a secret from two such perceptive kids would be well-nigh impossible. But for now he was pleased to have the drive to Charleston and the action-packed movie to divert their attention.

As far as his own thoughts were concerned, *Invasion from the Gamma Galaxy* could just as well have been some brooding black-and-white art film. While the screen blazed with exploding planets, marauding extra-terrestrials, and enough laser weapons to slice the Earth in half, Taylor's mind remained stubbornly focused on a certain pair of slate-blue eyes set in a smooth, oval face. God, he missed her! And she had been away for scarcely five days!

"That was great!" Matt proclaimed, loudly enough to be heard over the thunderous martial music.

Taylor was about to remind him to lower his voice when he blinked and realized that the movie was over. "Yeah, it was good."

"Boy, was that big ol' Mergatron *gross* or what?" Denny inspected his Matinee Monster Tub of popcorn and picked out the remaining kernels before pitching the empty carton into a trash bin.

Taylor had no idea what the Mergatron might have been, but he took Denny's word for its grossness. "I'll say!" he agreed.

Outside the shopping-mall theater, he pulled the boys to a halt. "Okay, fellows, I have an errand to take care of before we get something to eat. It'll only take a few minutes," he promised. "In the meantime, why don't you start thinking about what you'd like for supper?"

The boys nodded and dutifully fell into step with Taylor. They nudged and poked one another and pointed as they walked past the various stores, but Taylor did not allow them to sidetrack him. When they reached a small jeweler's shop at the end of the mall, he pulled the door open for them.

"Remember, no touching. And when I get through here, I expect a decision on whether we have pizza or tacos." Taylor delivered the command with a mock-serious frown.

"May I help you, sir?" The salesclerk quickly skirted the counter. Although she directed the question to Taylor, her eyes warily followed the two giggling youngsters loitering at the front of the store.

"I hope so." Taylor fished in his jacket pocket and pulled out a small blue-leather jewelry case. When he opened it, even the sharp-eyed clerk could not help but register her admiration. Lifting the antique diamond-and-ruby ring from its velvet bed, Taylor held it up for her inspection.

"A stunning piece." The clerk's voice had dropped to a confidential level.

"It's a family heirloom," Taylor explained modestly. "I need to have it sized."

The clerk gave him a smooth smile. "Certainly." Stooping, she pulled an order form and a brown paper envelope from beneath the counter. "And what size would that be, sir?"

"I don't know, but if you have a gauge I can show you."

The clerk shuffled through a drawer and produced a collection of bands in various sizes. Taylor studied the rings for a second before selecting one. He carefully slid the band over his pinky, nestling it against the first joint. "That size."

"Yes, sir." The clerk took the band from him and scribbled a few notations on the order blank, along with

Taylor's name and phone number. "Will there be anything else, Dr. Bowen?"

"I must have it no later than next Monday morning."

The clerk's eyebrows shot up in alarm. "Oh, dear! That's awfully fast, with the holiday and all. I don't know," she began. But something in Taylor's face must have made her reconsider. "Monday morning, then." She smiled broadly. "We try to accommodate special occasions."

On his way out of the store with Matt and Denny, Taylor wondered how she could have guessed the occasion would be so special.

"WHAT ON EARTH am I going to do with so much food?" Vanessa's mother hesitated in front of the open refrigerator.

Vanessa did not look up from the spaghetti sauce she was emptying into a pot. "Eat it, of course." One of her first self-assigned tasks that week had been to take stock of the pantry. Without consulting her mother—who always resisted any expenditures on her behalf—she had composed a gargantuan shopping list, driven to the nearest supermarket, and returned with $184.38 worth of groceries.

Shaking her head, her mother selected a tub of deli coleslaw and then pushed the fridge door shut. She was spooning the slaw into a serving dish when the doorbell rang. "Let's hope we have some lunchtime guests to help us eat up all this food," she quipped.

"Careful, Mom. Remember, most of that food you keep talking about is stuff like pancake mix and dry cereal." Vanessa grinned as she adjusted the burner and then hurried to the door. But when she recognized the generously rouged face smiling up at her, she had to stifle the urge to slam the door again.

"Well, I do declare! If it isn't a pleasant surprise to see you, Vanessa. Why it's been just *ages* since you've been down to see your mama." The short, portly woman gestured with the covered casserole she held, as if she intended to thrust it through the screen door.

"Hello, Mrs. Pence." Ignoring the woman's insinuation, Vanessa forced herself to smile, but as she held the door open she felt as if she were welcoming a swarm of wasps into her mother's home. Of all the townspeople who had witnessed her father's decline and fall, none had been less sympathetic nor spread more rumors than Harriet Pence.

Mrs. Pence's pale blue eyes darted around the living room, looking for trouble. "How is she?" she hissed loudly.

"Mother is doing very well. As it turns out, she was only reacting to a new blood-pressure medication," Vanessa said abruptly, begrudging the gossipy woman even that abbreviated information.

"Evelyn!" When Mrs. Pence spied Vanessa's mother standing in the hall doorway, she quickly deposited the casserole on the coffee table, flung open her arms, and rushed toward her. "I brought you a little something to eat, dear. I've been worried half to death, didn't sleep *all* night just thinking about you, you poor, sick girl!"

*I'm going to be sick if you keep this up,* Vanessa thought as she followed her mother and Mrs. Pence into the kitchen, keeping a careful distance. While her mother thanked their visitor for the chicken casserole and invited her to sit down, Vanessa hovered near the pantry, arms folded defensively across her chest. She tried to ignore the grating voice bombarding her mother with questions, but anything short of vanishing into thin air would have been an insufficient ploy to escape Harriet Pence's scrutiny.

"My daughter-in-law is moving to Richmond this summer. You'll have to look her up, Vanessa." When Mrs. Pence laughed, it reminded Vanessa of some of Emily's more exuberant vocalizations.

"I don't live in Richmond anymore." Vanessa's grip of her own arms tightened.

The penciled brows rose in alarm. "You don't? Did your husband get transferred?"

"I don't have a husband anymore," Vanessa told her coldly.

Mrs. Pence gasped and splayed a fat hand against her chest. "No! But how awful." The woman caught herself suddenly and uttered another ridiculous titter. "Well, enough about that! Silly me! Such a blunder!"

Vanessa walked to the stove and began to stir the spaghetti sauce. *Now that she has a juicy piece of gossip, maybe she'll be in a hurry to leave and spread it around,* she thought. Her hopes dimmed as she heard Mrs. Pence launch a battery of inquiries about Sandra.

"Medical school costs a king's ransom nowadays. I just read a magazine article about how much most new doctors owe by the time they get out. I forget the exact figure—I was never much good with numbers." She smothered a bleating laugh behind her hand before going on. "But it was something fearsome. I just hope it's worth it to your girl."

"It *is* quite expensive," Vanessa's mother conceded in a dejected tone that caused Vanessa to wheel around from the stove.

"My sister has wanted to be a doctor since she was a sophomore in high school, and as long as I'm alive, I'm going to see to it that she realizes her dream." Vanessa glared at the pudgy, painted face.

Mrs. Pence gave a short hiccuping laugh. "Well, of course you will, dear. Sandra is real lucky to have a sweet sister like you. And one who's so successful, too."

Vanessa shot a warning glance at her mother and was relieved to find her smiling serenely. The last thing they needed was for Harriet Pence to get wind of Vanessa's protracted unemployment, even if keeping that secret within the family required a few lies. Mercifully, however, Mrs. Pence seemed to have gotten her quota of news for the day. She lingered only long enough to bestow another round of lavish get-well wishes on Vanessa's mother before taking her leave.

"Good riddance!" Vanessa muttered under her breath after she had securely locked the door behind the nosy woman.

But try as she might, she was unable to shake the nasty aftertaste left by Mrs. Pence's visit. Vanessa did her best to enjoy the Easter ham that she and her mother shared; she tried to lose herself in the bittersweet memories stirred to life by the family albums they leafed through together on Sunday evening. Despite her best efforts, however, snatches of the town gossip's conversation kept floating through her mind.

As VANESSA PACKED her suitcase on Monday morning, she was still wondering what had bothered her the most: Mrs. Pence's pointed comments about Sandra's schooling, or her own bravado in squelching them. She had sounded awfully confident, swearing that she would see Sandy through school, come what might. Whether she would be able to deliver was another matter altogether. Back when she had a job, she wouldn't have given a second thought to stocking her mother's larder. Now, however, she was acutely aware of the dent even that modest expenditure had made in her bank account.

Vanessa managed to put on a brave face as she kissed her mother goodbye, but during the long drive to Parloe, her spirits seemed to sag deeper with each passing mile. At least Taylor would be waiting for her with comforting hugs and wine and a cozy dinner. But thinking about him only reminded her of how complicated the issue of finding a job had become.

She had no idea what demon possessed her to stop by the Parloe post office before driving to Taylor's house, but when she opened her box and recognized Henson and Knowles's trendy letterhead, she almost recoiled. This was it: Steve Czerny's embarrassed attempt to tell her gently that they wanted no part of her. *Salt on the wound,* she thought as she ripped the envelope open. Better to get it over with now—at least she had Taylor hovering in the wings to nurse her back onto her feet.

Dear Vanessa,
I've been meaning to fire this letter off to you for the past week. My apologies for the delay, but this place has been a madhouse since I saw you.

Poor Steve! For all his gruffness, he was a real softy. She could imagine him agonizing over the letter, trying to cushion the blow. Her eyes skimmed over the insider's jokes and platitudes, racing to the bitter conclusion.

Olsen really wanted you for his Lansing account, but he's just not the man to take on Jason McNair.

Vanessa swallowed and looked up from the letter. Well, that was as nice an excuse to offer as any she could think of.

McNair has enough clout with the Old Man to get just about anything he wants, and when he told Ham Knowles he'd finally found an account exec who could hang on to her cool under pressure, it was an open-and-shut case. Sorry, babe, but it looks like you're going to end up on Jason's team, not Olsen's, if you accept our offer. At least you know how to handle him! Seriously, although I can't tell you anything in an official capacity, you can depend on Jason to get you top dollar. Like I said, he may be a pain, but he has clout with a capital C.

The bank of post office boxes vibrated behind Vanessa; the speckled floor seethed beneath her feet as she reread the last paragraph. Henson and Knowles was making her an offer, and at the behest of Jason McNair! The very man who had put her on the spot over lunch had slugged it out for her; more importantly, he was apparently powerful enough to secure her enough money to solve her family's short-term problems! In a daze, Vanessa walked to her car and drove to Taylor's house.

TAYLOR EYED the thick bacon-wrapped fillet respectfully, giving the crimson surface a cautious poke. Maybe he should have enlisted Grace's help in the kitchen after all. Cooking wasn't his strong suit, and he wanted everything to be flawless tonight. Whatever the case, it was too late now. He slid the steak onto the broiler rack.

Shaky as his culinary skills might be, atmosphere he could manage just fine. A glance into the living room assured him that the lamps had been adjusted to a suitably mellow level; the pots of waxy white gardenias had been properly arranged near the sliding glass door where the breeze could catch their fragrance; the Burgundy was opened and breathing on the sideboard. Taylor had just selected a recording of lush Latin rhythms and slipped it into the CD player when the doorbell rang.

He turned to give the room a last split-second appraisal before rushing to the door.

"Wow, it's good to see you!" Taylor threw his arms around Vanessa and lifted her off her feet.

Vanessa steadied herself against his chest as he returned her to earth. "It's good to see you, too." She smiled—a little hesitantly, he thought—and reached for her handbag, which had slipped off her shoulder.

She had to be dead tired, with that long, tedious drive behind her. "How about a glass of wine? I have just a few last-minute things to take care of with dinner." Taylor nodded toward the kitchen and gave her a robust grin, as if he hoped to inject a little more pep into her waning smile.

"I'll help myself," Vanessa offered. As Taylor withdrew into the kitchen, he saw her bolt for the sideboard.

Was it just his own fluster over playing chef, or was Vanessa as nervous as he imagined? Taylor pulled the oven door slightly ajar and peered at the sizzling fillet. God, what if there *was* something seriously wrong with her mother, something she had been unwilling to tell him on the phone? She had sounded plucky enough when she had called him, he mused, sprinkling a handful of croutons over the salad. He stooped, just enough to peek through the pass-through between the kitchen and the living room. She was sitting in the middle of the sofa, clutching the glass of wine with both hands. With her knees pressed together and her eyes wide and serious, she looked like an errant school girl waiting outside the principal's office.

Well, whatever was bugging her—and Vanessa *did* have something on her mind, of that he was now certain—his job was to put her at ease, comfort her, show her how much he cared for her, would always care for her, for the rest of their lives. As he swung back to the oven to check the steak again, his hip bumped the counter, nudging the pocket where the diamond-and-ruby ring reposed.

"I hope this steak is up to par." Taylor deposited the platter on the table with a flourish and then stepped back, pulling a chair aside for her.

"It looks yummy!" Vanessa jumped up from the sofa as if propelled by an invisible spring.

Despite his earlier misgivings, the steak was cooked to a perfect medium-rare, but Taylor scarcely tasted the flavorful meat, so intent was he on drawing Vanessa out during dinner. He had never seen her so uneasy, but when he questioned her about her mother, her responses were uniformly positive.

"It was just her new medicine." Vanessa chewed vigorously for a second before adding, "Just one of those things."

While he was waiting for the coffee to brew, Taylor decided to take a more direct approach. This was not the mood he had envisioned for a romantic dinner, much less a proposal of marriage. He needed to find out what was preying on Vanessa's mind before he went any further tonight.

As it turned out, Vanessa broached the topic for him. When he leaned over the sofa to present her with a glass of liqueur, she looked up at him with such a pained expression he almost winced.

"I have something to tell you, Taylor." The glass shook slightly as her fingers closed around its fragile stem.

When people say that, what they really mean is "something bad," Taylor thought, but he forced himself to nod, just as he forced himself to smile.

Vanessa licked her lips before plunging in. "Henson and Knowles has offered me a job in Atlanta. I'll have to start in two weeks."

Through the ringing in his ears, he heard her low voice, rushing breathlessly into an explanation of what a golden opportunity this was, of how close Atlanta was, really, of how they would work things out and manage to see each other frequently.

"Congratulations." Could that be his own voice, so unnaturally calm and even and utterly lifeless? Taylor felt as if he were watching a grainy slow-motion film, one featuring a blond man with a stiff smile frozen on his face and a tall woman with enormous, stricken eyes. When their raised glasses met, the brittle clink sounded faraway, surreal. Only one thing seemed oppressively, inescapably real at that moment: the diamond-and-ruby ring lying in his pocket like a leaden weight.

## Chapter Twelve

The hammer fell in steady strokes, beating a dull cadence against the wood. Still clutching a crumpled ball of newspaper, Vanessa carefully parted the kitchen curtain to peek through. At the bottom of the back steps, Taylor was bent over a plank anchored beneath his knee. Crouched beside him, just out of the hammer's range, was Matt, acting as supervisor.

Vanessa let the curtain fall into place and turned back to the Provençal plates she was wrapping. There had been more to pack away prior to her departure for Atlanta than she had at first thought. Perhaps she had been foolish to bring so many things down from the attic in the first place, but she had wanted to make the place seem more like home.

*Well, it isn't home anymore.* The thought bored into her mind like one of the nails sinking beneath Taylor's hammer. Vanessa winced and then fought to control the stinging at her eyes. She turned her back to the window and found it helped to take stock of the disorderly kitchen. If a squeaky hinge had not betrayed him, she would not have noticed Denny slipping through the swinging door from the hall.

Vanessa looked up from the packing crate to smile at the little boy. "Were you helping the carpenters?"

Denny shook his head solemnly. "No." After a few seconds silence, he added, "I was just foolin' around."

When her smile widened, Vanessa felt as if her face were as fragile as the antique porcelain plates she had been wrapping. "Don't be misled by all that noisy hammering. I suspect Matt and Taylor are doing some fooling around themselves."

Denny worked his way along the counter's edge, carefully placing one sneakered foot in front of the other. "Yeah, I guess."

Vanessa had never seen the younger Burch boy so pensive, and she felt compelled to put aside her own somber musing to cheer him up. "Tell you what—I need a break from this yucky mess. Why don't we see if Emily would like a couple of carrots?" Not waiting for his response, she tossed the remaining wadded newspaper into the crate and headed for the refrigerator. She was bent over the vegetable bin, digging through the dwindling assortment of vegetables, when she felt a small hand gently graze her cheek.

"You've got some dirt on your face," Denny explained, stepping back behind the refrigerator door.

Without thinking, Vanessa reached up and touched her still-damp cheek. Then she glanced down at her blackened fingers. Thrusting the bag of carrots at Denny, she hurried to the sink. "It's that darned newsprint," she said over her shoulder, smiling. She wiped her face with a wet paper towel. "All gone?"

Denny nodded, but his brown eyes remained fastened on her face, taking her in.

"C'mon." Vanessa prodded his shoulder to propel him out of the kitchen.

They found the front lawn bathed in the shadowless light of the midday low-country sun. As they walked across the yard, the humid heat seemed to engulf them. In contrast, the kitchen had been cool, almost clammy. Vanessa rubbed her cold fingers along her bare arms, which were glazed with a film of sweat. Her whole body felt out of kilter, as if stricken by the upheavals in her life. The sidelong glance Denny gave her as he clambered over the paddock fence only confirmed her suspicion that she looked as out of joint as she felt.

A low-pitched snort greeted them from inside the garage, where Emily had sought refuge from the noonday sun. Vanessa followed Denny to the garage door and then paused to give her eyes a chance to adjust to the muted light.

When Denny held up the carrots, Emily bleated in anticipation. "We brought you a snack, girl," he informed the donkey. He pulled a particularly large specimen from the bag and held it out for Emily's inspection. The velvety nose snuffled the carrot for only a second before the soft gray lips seized it with practiced agility.

Hands latched into the back pockets of her jeans, Vanessa watched Denny pet the donkey's neck. Once she reached out to smooth Emily's forelock, but when the little creature tossed her head, Vanessa quickly retracted her hand. For the past several weeks, she had routinely brushed Emily, swatted the flies pestering her, and cleaned her feet, but now she felt strangely awkward even patting her soft fur.

"Do you think Emily's going to be lonely?" Denny's eyes continued to follow his hand's even strokes along the donkey's neck.

Vanessa pulled her hands free of her pockets and shifted from one foot to the other. "Oh, no, I don't think so. You know what Taylor said. Mr. White has lots of other animals to keep her company."

"Goats." When Denny glanced up, his mouth pulled into a sour downward curve. "She'll have to stay with a bunch of smelly old goats."

Vanessa shifted back to the other foot and cleared her throat. "Now, Denny, I don't know if goats are all that bad. Who knows? Emily might even like them."

Denny mercifully ignored her lame defense of Millard White's goats. "I bet no one will ever give her carrots or apples." A tremor rippled through the small voice.

Vanessa scooted around Emily and rested a hand on Denny's shoulder. "I'm really sorry I can't keep her, Denny. You know that. But I have to move."

Denny gave her a disconsolate nod. "Yeah, I know," he conceded. Stepping back from Emily, he brushed the loose hair from his palms. "Mom says we're gonna have to move, too, but we don't know where to, yet."

Just when Vanessa had thought her spirits had reached rock bottom, she felt them sink another notch. "I thought your mother was going to start working at the fish market this fall."

"She is, but she says that job won't pay enough to keep renting the house we're in, so she's gotta look for something on the mainland." Denny's reedy shoulders rose and fell in a sigh.

"Oh." *"Oh?" This little kid is feeling perfectly miserable, and all you can say is "oh?"* But as Vanessa stared down at the ruffled sandy head, her usual resourcefulness failed her. What could she tell him? To cheer up and think about all the new kids he'd get to know, after he'd adjusted to a new school? To look forward to a precarious existence made more so by the absence of familiar faces and surroundings?

Not looking up, Denny carefully pulled a cocklebur from the donkey's mane. "I'm gonna miss you, Emily," Vanessa heard him whisper.

On the surface, parceling Emily off to Millard White's pasture might seem trivial, but to Denny it represented yet another loss in a series of misfortunes. Vanessa ached to think that she had inadvertently contributed to this winsome little boy's unhappiness. Her hand stirred on his shoulder as she dug down deep within herself, vainly searching for any comfort she could offer him.

"Oh, Denny, I'm sorry," she began. "So sorry." Her voice caught.

Without warning, he pulled free of her hand and spun around. "I'm gonna miss you, too." The words were muffled in the hem of her blue work shirt as Denny buried his face against her.

Vanessa felt the small arms encircle her waist, holding on to her with a life-or-death ferocity. When a quiver passed through the child's narrow shoulders it seemed to carry through her own hands, sending a shudder down the length of her body. Standing there with his tousled reddish-brown head pressed against her, she suddenly felt very big—big and clumsy and helpless.

Cradling the boy's head in her hands, Vanessa dropped awkwardly to her knees. When she lifted his face, she found the freckled cheeks streaked with tears. In a gesture born of the purest nurturing instinct, Vanessa gently smoothed the moisture from the child's face. Only when she tried to speak did she realize how dangerously near crying she herself was.

"I'll be back, Denny." Vanessa's hand lingered tenderly on the flushed cheek. "And no matter how far away you live, I'll come get you, and we'll visit Emily and feed her all the carrots and apples she wants."

Denny stared at the packed-dirt floor, avoiding her gaze. Then he looked up and dug at one eye with his knotted fist. "Promise?" He sniffed.

Vanessa gave his chin a firm squeeze. "I promise."

"Denny?"

They both jumped to their feet as Taylor's voice carried from the yard. While Denny rubbed his eyes, Vanessa swabbed her face with her long shirttail.

"Time to go, son." Taylor blinked as he peered through the door. When Denny ran to his side, he settled a hand on the back of the boy's neck. Then he glanced back at Vanessa. "Those steps I replaced should hold up for a long time." His voice sounded unnaturally tight.

"Thanks." Vanessa forced a smile, but she hung back and let him lead the way out into the paddock.

"Why don't you help Matt gather up the tools?" Taylor gave Denny's shoulder a gentle nudge. He waited until the small boy had disappeared behind the house before turning to Vanessa. "If you find anything else that needs repairing before you leave, just give me a call, okay?"

"I will." Vanessa met his eyes, only to find them filled with an inexpressible sadness that mocked his casual remark. She quickly looked down to hide the treacherous tears welling in her own eyes.

"Vanessa. Listen to me, please." Taylor's low voice caught as his hand closed over her wrist. "We can call each other, as often as we like. And just as soon as you get settled, I'll come up to Atlanta to see you." He managed a shaky chuckle. "You know, I've already asked you to come back here for a visit."

*Don't ask me to visit. Ask me to stay—forever.* The impossible wish carried through her mind like a dying echo. For Taylor couldn't ask her to turn her back on Henson and Knowles, any more than she could ask him to abandon his hard-won veterinary practice. He was as committed to serving the forgotten people of Parloe as she was to providing for her mother and sister; all the reassuring platitudes in the world could not alter that fact.

"I'll come back to Parloe," Vanessa managed to murmur before her voice broke.

Taylor's hand tightened its hold on her arm. "We'll get through this," he began, but fell silent as Matt and Denny came racing around the house.

The Burch boys skidded to a halt a few yards short of the paddock. As if they sensed the two adults' discomfiture, they hung back, jostling one another and pretending to play.

Taylor cast an uneasy glance at the boys and then released his hold on Vanessa's wrist. "I hate to run off now, but I really need to get these guys home. I'd almost forgotten about the Committee meeting tonight."

Vanessa nodded. "Give Cora and Ray my regards." While Taylor stowed his toolbox in the rear of the Jeep, she hustled Matt and Denny into the back seat. Mercifully, Taylor did not offer to kiss her goodbye, but only gave her hand a brief, intense squeeze. Vanessa watched the Cherokee bounce down the drive and then turn onto the road. Her eyes held on to the vision of Denny waving steadily through the rear window until the hanging moss blotted out the jeep.

When Vanessa walked back into the house, its stillness seemed to amplify her reeling thoughts. For so long, she had privately bemoaned her professional setback, had wrestled with all the self-doubt and uncertainty that went along with that and her divorce. With the help of Henson and Knowles, she had at last slain those dragons; by all accounts, she should now feel competent and strong, capable not only of supporting herself but also of helping her family. Yet as Vanessa sank onto the bottom of the stairs, she had never felt less in control of her life.

She had talked herself into a high-powered job, yet she couldn't even carry on an honest conversation with the man she loved. She was about to be entrusted with six-figure advertising accounts, yet she couldn't even satisfy a small boy's wish for a pet. Executives would seek her counsel on sophisticated marketing strategies, yet she could do nothing to alleviate the Burch family's problems.

Or perhaps she *could* do something, at least for the Burches. As a nebulous thought began to crystallize Vanessa lifted her face from against her knees and stood up. Of course, Grace was extremely proud, she reminded herself as she marched to her car. She would have to approach her carefully. Vanessa tried to organize a bullet-proof argument supporting her idea; after all, it was a plan that would help both of them. But when she pulled up in front of the brown-shingled bungalow, she felt very awkward.

Grace had apparently spotted the dark blue Thunderbird, for she was already holding open the front door as Vanessa came up the walk.

"Well, this sure is a pleasant surprise. I'm lucky I got home from work a little early today." Grace welcomed Vanessa into the house. "Matt tells me you got your back steps all fixed up," she remarked, pausing to hook the screen door behind her.

Vanessa smiled, acknowledging the pleasantries, but when Grace gestured cordially toward the sofa, she shook her head. "Grace, I need to talk with you."

Grace's keen dark eyes regarded her closely. Then she strolled to the kitchen door and leaned inside. "Boys, Vanessa and I want to visit. I'd like for you to clear away that game of yours and go play in the yard for a while."

Vanessa heard rubber-tipped chair legs skid across the linoleum floor, followed by scuffling feet; in a few seconds Matt and Denny trooped through the living room, with bat and catcher's mitt in hand. When they saw Vanessa, they dawdled in the door, but Grace promptly shooed them out.

*Here goes,* Vanessa thought as she followed Grace into the kitchen. She seated herself at the table while her hostess filled glasses with iced tea from the refrigerator. When Grace slid into the chair opposite hers, Vanessa took a deep breath.

"Grace, I want to discuss a business proposition with you." Vanessa clutched the clammy iced-tea glass with both hands.

Grace's dark brows rose in surprise. "Business?"

"It's about Great-aunt Charlotte's house. Ever since I accepted the job in Atlanta, I've been worrying about what will become of the place when I leave. The tenants I've had in the past have been pretty careless, and you know how hard I had to work to get the house back into decent shape. It really bothers me to think that someone is going to move in after me and tear everything up again."

When Vanessa paused for breath, Grace leaned across the table slightly. "I understand. But to tell you the truth, I don't know of anyone looking to rent who could afford such a big house. I'm sorry 'cause I'd really like to help you out."

Vanessa stirred her tea carefully. "You *can* help me, Grace, if you're interested in this business arrangement I have in mind." She deposited the iced-tea spoon on a folded paper napkin and then looked directly at Grace. "I'd like you to manage the place for me. Now, I know you might want to think this over. You're probably satisfied in this house, and if you took me up on this deal, you and the boys would have to move into the house."

Grace was visibly shaken. "Move into *your* house?"

Vanessa nodded as she rushed ahead. "I know it sounds like a lot of work, but I've managed to make the major repairs, so you'd only be keeping the yard tidy, the house clean." She laughed briefly. "Things you'd do in your own home anyway. There is one problem. I can't afford to pay you anything right away, since I wouldn't be getting any rent on the place."

Grace was staring down at the table, frowning. "Wait a minute, now. If I've got this straight, what you're really saying is that you want me to live in your house and not pay you anything for it. Now I know it may look like the boys and I are having some hard times..."

Vanessa pushed the tea aside and clasped her hands on the table. "That's not it, Grace. It's something much more personal. For me." Her voice dropped, underscoring the urgency of her plea. "Back in March when I first came to this island, I felt that house was all I had

left. Living there helped me put some things back together for myself, and..." Her voice quavered and she
paused, staring at her tightly folded hands. "It's hard
for me to leave now, but I think it would be just a little
easier if I knew good friends were living in the house
who would love it as I do."

When Grace's strong-boned hand settled over hers,
Vanessa looked up. Her eyes were brimming, but she
managed to smile. "Do you understand? It would mean
so much to me. And our special arrangement would be
just between us. No one else would have to know."

Grace smiled slowly. "Since you put it that way, I
reckon I can't say no."

Vanessa swallowed, pressing her lips together to still
their trembling, and then leaned back in her chair.
Gently extricating her hands from Grace's comforting
grasp, she stood up. "There's one other thing I need to
discuss with Matt and Denny. Especially Denny."

Grace looked puzzled, but before she could say anything, Vanessa walked to the front porch. Matt was at
bat, and Denny had just wound up for the pitch, but
when he spotted Vanessa, his little arm froze in midro-
tation. As she approached their improvised baseball
diamond, they ran to meet her.

Vanessa crouched and placed a hand on each boy's
shoulder. "Fellows, your mom and I have just been
talking about her helping me out while I'm away, but
there's a small matter that's still worrying me."

The boys exchanged baffled glances, not fully com-
prehending her meaning.

"I've decided not to let Mr. White have Emily after
all." Vanessa imagined that Denny's shoulder quivered
at this announcement. "But the only people I can think
of who would treat her as well and love her as much as

I do are you guys. So what do you say? Will you be willing to take care of her for me?''

Matt's eyes bugged. ''Wow! You betcha'! Will we ever!'' he exclaimed.

But Denny said nothing. Not that he needed to. The hands clasped around Vanessa's waist—one of them still encased in an enormous baseball mitt—were answer enough.

## Chapter Thirteen

Handing Grace Burch the keys to Great-aunt Charlotte's house proved to be the single memorable moment in Vanessa's otherwise uneventful departure from
Parloe. So much had happened during the previous two
months, she felt strange simply climbing into her car
and driving off. But in the end that was precisely what
she did.

Vanessa was unsure whether to praise the gods or rail
against them for allowing Taylor's trip to Columbia to
coincide with her departure; whatever the case, they
said their goodbyes two days earlier, after a Contained
Growth Committee meeting.

"Take care of yourself." Taylor's hand had trem-
bled a little when he touched her hair. As if he mis-
trusted his own reflexes, he had quickly repocketed the
hand. "I expect to see you in fine fettle the next time we
get together. And that had better be soon," he had
added with a shaky grin.

Vanessa had mirrored his nervous smile. "Very
soon."

They had sealed their pact with a brief kiss and a
slightly more protracted hug. She had wished him suc-

cess in Columbia; he had admonished her to drive safely, and they had parted ways.

When Vanessa arrived in Atlanta, she felt grateful, for the first time in her life, for having too much to do. The scramble to get settled before starting her new job left her little time for brooding over her relationship with Taylor. After looking at three houses to lease, she decided on a redbrick bungalow near Emory University. The house was small enough to be practical for one person and only a fifteen-minute drive from her office. Privately, Vanessa realized that her decision had been influenced by less rational factors. The old-fashioned detached garage had reminded her of Emily's stable, and the transom over the dining-room door was fitted with leaded-glass inserts similar to those in Great-aunt Charlotte's house.

*No harm in indulging in a little nostalgia,* Vanessa told herself. But as she tacked sheets over bare windows and measured for furnishings, her spirits stubbornly refused to rally. In time, the rental house could be made to look like a home, but she knew it would take more than well-chosen pictures and cozy furniture to fill the void within her. Wandering through the empty rooms, Vanessa realized how much she missed Taylor, missed him in a deep aching, way. She was relieved when Monday morning at last dawned, forcing her to put aside her personal problems so she could grapple with the workaday world.

Although Henson and Knowles did not officially open for business until nine o'clock, Vanessa made a point of arriving a good forty-five minutes early on her first day. The receptionist hailed her before she had even stepped off the elevator.

"Mr. McNair is looking for you, Ms. Dorsey." The young woman's voice trailed off, and her eyes darted to the corridor.

"Well, you're here at last!" Jason McNair glared at Vanessa as he charged into the foyer and dumped a handful of legal-size yellow sheets into the reception-ist's in-box. Not waiting for a reply, he turned on his heel. "Come on. I'll show you to your office. The Bay-berry Soup people will be here at noon. Ham Knowles is joining us for lunch, and I want to present the results of Bayberry's latest focus group." Jason paused to ges-ture toward a woman seated at an alcove desk. "Pau-lette Mason will be your secretary. Paulette, see that Vanessa gets the results of the Bayberry Condensed Turkey Gumbo market-research tests. And while you're at it, make copies of the Whitney-Spawn file for her."

Paulette Mason's round dark eyes registered dismay. "The whole file?"

"Of course!" Jason gave Paulette a glance acid enough to wither the potted fern on her desk. Having effectively silenced the secretary's protest, he redi-rected his cold-eyed attention to Vanessa. "This lunch meeting is critical. We need to have everything in or-der, *everything*. Stop by my office at eleven, and we'll discuss your analysis of the gumbo tests."

"Sure." Vanessa forced an undaunted smile. Al-though she had no idea how complicated the market-research reports might be, right now her main concern was getting rid of Jason and barricading herself safely behind her desk. She waited until he had disappeared down the corridor before retreating to her office.

Paulette Mason caught her in the doorway. "I'm in the middle of typing a big report, but I'll do my best to copy the Whitney-Spawn stuff this morning." The secretary eyed her cautiously, trying to decide, Vanessa guessed, if her new boss were a clone of the demanding Jason.

"Just get to it when you have time. I'm going to be buried in these gumbo stats all morning and probably won't have a chance to look at anything else right away." Judging from the secretary's relieved expression, Vanessa felt confident she had just gained an ally.

One peek inside her office, and she knew she was going to need all the support she could get, from any quarter willing to give it. Barring divine intervention, Vanessa had no idea how she would manage to sort through the folders, files, memos, annual reports, and assorted correspondence piled on her desk, much less marshal the information into any kind of coherent presentation.

If Jason had only warned her in advance that she was expected to attend an important meeting today, she could have come in over the weekend and familiarized herself with the material. But then he wouldn't have had the chance to test her—again. Now she had no choice but to plow through the mountain of paper as best she could. Sinking onto the desk chair, Vanessa scowled at the closed door before reaching for a pen and a fresh legal pad.

She had filled five pages with notes and was bent over a graph when a scratching sound intruded on her concentration. Vanessa looked up to see Paulette Mason peeking around the door.

"Sorry to bother you, but I have the Whitney-Spawn copies." The secretary pushed the door ajar with the manila folders she carried.

"Thanks a lot." Vanessa tried to inject some enthusiasm into her voice for Paulette's sake. "Just put 'em anywhere."

If she had had any doubts about how she would spend her evening, the massive stack of data her secretary had just delivered had settled the issue. Vanessa tried to ignore the bulging folders as she skimmed another gumbo taste-test summary, but her eye kept drifting back to a full-color brochure protruding from one of the files. Even viewed upside down, the cover photograph was clearly that of a sun-drenched beach. Vanessa finally yielded to curiosity and pulled the brochure from the file.

*Paradise Isle*. To judge from the lush photographs, the name was appropriate for the location if not for the huge complex of condominiums the brochure promoted. In fact, the setting reminded her very much of Parloe. In spite of herself, Vanessa raced through the text until she found the name of the island. Thank God, it was Montcrief Point and not Parloe. Her relief was only momentary, however, for as she scanned the brochure, a queasy feeling began to grow in the pit of her stomach. Although she had never seen Paradise Isle, there was something all too familiar about it. The sprawling marina, the golf course carved out of reclaimed marshlands, the multistoried buildings that towered over the beachfront—every aspect of Whitney-Spawn's project echoed the developments that the Committee for Contained Growth had opposed so vigorously on Parloe.

Vanessa closed the brochure and stared at its glossy cover for a long moment. She had known, of course, that Whitney-Spawn was involved in a variety of real-estate ventures, but her background reading had led her to believe that the firm concentrated on shopping malls and office parks. The Paradise Isle brochure was sobering proof to the contrary. Only a few weeks earlier, all her energy had been focused on opposing just such a project; now she was expected to devise a marketing strategy for an organization that bore more than a passing resemblance to her opponents on Parloe. But how could she honestly represent people whose interests might someday conflict with her own principles?

Based on past experience, she imagined that Jason McNair would take a dim view of her scruples. She would have to present her argument from a business viewpoint, stressing that she should be taken off the Whitney-Spawn account simply because she was not the best person to represent that client. Vanessa tried to build a persuasive case in her head, but her attempts to second-guess Jason's response only added to her apprehension. *All the more reason to get it over with now.*

Without giving herself a chance to falter, Vanessa snatched up her notes on the soup market research and headed straight for Jason's office. She found him barking dictation into a microphone, but when he saw her in the doorway he immediately snapped off the recorder.

"Let's see what you've come up with." Jason reached for the notes Vanessa was clutching, but she stepped back, holding them out of his grasp.

"There's something I need to discuss with you first." Seeing a protest brewing in his steely eyes, she hastened to add, "It's about Whitney-Spawn."

"What about them?" Jason looked surprised, and Vanessa rushed to take advantage of having him off balance, if only momentarily.

"I had a chance to look over some of their material, and..." *Oh God, this is going to be worse that I thought.* "I just don't think I'm the right rep for that account."

"Why?" Jason demanded.

"As you know, I lived on Parloe Island for a while. I still own a house there. Some of my fondest childhood memories are of that island, and the place means a lot to me."

Jason leaned back in his chair and fingered the microphone impatiently. "Vanessa, I can't believe you came in here to tell me your life story."

Vanessa straightened herself and squelched the urge to fiddle with the papers she held. "I didn't, Jason. But since I've looked over some of the Whitney-Spawn file, I've had to ask myself how I would feel if they wanted to build another Paradise Isle next to my house on Parloe."

Jason tossed the mike onto the desk. "Just what are you getting at?"

"Perhaps I'm not the best person to work with Whitney-Spawn, at least on their resort projects."

"So, what are you suggesting—" Jason's voice took on a patronizing whine "—that I tell them you can manage an office complex, but hotels upset your tummy?" He snorted contemptuously. "Be serious, Vanessa. You're either part of this team or you aren't, period. I need an account exec who gives one-hundred-and-ten percent *all the time, every time*. I don't have time for this nonsense about how you *feel* about a project—I just expect you to get the job done. If you want the job," he added, suddenly leaning across the desk. "Have I made myself clear?"

"Yes, you have." Vanessa was struck by how foreign her voice sounded, as if it echoed from a dream. But as she sank onto the chair next to Jason's desk and began to thumb through her notes, she realized that her dream—that bright fantasy of making everything right for her mother and Sandra—had suddenly turned into a nightmare.

"TAKE IT EASY, FELLOW." Taylor stroked the shelty's ruff while his other hand held the dog firmly pinioned on the examining table. "Dad, can you come out of retirement for a sec and take a look at this little guy's leg?"

Stewart Bowen was regarding the collection of framed photographs arranged along the wall. He paused for a closer look at one of them—a fading snapshot of a mule with a note scribbled by its grateful owner—and then turned to join Taylor at the table. "Just looking at those pictures takes me back to the old days. I'm glad some of my clients were as sentimental as I am."

"People often give me pictures of my regular patients, too," Taylor assured his father before bending over the dog again. His finger gently delineated the rim of the cast immobilizing the animal's right foreleg. "I think the fracture is healing okay, but this swelling concerns me a little. Feel it?"

Stewart Bowen frowned as he carefully palpitated the shelty's leg. When the animal whimpered, he gave its head a soothing pat. "If I were you, I'd keep him here another couple of days, treat the swelling, and then see."

Taylor nodded his agreement. "That's what I thought, but I wanted your opinion." He scooped the shelty into his arms and carried it to one of the large recovery cages. When he turned back to the examining table, he found his father flipping through a lab report.

"I'm glad you don't mind a doddering old man dropping in now and then for his dose of nostalgia." Stewart shook his head and chuckled as he returned the report to the standing desk file. "How things change! I never thought I'd see the day when this clinic treated more dogs and cats than mules."

Taylor rounded the table and paused by the file. His fingers slowly walked the edges of the folders until they landed on one labeled "Feline Leukemia." "I'm grateful for the increase in small-animal business. You know, that's what most vets look for these days." A curious tightness grabbed at his throat, causing him to swallow hastily.

Arms folded across his chest, Stewart Bowen wandered back to the wall of photographs. "If doctoring sand fleas would help you find a partner, I'd be all for it. I know you run yourself ragged most of the time. I remember hoping the day would come when folks on Parloe would be well-off enough just to pay me regularly. Who knows? Maybe someday this practice will be able to support a second full-time vet."

Taylor pretended to scan the lab report. "I wasn't talking about sharing the practice."

"To look at this old plow-horse, you wouldn't guess she'd have enough fire in her to kick flies, much less..." Stewart Bowen broke off and abruptly turned his back on the pictures. "You weren't?"

Taylor was bent over the standing file, and he took his time straightening himself. "What I'm trying to say is that I've been thinking about selling the practice.

Back when most of our patients were colicky mules with
owners too poor to pay us for six months, we would
have had a hard time giving the clinic away. But the
economy on Parloe has changed—enough, I think, to
make the practice a fairly attractive business. I know
this is probably hard for you to hear, with all the hard
work and sacrifice you've put into the clinic . . ." Taylor fell silent as his father's hand settled on his tensed
shoulder.

"This has something to do with Vanessa, doesn't it?"
Stewart Bowen asked gently.

Taylor nodded. "Since she moved to Atlanta last
week, I've been thinking a lot—how constructively, I'm
not sure. But I know we can't go on like this. Everything is so up in the air—neither of us knows what to
say to the other." He paused, clasping his arms tightly
across his chest. "Hell, I don't even know what to tell
myself most of the time. I guess this sounds pretty
muddled, doesn't it?"

Stewart Bowen gave his son's shoulder a sympathetic
squeeze. "Not to someone who's been in love himself.
You're really serious about her, Taylor. I've known that
for a long time." When Taylor looked at him questioningly, he shook his head and smiled. "Don't ask me
how—I've just known. And I can tell you, if I'd had to
pull up roots and go somewhere else to make things
work with your mother, I would have done it in a flash.
You don't have to apologize to me for your feelings."

Taylor kept his eyes fixed on the hand that rested on
his shoulder. He was struck by how strong and capable
that hand looked, a hand that belonged to a person who
could make decisions, someone you could depend on,
trust with your innermost thoughts.

"Everything seemed to evolve so naturally with Vanessa, right from the start. We understood so much about each other, without even talking. It was as if our paths had been converging all those years, and now we'd each suddenly found the other, found the right person. At one point, I thought we were ready to consider a more permanent relationship." Taylor paused and shifted his shoulders uneasily.

"It's called marriage," his father prompted delicately.

Taylor nodded, staring across the room at the row of cages. "But now Vanessa seems focused on another world, somewhere out there far, far from what we had here." He gestured broadly and then let his hand drop. "I often wonder if we still share the same goals, still want the same sort of life. Occasionally, I wonder if we ever did. And . . . well, I just don't know. Sometimes, I think she'll tell me I'm crazy to suggest marriage. Other times, I get the impression she's just waiting for me to bring it up. I wish I knew how she felt."

"There's only one way you're going to find out, son. You have to ask her," Stewart advised him matter-of-factly. When Taylor shifted his gaze, he found his father smiling at him warmly. "Have you told Vanessa that you were thinking of looking for another practice?"

Taylor shook his head. "Not yet, but I plan to, just as soon as we can arrange to see each other again." *If I can find the guts to tell her how important she is to me.*

Stewart Bowen gave his son's shoulder a parting tap. "I know the situation may look complicated, but you and Vanessa will work it all out. Trust me, Taylor. I expect I know you better than just about anyone, and you've never been this serious about a woman before.

You and that lady belong together, wherever it may be."
He drew a deep breath, and his eyes traveled to the rows
of framed pictures. "And if it's not on Parloe, then
that's just the way it was meant to be."

## Chapter Fourteen

If there was anything worse than being cooped up with complete strangers on a commercial airliner, it was being trapped with your business associates on a corporate jet. At least the airlines let you hide behind magazines as you quietly accumulate Frequent-Flyer miles. Vanessa had neither consolation during the flight from Atlanta to Charleston. She scarcely knew the two representatives from Whitney-Spawn; in fact, she had mixed up their names once—fortunately, out of Jason McNair's earshot. As for Jason, she could feel him breathing down her neck, evaluating her every move.

Thank God there would be a lot of other people attending the seminar at White Dunes, she told herself after their party had picked up a rental car at the airport and headed for the coastal golf-resort. For once, she was relieved to walk into a hotel lobby and find it swarming with name-tagged conventioneers. Besides providing a buffer from Jason, a large gathering would make it easier for her to slip away for some private time with Taylor. When he had called and insisted they meet that weekend, she had been so startled she had at first fumbled for words.

"It's really important that we sit down and talk." He had sounded so earnest, she had been tempted to hop a flight to Charleston that very night.

Instead, she had promised to call him after she had arrived at White Dunes and had a better look at the seminar schedule. True to her word, Vanessa had skimmed the roster of panel discussions, lectures, and obligatory luncheons by the time the bellboy had delivered her bag. When she phoned the Parloe Island Animal Clinic, Mary Beasley put her on hold and paged Taylor.

"Well, I'm glad I caught you in the office," Vanessa began when he picked up the phone.

"God, I've been waiting for this call all day!" She could almost feel the vibrancy in his voice. "When can we get together?" he asked without further ado.

"The people who organized this seminar have managed to program every waking moment, but there's a cocktail party and buffet tomorrow night that I can afford to skip. How should we work this? Shall I rent a car and drive down to Parloe, or..." She broke off at the sound of an insistent rapping. "Excuse me a second, but there's someone at the door."

Vanessa laid the receiver on the nightstand and walked to the door. She squinted through the peephole, expecting to find a solicitous maid smiling up at her. Instead, she discovered Jason McNair's jowly visage. Vanessa pulled a face before unlatching the lock.

"Hi, Jason." She deliberately left the chain lock hooked, blocking his entry to the room. "I'm on the phone right now. Can we talk later?"

McNair scowled over her shoulder, his rapacious eyes scouring the room for the offending phone. "That won't be necessary. I just wanted to be sure you had the Whispering Pines market-research stats with you."

Vanessa nodded, a trifle impatiently. "I do," she assured him, just as she had a half-dozen times since they had left Atlanta.

"Good. Pierce just told me that a few of the Stanford Bank and Trust people are coming to this reception tomorrow night, and I want to be ready. This is our chance to make a big killing. I'm counting on you, Vanessa." His gaze was steely, his voice calculated to stiffen backbones. Vanessa felt as if she were being psyched up for a commando raid instead of a cocktail party.

"Okay, Jason. Fine. See you later." With each word, Vanessa edged the door a little closer shut.

"Sorry," she apologized to Taylor when she picked up the phone again. "That was Jason, giving me my marching orders. It looks as if I'm expected to attend this thing tomorrow evening after all." She sighed and reached for the seminar brochure lying on the bed. "Let's see," she mumbled, running her eye down the schedule. "Well, 4:00 a.m. Sunday looks great."

Taylor chuckled. "I can drive up anytime, you know. What about after the party Saturday night?"

"That's a thought, although it's hard to say how late I'll be 'encouraged' to stay there," Vanessa murmured. "Wait a second. This reception invitation says 'and guest.' That means I can bring someone. Are you game?"

"If you are. I don't know how well I'll fit in with these real-estate types. You said earlier that this place was going to be swarming with salivating wolves, crouched to pounce on places like Parloe."

Vanessa swallowed and hesitated. Yes, she had told him that all right; what she had failed to mention was that she was now working with one of the wolf packs. "That's true," she began. "You know, now that I've thought about it, this might be a good chance for you to meet some influential people socially. They aren't all greedy ogres—a lot of them would be interested in hearing what you have to say." She tried to sound positive, in part to quiet her own still-unresolved misgivings.

"Okay," Taylor agreed with a dubious laugh. "I'll wear my three-piece lobbying suit for the occasion."

"Great! I'll meet you in the White Dunes courtyard tomorrow at six."

THE FOLLOWING EVENING Vanessa congratulated herself on two counts: first, for bringing the stunning electric-blue silk cocktail dress; second, for skillfully eluding Jason McNair by taking the service elevator down to the resort restaurant's open-air courtyard. She found Taylor waiting for her by the fountain, looking not in the least ill at ease as he surveyed the milling crowd. When he spied her, he hurried to meet her.

"You look wonderful!" His lips moved against her cheek, forming a kiss decorous enough for the public setting, intense enough to convey lustier undertones. His hands felt warm, sensual as they clasped her bare arms for a lingering second.

"You do, too." Vanessa beamed and stepped back to give him another approving look. "I like this three-piece lobbying getup."

Taylor adjusted his lapels and grinned. "Never can tell who you're going to meet at a function like this."

"Uh-oh. I think you're about to meet one of the more questionable attendees right now." Vanessa gave his arm a furtive poke at the sight of Jason McNair bearing down on them.

"I've been looking all over for you," Jason greeted her abruptly.

"I've been keeping an eye peeled for you, too," Vanessa managed to say without a trace of a smirk. "Jason, I'd like you to meet Taylor Bowen. Taylor, this is Jason McNair."

"I've heard so much about you, I almost feel as if we'd already met." Taylor was smiling, but he avoided looking at Vanessa as he locked hands with Jason.

With the bare minimum of civility taken care of, Jason immediately turned back to Vanessa. "You've got those Whispering Pines stats, I hope."

Vanessa lifted her minuscule silver-mesh evening bag pointedly. "They're upstairs in my room. In any case, no one is going to want a computer printout thrust under his nose while he's reaching for the clam dip."

Jason's heavy face darkened. "Vanessa, I thought we had discussed this," he began, but before he could start a verbal tug-of-war, the two Whitney-Spawn reps came to the rescue.

Like a seasoned quick-change artist, Jason immediately put aside his drill-sergeant persona and glided into the role of unctuous account manager. He hailed the two reps as if they were old pals. "Pierce! Frank!"

With her contentious boss now in high gear, Vanessa stood aside and let him handle the introductions. She watched Taylor closely as he traded handshakes with the two men, but if he felt any aversion, he kept it well hidden beneath a cordial smile.

After their party had collected drinks from the bar, Vanessa managed to cull Taylor and Frank Melrose away from the group. She felt comfortable with the easygoing Melrose and sensed that he would make a far more sympathetic impression on Taylor than his hyper cohort, Pierce Steadman.

"You said you live on Parloe Island, right?" Frank asked, gesturing with his highball. When Taylor nodded, he went on. "Beautiful place, that island. Like a little bit of paradise the twentieth century somehow overlooked."

Taylor smiled down into his wineglass. "I fear the twentieth century has at last found us."

*Easy does it, Taylor. Give the guy a chance.* Vanessa had never felt psychically gifted, but if she had any telepathic skills, she intended to use them now.

"Yeah, I know what you mean. *Mucho* development going on down there these days." Frank jiggled the ice cubes in his glass before tossing off the dregs. "You know, my outfit is looking at some of those old houses on Parloe. We're not interested in a big complex like White Dunes." He swept an arc with the empty glass.

"That's good to know," Taylor mumbled, still smiling.

Vanessa swiftly stepped in. "What exactly do you have in mind, Frank? I'm only familiar with your Whispering Pines project near Hilton Head."

Frank turned to her, obviously eager to talk. Vanessa tried to ignore Taylor's maddeningly enigmatic smile as she listened to Melrose's plan to convert a historic home into a guest house.

"We want to restore the house as closely as possible to its original condition—you know, period wallpaper, furnishings, drapes, the works. It'll be a place where guests can go back in time without sacrificing modern comfort. Everything will be first-class *and* homey. Needless to say, the problems with such an undertaking are enormous."

"I can imagine," Taylor interposed. His amused expression reminded Vanessa of a cat playing with its prey.

The unsuspecting Melrose wheeled, shaking his head in exasperation. "Restoring the house is the least of them, too. Finding good staff is pretty hard in an out-of-the-way place like Parloe. And then there's always a zoning hassle."

At the buzzword "zoning," Vanessa thrust her empty wineglass between the two men. "Shall we hit the bar again?"

Frank looked a little startled by the glass looming right in front of his face. "Well, I guess so. What about you, Taylor?"

Taylor shrugged, agreeably enough, but before he could answer, Pierce Steadman charged onto the scene, red faced and wild eyed. "How's it going, Frank?" he asked. Not waiting for a response, he glanced rapidly from Vanessa to Taylor and back again. "I just ran into one of the guys who developed this place. Any of you know Bill Butler?" Not even pausing for breath, much less an answer, he rushed on. "Man, we could learn from Butler's people. He was telling me how they drained the marsh, just filled in the whole damned thing." His big hands made expansive draining and filling gestures in the air. "They literally carved this place out of nothing."

"I wouldn't call coastal marshlands nothing." Taylor's smile had dimmed noticeably, along with the geniality in his voice.

Vanessa struggled to keep calm, but it was not an easy task. Pierce Steadman's monologue had given her a case of motion sickness, and now with Taylor's hackles rising alarmingly, she felt pressured to defuse the mounting tension. "Jason and I would really appreciate your introducing us to Bill," she interposed. Having momentarily derailed Pierce, she glanced quickly from

Frank to Taylor. "Why don't we see about those drinks?"

To her relief, the three men pivoted in unison toward the bar. She had succeeded in inserting herself between Taylor and Pierce and had initiated a discussion of White Dunes' upcoming golf tournament when she spotted Jason, impatiently elbowing his way through the crowd toward them.

Jason gave both Whitney-Spawn men a slick smile, but when he turned to Vanessa his eyes were as hard as black marble. "Joe Carmichael of Stanford Bank is holding a table for us outside. I said I knew you'd want to be in on our discussion."

Vanessa glanced reflexively at Taylor; he looked back at her without registering the slightest emotion. "Well, I guess so. Sure."

"I'll catch you later." Taylor's voice had all the warmth of a recorded greeting as he waved her away with his wineglass.

Following Jason across the courtyard, Vanessa looked over her shoulder to see Frank Melrose wander off by himself to the buffet. Her heart sank when she spotted Taylor and Pierce still lingering at the bar, engrossed in conversation. Heaven only knew what horror stories of ravaged beachfronts and gentrified backwoods Pierce had in his repertoire; heaven only knew, too, what sort of barbed rejoinders Taylor would come up with. Whatever the case, she was helpless to do anything about it. She had no choice now but to put her best foot forward with the Stanford Bank people, and leave Pierce and Taylor to their own devices.

Still, Vanessa found her mind wandering as she sat at the terrace café table, talking with Jason and the two Stanford Bank and Trust representatives. She was relieved when Joe Carmichael finally suggested that they serve themselves from the buffet.

"I'll catch up with you in a moment, but first I want to ask my friend to join us for dinner." Vanessa excused herself and then hurried back to the bar. Pausing by the fountain, she scanned the room. She jumped when Frank Melrose slipped up behind her.

"Oh, hi, Frank. You haven't happened to run into Taylor, have you?"

Frank motioned toward the buffet. "Last time I saw him he was standing in line at one of the tables. I think Pierce got him a little hot under the collar," he added quietly.

"Oh, dear!" *You will not panic. I repeat, you will not panic.*

"I don't think it was anything serious," Frank went on in his easygoing way. "Pierce gets to everybody sooner or later. Even me." He chuckled.

Vanessa managed a dubious smile, but her eyes darted frantically to the buffet tables arranged in a U-shape at the far end of the courtyard.

"C'mon. Let's see if we can find everybody." Frank prodded her elbow gently.

Vanessa let Frank pilot her between scurrying waiters and around potted palms. At the buffet, they found Taylor forking a slice of smoked turkey onto his plate.

"Well, I see you beat me to the food for once." Vanessa tried to sound teasing, but she glanced uncertainly at Taylor's filled plate.

Taylor replaced the silver fork on the edge of the turkey platter. "I wasn't sure what you had planned, so I decided to go ahead and eat." Without looking up, he reached for a stick of stuffed celery.

"I planned to eat with you, of course!" Vanessa tried to mask her nervousness with a light laugh.

Taylor nodded. "Okay, so let's eat."

He sounded so abrupt, Vanessa could only stare at him for a second. She waited for him to turn, to smile, to do something to ease the awkwardness of the moment, but he only continued to look over the assorted condiments. "I can't eat until I get a plate," she announced for want of anything better to say.

"They're down at the end." He jerked his head toward the end of the table and spooned a dollop of horseradish sauce onto his plate.

"I'll get one." Vanessa turned on her heel and marched down the table. As she edged past Frank, who was now bent over a tray of oysters Rockefeller, she tried to mask her irritation with a smile.

Pierce Steadman wasn't her fault, damn it! None of this was her fault! She should never have invited Taylor to this idiotic affair in the first place. And she never would have, had she not felt so guilty about sidetracking their relationship with her move to Atlanta. As if her qualms about working with Whitney-Spawn hadn't saddled her with enough guilt!

Vanessa's mouth was set in a tight line as she snatched a plate and napkin and then moved along the buffet. When she caught up with Taylor, she deliberately reached in front of him to seize a serving fork. "Jason is saving places for us," she mumbled, shaking the fork to dislodge the olive skewered on its tines. When he made no comment, she added, "Are you ready?"

Twisting his mouth to one side, Taylor looked at his plate. "I guess I've had enough."

She wouldn't even try to interpret *that* remark, Vanessa thought as she led the way to the table where Jason and the Stanford Bank people were sitting. After performing another series of perfunctory introductions, she slid into one of the vacant chairs. Taylor's sleeve brushed her arm as he scooted in beside her.

To his credit—and in spite of Jason's obvious consternation—Joe Carmichael guided the conversation away from business to more universally interesting topics. It was a gracious gesture, and one Vanessa was sure had been made on Taylor's account. But if Taylor recognized the concession, he stubbornly refused to utter more than five consecutive words for the entire meal.

"Are you much of a golfer, Taylor?" Joe interrupted his discussion of the White Dunes tournament to ask.

Taylor took his time swallowing. "Played a few times." He took a sip of wine. "I'd rather sail or ride." He speared another chunk of turkey.

Vanessa made a valiant effort to carry the conversation for their side of the table, but when Jason brought up resort-marketing strategy, she was only too willing to let him draw the Stanford Bank people into a huddle. With Taylor doing a silent, methodical job of cleaning his plate to her right, she turned her attention to Frank Melrose on her left.

Frank was still eager to talk about his guest-house scheme. When he mentioned the staffing problem again, Vanessa was quick to tell him that she knew someone on Parloe who was skilled in both restaurant work and the management of old houses. At least she had been able to put in a plug for Grace Burch; she took what satisfaction she could in that thought as they finished their coffee and then prepared to break up for the night.

The handshaking and parting pleasantries seemed to take forever, probably because Vanessa dreaded what was to follow. Inevitably, the moment came when she and Taylor were left alone. Vanessa took a deep breath before turning to face him.

"Well, shall we take a walk outside?"

Taylor gave her a look that registered either surprise or amusement—Vanessa could not be sure which. "All right." He unfolded his arms and then wheeled toward the terrace sloping down from the courtyard. The steps etched into the slope were well lighted, but tricky for someone wearing high-heeled evening slippers. Taylor had already reached the parking lot and was waiting beneath a vapor torch when she caught up with him.

"Are you really in such a hurry?" She hadn't meant to snap; the words had just come out that way.

Taylor purposely gazed across the parking lot before fixing her with an icy stare. "All good things must come to an end."

Vanessa felt her lips tighten. "Look, Taylor, I'm sorry if you didn't enjoy yourself tonight. I had hoped this would give you a chance to make some valuable contacts for the Committee."

"So had I." His mouth pulled into a curve that dangerously resembled a sneer.

Vanessa felt her temper rise another degree. "Frank and Joe went out of their way to include you, but you did nothing but grunt at them all evening. You know, you can't just bulldoze your way through and expect people to take you seriously."

"No? Seems to me that's exactly what that vulture Steadman has in mind for any marsh that gets in his way. Sorry if my performance didn't pass muster with your Madison Avenue cronies, Vanessa. I guess I just don't have your flair for playing both sides of the fence."

"What do you mean?" Vanessa demanded. She felt her body grow rigid, and she fought to control herself.

"You know what I mean," Taylor shot back at her, at last peeling the barely polite veneer from his anger. "You talked so big about saving Parloe and helping the Committee, and now you're cozied up with the likes of Steadman and his gang."

"That's the grossest oversimplification I've ever heard in my life," Vanessa sputtered. "Whitney-Spawn is my advertising client, period. My interest in Parloe hasn't changed one bit since I left the island, and...and it's unfair and manipulative of you to imply that it has."

Taylor gave a brief, derisive snort. "Well, excuse me, but that's not the way it looks. You were fawning all over Mr. Primrose or whatever his name was all night. Every time he so much as yawned, you jumped in to score a marketing point."

"Frank Melrose happens to be a very decent human being, which is more than I can say for some people." Vanessa caught herself before she went any further.

"I couldn't believe you actually sat there and tried to sell him on hiring Grace Burch as a *maid*." Taylor spat out the words as if they were laced with poison.

Vanessa's eyes grew livid. "I never said anything about Grace working as a maid!"

"Of course, I'm sure you only had her best interests at heart." Taylor's chilling sarcasm contrasted with Vanessa's shrill tone. "After all, she needs to earn enough to pay you rent."

For a split second, Vanessa could only gape at him in speechless disbelief. "Let's just leave Grace out of this, okay?" she finally managed to get out.

One brow rose a scant millimeter on Taylor's otherwise stony face. "Along with all those phony gestures you made to the Preservation Committee? Thanks, but if weaseling Whitney-Spawn onto the island behind our backs is your idea of giving us a hand, I think we can do without your help."

Vanessa took a step forward and glared directly into his eyes. "That's a cheap shot, Taylor, and you know it!" When he only continued to look at her with that implacable stare, she raised her voice. "I have to earn a living, and I haven't done anything underhanded along the way. And I've done nothing to deserve your smug insults! You think you know everything about me, but you don't!"

"You're right; I don't. But I've learned enough from the company you're keeping. I'm afraid I don't have the stomach to learn any more." She had never heard him shout before, and she was stunned by the angry resonance in his voice.

Vanessa flung her arm out, striking blindly at the air. "Then go! Leave! Take all your self-righteous pride back to *your* island with you, and leave me alone!" She gestured wildly again, but he had already spun around and was headed across the parking lot.

Vanessa stumbled back toward the steps. As she watched his retreating figure she was vaguely aware of how hard she was now breathing. She felt a queer constriction in her throat; at the same time, her eyes began to sting. She was a hair's breadth from losing control of that raging reservoir of tears; the best she could hope for was to reach her room before the floodgates burst open.

Mindless of the treacherous evening slippers, she jogged up the steps. Backed into the corner of the service elevator, Vanessa bit her lip and counted the floors. Her jaw ached, and her nose felt as if it had swelled to cover half her face by the time she reached her room. The first shuddering sob tore from her as she slammed the door behind her.

She had been wrong before in her life, but never as wrong as she had been about Taylor Bowen. Vanessa paced around the room, alternately cursing him and running into the bathroom to grab a Kleenex. As if to fill the dull void growing inside her, she flipped on the TV. A colorized movie—one with hordes of high-kicking dancers in top hats—flooded the room with inanely cheerful music. Vanessa twisted the volume down before flinging herself across the bed.

Smearing diluted mascara across her cheek, Vanessa tried to recall all the hurtful things Taylor had said that evening. But somehow, the more she thought, the less distinct those thoughts became. Against her will, a flood of old memories from a happier time surged into her mind—Taylor leaning over in the saddle to comfort her, Taylor bracing himself against the wind as they sailed with the Burch kids, Taylor leading her into their solitary dance on the veranda, Taylor loving her.

When Vanessa turned onto her back, a toilet-bowl cleaner had replaced the exuberant dancers on the television. God, how she hated commercials! She was pulling herself to her feet, intent on cutting short the advertiser's thirty-second invasion of her privacy, when another image flickered onto the screen. It was an obviously low-budget spot, probably a public-service announcement, shot in a schoolyard on videotape, but there was something endearing about the unrehearsed antics of the children shooting baskets in the background, something wistfully appealing about the tall man ambling into the foreground with two little boys at his side.

Vanessa started when the Big Brothers logo rose on the screen, but she kept her eyes trained on the TV set until the tall man looked up at the camera. Taylor smiled directly at her, as he had so often in the past, but the smile was like a knife in her heart tonight. As his lips moved in a silent plea, she twisted around to bury her own wordless cry in the pillow.

## Chapter Fifteen

"Just one more time, please!" Matt leaned forward in the saddle as far as his short legs would permit and implored with every inch of his small frame. *"Pleeease!"*

Taylor ducked through the fence and then straightened up. "That's what you said before you trotted Knight around the paddock the last time."

Sinking back in the saddle, Matt frowned down at the reins threaded through his fingers. "Yeah, but I'm just now gettin' good at it."

Steadying the horse by the bridle with one hand, Taylor reached up to jostle Matt's knee with the other. "We'll ride next weekend, I promise. But now you need to get Knight groomed before your mom gets here."

As the boy reluctantly swung a leg over the horse's rump, Taylor grabbed him around the waist and lifted him from the saddle. He paused to unsaddle Knight before handing Matt the reins. "Walk him around for a few minutes to cool him down, and then tie him up by the trough and brush him. You, too, pardner." Taylor nudged Denny, who had been observing his brother's riding lesson from atop the fence rail. Denny grinned and obligingly jumped to the ground.

Taylor watched the two boys lead the big horse along the fence before he hefted the saddle over his shoulder and walked to the stable. Both Matt and Denny were such enthusiastic young horsemen, he was usually happy to indulge them. He always insisted, however, that the boys take responsibility for grooming Knight after a ride, and he wanted to have them ready to go when Grace arrived.

It was just as well that Grace had planned to drop by his house and fetch the boys today, Taylor thought as he shook out the saddle pad and hung it on its rack. These days driving up to the Dodderidge house held all the charm of a descent into hell. Every time he was reminded of that catastrophic evening at White Dunes, he got angry—angry at Vanessa for getting mixed up with that bunch of vultures, angry with the trick of circumstance that had intruded on the fantasy he had built around his relationship with her, and, most of all, angry with himself for spinning the fantasy in the first place.

Scowling, Taylor gave the soiled girth-straps a furious scrubbing, as if he hoped to blot out a far deeper stain than the gray streaks of dried horse sweat. He had just laid the girths across the oat barrel to dry when he heard Grace's Beetle grinding its way up the drive. Taylor took a minute to wipe his hands and adjust his forbidding expression before walking outside.

"Got 'em ready for the Kentucky Derby yet?" As she shoved the car door shut, Grace nodded toward the fence where Matt and Denny had tethered Knight. Armed with brushes and curry combs, the boys were now busy giving the animal a head-to-hoof grooming.

"Maybe next year." Taylor shrugged affably, but looking into Grace's piercing dark eyes, he felt his grin waver.

Although Taylor had responded to Grace's inquiries about his visit to White Dunes with only the sketchiest of replies, he had detected a subtle alteration, a faint chill in her manner of late. Then, too, he could not be sure what Vanessa might have told her; after all, Grace probably communicated regularly with her landlady. In spite of himself, he felt a ripple of distaste at the word's pejorative connotation.

"You certainly look nice today," Taylor commented, as much to shift his own focus as to compliment Grace. She did look quite attractive in her bright tropical-print sun dress; with her thick hair cut in a becoming short wedge and a smattering of make-up accenting her high cheekbones, Grace Burch's strongly boned face bore a startling resemblance to those that regularly grace fashion magazine covers.

Grace smiled briefly, but she brushed off the compliment. "Thank you. I figured I ought to look my best if I wanted to get a decent job."

Taylor blinked in surprise. "You had a job interview?"

"Better than that—I had an offer." Grace shaded her eyes with one hand and watched the two boys energetically combing Knight's tail.

"I thought you had decided to try working at Dub McCarthy's fish market for a while."

"That was just until something better turned up." If he had not known Grace better, Taylor would have sworn that brief glance she gave him was one of contempt. She sniffed as she looked back at her two sons.

"Of course," Taylor hastened to agree. "So tell me about this other job." Grace's evasive answers were beginning to make him feel as if he had been unwittingly drawn into a very tedious parlor game.

Grace pursed her lips, and for a moment Taylor wondered if she were going to offer him any answer at all. Finally, she sighed. "This fellow called me the other day, just out of the blue, and said he was going to be down here this weekend looking at some old houses. Seems his company's had its eye on Bellemere.''

"Bellemere? That old place is nothing but a termite colony."

Grace shot him another of those questionable glances before going on. "Well, he seems to think the house can be salvaged, and I expect he knows more about these things than either of us. Anyway, these folks are going to fix Bellemere up and turn it into one of those guest houses, like they have in Charleston, you know. And . . ." Still gazing across the yard, Grace paused to draw a deep breath. "Mr. Melrose—that's this fellow's name—wanted to know if I'd be interested in running the place for them."

As a veterinarian, Taylor was accustomed to getting a grip on his nerves in a crisis, but now he could only stand by helplessly and let the flush creep unchecked up his neck to his ears. "That sounds really great," he gulped.

"Yes, it does, doesn't it? Thanks to Vanessa, I just might get a chance to do something besides scale fish all day for the rest of my life—without leaving the island."

"Come to think of it, I do remember Vanessa mentioning your name to Mr. Melrose," Taylor conceded weakly. How could he forget? Every moment of that wretched evening was indelibly stamped in his mind. "I'm glad he called you."

But if Taylor had counted on placating Grace with such feeble comments, he had sadly miscalculated. Fists anchored on her hips, she now faced him in the uncompromising stance of a prizefighter. Her dark eyes gouged through him like two shards of flint. "Taylor, I'm going to tell you something. I don't know what happened up there at that fancy golf place, and since you're too proud to tell me and Vanessa's too kind, I guess I never will. But I've got two eyes in my head, and I know a mess when I see one. I also know a fool, and that's just what you are, Taylor Bowen, if you sit down here on this island and let that woman slip out of your life."

Taylor's mouth must have dropped open—at that point, he was too stunned to keep track of his body's reactions—but Grace rushed on to head off any defense he might have offered. "I don't pretend to know everything about your business—or Vanessa's, for that matter—but to my mind there's not a sweeter, more generous woman on the face of the earth than Vanessa Dorsey. As bad as she needs money to help her poor mama and put her sister through school, she still wouldn't take a dime's rent from me for that house of hers." When Taylor's eyes widened, she nodded smartly. "That's right, not one penny."

"I had no idea," Taylor gasped. "I mean, about the house."

"No, I suppose you didn't. Vanessa wanted to keep our arrangement just between us. I guess she wanted to spare my pride." Grace lowered her voice without dulling its defiant edge. "I confess to having my pride, too, Taylor, but I'll be damned if I'll ever let it ruin my life. And that's exactly what you're doing to yourself."

Listening to Grace's revelations, Taylor felt as if the carpet of mossy earth had suddenly been pulled out from under his feet, leaving him suspended in midair. He was still floundering to regain his footing when Matt and Denny came running up.

"All done?" Grace asked in a deceptively light tone.

Denny nodded emphatically, while Matt pointed to Knight, who was now lazily cropping clover in the paddock. "Doesn't he look good?"

"He looks just like a prize show horse," Grace assured them. "Come on now, boys. We've got to pick up some groceries at the One-Stop on our way home." She gave their backs a gentle prod in the direction of the rusty Beetle. "Be sure to thank Taylor for the good time you had."

The boys chorused their agreement on that point. But as Grace herded them toward the car, Denny frowned up at Taylor with eyes that were disconcertingly reminiscent of his mother's.

"Is something wrong, son?" Taylor fought to suppress the uneasiness in his voice.

"Your ears sure got sunburned."

Taylor's hand shot up to his ear, but he managed to wave at the departing Beetle. Long after the sound of its tinny engine had petered out in the distance, he stood staring down the drive. At last he turned slowly and walked back to the empty stable alone.

WHEN YOUR PERSONAL LIFE falls apart, lose yourself in your work. Since her disastrous encounter with Taylor at White Dunes, Vanessa had frequently repeated that late-twentieth-century axiom to herself—without any noticeable healing effects. Maybe if she had not felt so ambivalent about her primary account she could have seen her job as more than just a trade off for a hefty paycheck. Maybe if she had been working with someone more compatible than Jason she could have approached each workday as a challenge and not as an ordeal to be endured. Unfortunately, her position at Henson and Knowles was inextricably bound to those two bothersome factors, and neither showed any inclination to vanish.

If she could do nothing about the disarray in her own life, at least she had been able to have a positive effect

on Grace Burch's situation. Vanessa consoled herself
with that thought one afternoon as she took the long
route from the coffee room to her office and reread a
note she had just received from the spunky widow. After thanking Vanessa again for recommending her to
Frank Melrose, Grace had delicately broached the subject of Great-aunt Charlotte's house. As the future
manager of Bellemere, Grace would be required to attend a hotel-management course in Florida in two
weeks. Her pride that her new employer was investing
in her training was tempered by her reluctance to leave
the Dodderidge house untended for a whole week. Vanessa smiled to herself as she made a mental note to
phone Grace that evening and allay any misgivings she
might have.

Her smile faded when Paulette Mason intercepted her
in the corridor.

"Big trouble?" Vanessa took a quick sip of the luke-
warm coffee to fortify herself.

Paulette grimaced. "Both Whitney-Spawn reps called
to complain about an undelivered storyboard. Jacque-
line dropped off the final figures for the Burberry Bay
TV commercial, said it's *only* $25,000 over budget.
And—" she released a heavy sigh "—Jason is chomp-
ing at the bit to see you. Hope you're wearing your
bullet-proof vest," the secretary warned her as she
handed Vanessa Jason's scrawled note.

Vanessa opened her jacket and pretended to study her
white silk blouse. "I knew I'd forgotten something,"
she kidded Paulette. But as she approached McNair's
office, she could feel the tension mounting within her.
She was sturdy enough as human beings go, but she
simply was not built to withstand a lot of fighting. In
the wake of that hideous blowup with Taylor two weeks

ago, she knew she could not go more than one round with Jason.

Jason was bent over his desk, examining slides through a hand viewer, and he did not look up when she rapped on the door frame. "Come in, Vanessa. Have a seat." Still squinting over the viewer, he waved carelessly toward the chair facing his desk.

Vanessa eased into the chair, but she stiffened when he suddenly looked up and snapped off the viewer light. "Paulette said you wanted to see me."

"Right." Jason swiveled in his chair and dug through a disgustingly neat standing file. When he whirled back around, he slapped a flyer on the desk in front of her. "Just what is *your* name doing on *that*?"

Vanessa took a moment to examine the flyer, but before she had even touched the pale blue paper, she recognized the Parloe Island Committee for Contained Growth's newsletter. The columns of Committee news and development data blurred before her eyes, drifting out of focus, while Jason's jackhammer voice pummeled her senses.

"Somehow this thing ended up in Pierce's hands, and he phoned me yesterday evening at home. We can't have this, Vanessa."

"If you recall, Jason, I once tried to discuss with you my reservations about working with Whitney-Spawn," Vanessa reminded him in a deliberately level voice.

Jason dismissed her comment with an impatient shake of his head. "To hell with your reservations! Your association with a group like this is more than an embarrassment. It jeopardizes the agency's relationship with Whitney-Spawn! Fortunately, Pierce seemed satisfied with my assurances that you had completely disassociated yourself from this outfit."

Vanessa looked up from the newsletter and blinked. "But I haven't, Jason," she said quietly.

"Pierce needn't know that. I was merely buying us time until you could make the break. Which you will do immediately, of course." The room was silent save for the crotchety squeak of Jason's chair as it swiveled to and fro like a pendulum.

Vanessa carefully folded the newsletter and placed it on the desk. "And if I don't?"

"What kind of question is that?" The irritating squeak abruptly ceased, and Jason leaned across the desk. "It's clearly a conflict of interest to represent Whitney-Spawn while you're mixed up with a crackpot group like this."

Vanessa ignored Jason's crude slur. Like a beneficent soft cloud, a strange calm had descended on her, steadying her voice. "Not necessarily. The Committee is not opposed to development per se—we only want some leverage in what happens to Parloe."

In contrast to Vanessa's cool demeanor, Jason was growing more livid by the second. The thick flesh rising from his collar was now marked with red striations, and his eyes were bulging. "I've tried to be fair with you, Vanessa, but I'm warning you. Get... out... of... that... group." His fist beat a doleful cadence with each word.

He was standing now, and Vanessa rose to look him in the eye. "And if I don't?"

"You have a choice—this idiot group or your job." His tone was menacing.

"Then you'll have to accept my resignation. Two weeks' notice, of course, and I'll do everything I can to insure a smooth transition." A heady exhilaration zoomed through her, as if she had just sprung from a plane and was waiting for her parachute to open.

"Have you lost your mind?" Jason was roaring as he followed her out of his office.

"No. I think I've just recovered my senses." As Vanessa marched down the hall, she was aware of curious heads popping out of doorways, but she did not stop until she reached her own office. She ignored Jason, who was hovering at her side as if he were a freshly exorcised demon, and paused to stuff a few folders into her briefcase. "Paulette, I'm going home for the day. I'll phone in later for my calls. And I'll have a cassette of dictation ready for you in the morning." Vanessa turned to the now dumbstruck McNair. "Excuse me."

For the first time, Jason politely stepped aside to let her pass.

Vanessa was breezing through the reception area just as Nikki Pappas stepped off the elevator.

"Whoa there, Van! Is there a fire up here or something?" Nikki pretended to jump out of Vanessa's path.

"No, I'm just on my way out."

"Yeah, well, you look as if it's for good," Nikki joked.

Vanessa gave her a grim smile just before the elevator door glided shut. "It is."

HER PLAN WAS SO BOLD yet so simple, Vanessa was startled that she had not thought of it earlier. Back when she had lost her job in Richmond, she supposed sentiment had been weighted against it. Also, the wounds left by the divorce had not yet healed, and she had been too desperate for a safe haven even to consider selling Great-aunt Charlotte's house. Even now, as she pulled into the drive of her rented bungalow, she winced at the thought of surrendering her right to the beloved mansion forever. Still, the house was the most valuable asset that she and Sandra possessed; with both of them now in straitened circumstances, converting it into cash made perfect sense.

Despite the ironclad argument she had forged in her mind, Vanessa did not risk giving herself time to falter. When she walked into the house, she went straight to the phone and called Sandra. As usual, her sister was buried in a medical text but glad to hear from her.

Sandy's easygoing tone altered markedly when Vanessa made her earthshaking announcement. "You *what*?"

"I said I quit my job today. I mean, I didn't just walk out—I'll be going back in until they find a replacement."

Sandy was quiet for a long moment. "Well, you did say your boss was a real pill. You've probably made the right decision."

"And don't start worrying about your tuition," Vanessa quickly assured her. "I have a plan that will take care of that."

"It's not the tuition that's bothering me." Sandra sounded a trifle annoyed, but then her tone softened. "You're the greatest sister in the world, and I love you, but sometimes I wish you wouldn't fret over me so much. Now that I have this summer lab job nailed down, I'm home free for next year. I was just thinking of you, of how hard you looked for a job. I just hope you won't regret your decision to resign."

"I won't," Vanessa told her firmly. "But there's another matter that I can't decide alone, not without you. Would you agree to sell Great-aunt Charlotte's house?" Hearing Sandy gasp, she rushed on. "I know we've never even dreamed of parting with it, but chances are neither of us will ever live there permanently." Her voice caught on those words, and she swallowed hastily. "An old house like that requires loads of maintenance, and we haven't had the best luck in the world with tenants. And we could both use the money.''

"You sound as if you've really given this a lot of thought," Sandra began carefully.

"I have," Vanessa fibbed. "And I think we ought to put it on the market immediately."

She could hear Sandy slowly swallow on the other end. "I'll agree to whatever you want. Somehow I've always felt the house meant more to you than it did to me, but if you're willing to sell, I won't object—on one condition. You have to swear to me that you're not selling it just to pay my tuition."

"I swear, Sandy. I'm doing this to bail myself out. Believe me, when we have the cash in hand, I think we'll both be amazed we didn't sell that house years ago."

PERHAPS SHE AND SANDY would wonder why they hadn't unloaded the crumbling old house sooner once they found a buyer, but until that merciful day Vanessa steeled herself for an onslaught of doubt. As she had anticipated, Grace Burch was shocked when Vanessa called to give her the news and assure her that the sale provisions would allow the Burches to live in the house until their move to Bellemere. Vanessa's mother had guardedly urged her to reconsider, and Nikki Pappas had told her that she was flat-out crazy. In fact, the only person who had greeted the news with unreserved approval was Mr. Paul Tate of Tate Realty.

"I'll have you a fantastic offer before the summer is over," he had assured her over the phone.

As it turned out, Paul Tate called her with a serious prospect within the week. Vanessa had not expected such a rapid turnaround, and for a moment she was gripped with the insane urge to tell him she had changed her mind. Before her emotions got the best of her, she thanked him for his efficiency and promised to meet him at the house on Friday. With the house still requiring significant repairs, the realtor wanted Vanessa on hand to approve any negotiations. Much as she dreaded the ordeal of returning to Great-aunt Charlotte's estate and reviving a host of wrenching memories, she was grateful that Tate's buyer had surfaced this particular week. With Grace Burch in Florida, Vanessa hoped to slip onto Parloe without seeing anyone she knew, consolidate the deal, and then draw a curtain on that painful episode in her life.

When Vanessa turned into the drive leading to Great-aunt Charlotte's house the following Friday morning, she was doubly grateful that no one would be there waiting for her. With no witnesses about, she did not have to worry about restraining the moisture that had been welling in her eyes since she had crossed the Intracoastal Waterway. When she spotted the For Sale sign planted squarely in the center of the front lawn, the dam at last broke, flooding her cheeks with hot channels of tears.

Blotting her eyes clumsily with a tissue, Vanessa rushed past the suddenly obscene sign to the front porch. She fumbled with the key and then flung open the door. The house was quiet, filled with a stillness as eerie as the hush that had greeted her on that day in March when she had first returned to the island. Taylor had been with her then, had tried to cheer her. A sob broke from her throat at the memory.

"Get hold of yourself!" Vanessa muttered between gasping breaths. Jerking a fresh tissue from her handbag, she fiercely mopped her cheeks. She hadn't driven all the way up here just to frighten away a potential buyer with her swollen eyes and red nose.

Vanessa hurried into the study and began to adjust the curtains. As the room brightened, she spotted a note from Grace tucked beneath the telephone.

So sorry I'll miss your visit, but I told everyone you're coming back. Cora and Luke are anxious to see you. In fact, just about everyone on the Committee is. That TV reporter, Jack Marshall, wants you to call him. The boys are staying with Taylor.

*Taylor.* Vanessa pressed her lips together and stared at the phone. She could, of course, call him; any woman gutsy enough to walk out on a job in the wake of five months' unemployment was certainly not too fainthearted to call a miffed lover. But did Taylor actually qualify as a miffed lover? In happier days, when Vanessa had felt really close to him, their love had seemed too special, too personal, too entirely theirs to fit the ordinary definition. And, conversely, the rift that had torn them apart was far too profound to be laughed off as a lovers' quarrel. Even now that she had severed her connection with Whitney-Spawn—for strong, personal reasons of her own—she feared that only a miracle could restore trust between her and Taylor. And miracles seemed to be in short supply these days.

Her somber musings were interrupted by the sound of two cars on the drive. Vanessa hesitated long enough to take one last swipe at her damp eyes and then jogged to the door. Paul Tate had already climbed out of his car and was surveying the lawn like a general reviewing his troops. Only when she reached the steps did Vanessa see the charcoal-gray Cherokee pulled up behind the realtor's Riviera.

As Taylor rounded the vehicle, his expression was impossible to interpret. Whatever his frame of mind might be, however, Vanessa knew this was not the right time to talk with him, not with a critical business transaction hanging in the balance.

"Good morning, Miss Dorsey!" Paul Tate fairly bounded up the walk to greet her.

"Good morning, Mr. Tate." Vanessa tried to smile, but her eyes drifted against her will back to Taylor. "Uh, Mr. Tate, if you'll excuse me for a moment, I have an unexpected guest I need to talk with."

"Certainly," the real-estate agent agreed brightly. "I'm sure Dr. Bowen won't mind the wait. He's really excited about buying this place of yours."

Vanessa's lips moved in wordless amazement before she finally gasped, "*He* wants to buy my house?"

Paul Tate's eyes blinked rapidly behind his thick horn-rims. "Well, yes," he stammered.

"But that's ridiculous!" Vanessa blurted out.

Taylor had been watching the exchange in silence, but he now stepped around the dumbfounded realtor. "Not as ridiculous as your selling a piece of your heart. And that's just what you'll be doing if you part with this house. I'm going to buy it, Vanessa, and someday, when you come to your senses, I'll sell it back to you."

"I can't let you do that!" Vanessa took a step forward as she met Taylor's challenging gaze.

Taylor raised a skeptical brow, but stood his ground. "Why not? I'm a legitimate buyer, and the house is for sale."

"Maybe it isn't," Vanessa shot back without thinking.

"Wait a minute, Vanessa." Taylor's voice was maddeningly calm and reasonable. "You've signed a contract with this gentleman. That sign says For Sale just as big as day."

Vanessa pushed past the two men and dashed across the lawn. She yanked the realtor's sign out of the earth and then turned to face them. "I've changed my mind."

"You can't pull the rug out from under an interested buyer, just like that," Taylor protested, but Vanessa thought she recognized a slight twinkle in his green eyes.

"Dr. Bowen is right," Paul Tate ventured to suggest, but Vanessa's stern glance sent him retreating to his car. "On the other hand, maybe I should just let you two handle this." He scooted behind the wheel and carefully locked the door before grinding the ignition.

Vanessa's eyes were fastened on Taylor as he walked toward her and took the sign from her unresisting hand. Flinging it onto the ground, he smiled for the first time that morning.

"Well, at least that's one mistake I've managed to nip in the bud." Taylor's voice was husky yet insinuating.

"I've made some pretty big ones lately, haven't I?" Vanessa said softly, but Taylor lifted his hand to silence her.

"Yours were nothing to compare with mine. I'm not used to telling myself I'm wrong, Vanessa, but since I left White Dunes that night I've had plenty of practice. Now I realize you were sincerely trying to bring everybody together in the island's best interest. In fact, I'm ashamed to admit that I probably realized it that night. But I let my own insecurity get the best of me. I guess I was just so in love with the woman I'd gotten to know on Parloe, the one with ratty blue jeans and a leaky roof, that I didn't quite know what to do with the big-city ad lady. I should have trusted you, but the part of me that longed to comfort and protect you started to fear that you might not need that anymore."

"I'll always need comfort and protection," Vanessa managed to interject.

Taylor nodded. "I guess what I really mean is that I've come to beg your pardon, and . . ." He hesitated. His broad shoulders rose and fell as he took a deep breath. Then he glanced across the lawn as if he were searching for a misplaced cue card. "Hell, I rehearsed what I was going to say all the way over here, and I'm still going to blow it." Taylor suddenly gripped both of Vanessa's arms. "Vanessa, I love you with all my heart, more than I've ever loved anyone, better than any man can ever love you." He released his hold on one of her arms and dug inside his pants pocket. When he pulled out an exquisite ruby-and-diamond ring, Vanessa could only stare. "I want to marry you, Vanessa . . . Will you marry me?"

Still too stunned to speak, she watched him slide the ring onto her finger. The warmth of his hands clasping hers assured her that this was no dream, but blissful reality. "Oh, Taylor!" Vanessa suddenly threw her arms around his neck. "Yes! Yes! Yes!" She punctuated each word with a kiss before surrendering to the strong arms that locked around her turning now into forever.

TAYLOR SNUGGLED HIS FACE into the thicket of dark curls on the pillow beside him. A whisper of Vanessa's perfume clung to her hair, enticing him even closer. The midmorning sun had already stained the drawn white blinds a pastel rose, hinting at the clear summer day that was now in full bloom outside the bedroom. At the moment, however, Taylor could think of nothing compelling enough to force him out of bed—not with the woman he loved so tantalizingly close at hand. Pushing himself onto one shoulder, he let his lips wander across her hairline and down her cheek.

Vanessa murmured contentedly. When her eyes fluttered open, he paused and smiled down at her. "Don't stop," she protested. Slipping her hands around his neck, she pulled him down until his mouth hovered close to her own. The sensitive skin of their lips had barely touched when the phone jangled, halting them in midkiss.

Still holding on to him, Vanessa eased up on the pillow reluctantly. "I suppose I should get it. It's probably Sandy, wanting to know how the prospective buyer panned out." She grabbed his shirt and slipped it on as she climbed out of bed.

"She'll probably laugh when you tell her about our 'deal.' I'll make some coffee while you're on the phone." Taylor leaned over the side of the bed to grab the khaki pants that were still lying exactly where he had stepped out of them last night.

In the big, rambling kitchen, he shuffled through cabinets and drawers until he had assembled the necessary ingredients for a pot of coffee. But as he measured water and poured it into the percolator, he could not help but overhear snatches of Vanessa's conversation in the hall.

"Well, this *is* quite a surprise!" she was saying with an elated little titter. "No kidding?"

There was a pregnant pause before she spoke again. "So soon? Oh, of course I can interview right away. No, I wouldn't have any trouble with that start date." This time she erupted into a full-blown laugh. "This is really great!" Another pause was followed by another laugh. "Thank *you!*"

Taylor had never enjoyed guessing games, but he had picked up enough clues from Vanessa's one-sided responses to know two things: someone had called her about a job, and she was excited about it. As he heard her wander into the kitchen, he deliberately kept his back turned and pretended to check the coffee's pro-

gress. Although he was still as committed as ever to re-
locating his practice if need be, her resignation from
Henson and Knowles had been a reprieve for him, a
chance for them to spend some time together on Parloe
and simply *live*. Still, he wanted to hide his disappointment and congratulate her on her good fortune.

"Who was that?" he asked as casually as possible.

"Some people who might have a job for me." Vanessa was obviously trying to sound apologetic. Her
hand slipped through the crook of his arm and tugged
timidly.

"Well, that's great." Taylor yielded to the pressure of
her hand to turn and give her a big smile.

Vanessa looked down at the counter. "Oh, I guess
so."

Taylor chafed her arm gently. "Is there some problem with the job?"

She shrugged. "No, not really. I just wasn't planning on ever working in this particular city."

Taylor clasped her by the shoulders, forcing her to
look up at him. "Now listen to me, Vanessa. You don't
have to take the first thing that comes along. We have
each other now, remember? That means we can help
each other." He stopped as her shoulders began to
shake beneath his hands. "What's so funny?"

"I just wasn't expecting to ever turn up a job in
Charleston," she managed to get out through her
laughter. "That was Jack Marshall. It seems his television station is looking for an advertising sales manager, and he recommended me. He remembered our
work together on the feature. When he phoned here last
week, Grace told him I had left H and K and was back
in the market for a job. I still have to woo the powers-
that-be at the station, of course, but Jack thinks I'm a
shoo-in."

"That's wonderful news!" Taylor squeezed her shoulders, lifting her off her feet for a second.

"Isn't it?" Vanessa was beaming, but she sobered slightly. "But right now the best news is that we have the rest of the weekend together."

Taylor shook his head solemnly. "No, Vanessa. The best news is that we have the rest of our lives together. This is one time I'll insist that I'm right, and you're wrong!"

Taylor quickly sealed her smiling lips with a kiss, but Vanessa would have been the last person in the world to disagree.

# *Harlequin American Romance.*

*Gull Cottage*

## *SUMMER.*

The sun, the surf, the sand...

One relaxing month by the sea was all Zoe, Diana and Gracie ever expected from their four-week stays at Gull Cottage, the luxurious East Hampton mansion. They never thought they'd soon be sharing those long summer days—or hot summer nights—with a special man. They never thought that what they found at the beach would change their lives forever. But as Boris, Gull Cottage's resident mynah bird said: "Beware of summer romances...."

Join Zoe, Diana and Gracie for the summer of their lives. Don't miss the GULL COTTAGE trilogy in American Romance: #301 *Charmed Circle* by Robin Francis (July 1989), #305 *Mother Knows Best* by Barbara Bretton (August 1989) and #309 *Saving Grace* by Anne McAllister (September 1989).

GULL COTTAGE—because a month can be the start of forever...

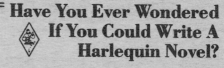

# Have You Ever Wondered If You Could Write A Harlequin Novel?

Here's great news—Harlequin is offering a series of cassette tapes to help you do just that. Written by Harlequin editors, these tapes give practical advice on how to make your characters—and your story— come alive. There's a tape for each contemporary romance series Harlequin publishes.

Mail order only

All sales final

----------------------------------------------------------------

TO:   **Harlequin Reader Service**
      **Audiocassette Tape Offer**
      **P.O. Box 1396**
      **Buffalo, NY   14269-1396**

I enclose a check/money order payable to HARLEQUIN READER SERVICE® for $9.70 ($8.95 plus 75¢ postage and handling) for EACH tape ordered for the total sum of $_____*
Please send:

| | Romance and Presents          |   Intrigue
| | American Romance              |   Temptation
| | Superromance                  |   All five tapes ($38.80 total)

Signature_____
                                            (please print clearly)
Name:_____

Address:_____

State:_____ Zip:_____

*Iowa and New York residents add appropriate sales tax

AUDIO-H

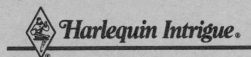

# Harlequin Intrigue ®

## High adventure and romance—
## with three sisters on a search . . .

Linsey Deane uses clues left by their father to search the Colorado Rockies for a legendary wagonload of Confederate gold, in #120 *Treasure Hunt* by Leona Karr (August 1989).

Kate Deane picks up the trail in a mad chase to the Deep South and glitzy Las Vegas, with menace and romance at her heels, in #122 *Hide and Seek* by Cassie Miles (September 1989).

Abigail Deane matches wits with a murderer and hunts for the people behind the threat to the Deane family fortune, in #124 *Charades* by Jasmine Crasswell (October 1989).

*Don't miss Harlequin Intrigue's three-book series The Deane Trilogy. Available where Harlequin books are sold.*

DEA-G